Joy Martin was born i[...]
journalist and worked o[...]
moved to writing news[...]
Corporation and the BBC[...]
She has also broadcast on [...]
Africa and Britain. She is th[...] author of *A Wrong to Sweeten* and *The Moon is Red in April* and is at work on her next novel, *A Heritage of Wrongs*.

By the same author

A Wrong to Sweeten
The Moon is Red in April

JOY MARTIN

Ulick's Daughter

Grafton Books

A Division of HarperCollins*Publishers*

GraftonBooks
A Division of HarperCollins*Publishers*
77–85 Fulham Palace Road,
Hammersmith, London W6 8JB

Published in paperback by GraftonBooks 1991
9 8 7 6 5 4 3 2 1

First published in Great Britain by
GraftonBooks 1990

Copyright © Joy Martin 1990

The Author asserts the moral right to
be identified as the author of this work

ISBN 0-586-20738-4

Printed in Great Britain by
HarperCollinsManufacturing Glasgow

Set in Palatino

All rights reserved. No part of this publication may be
reproduced, stored in a retrieval system, or transmitted,
in any form or by any means, electronic, mechanical,
photocopying, recording or otherwise, without the prior
permission of the publishers.

This book is sold subject to the condition that it shall not,
by way of trade or otherwise, be lent, re-sold, hired out or
otherwise circulated without the publisher's prior consent
in any form of binding or cover other than that in which it
is published and without a similar condition including this
condition being imposed on the subsequent purchaser.

For the family at Oakfield

Acknowledgements

My gratitude to the following whose research has helped me in writing this book: Olive Sharkey, Reverend Father Cathal Stanley, P.P., Desmond Roche, P.K. Egan, M.J. Shiel, Jim Fahy, Thomas J. Page, Thomas Feeney, Padraic O'Farrell, Ruth Delaney, John Bergamini, Harvey Pitcher, Michael Ignatieff, Olga Davydoff Dax and Jacqueline Onassis; *The Times*, and *We Thundered Out* by Philip Howard, published by Times Books.

I would also like to thank Mrs Guin Lerner, Secretary, Great Britain–USSR Association, Miss Rosemary Ashbie, Archivist, The Savoy Hotel, and Olga and Lena, my guides and translators during my time in Russia.

Prologue

From the lake shore with Spa Island South at his back he could see only a portion of the thatched roof of her house and that bit of the side wall where the rain, trickling from the ill-constructed overhang, had created a green stain. Otherwise the cottage was concealed by an anarchic tangle of blackberry bushes, ferns, overgrown grasses and balding thistles.

When he had suggested that she cut back a bit of this jungle she had said she liked it the way it was; that it made a hidey-hole out of the house, allowing her to look out on to Lough Derg without any fear that a man out of one of the boats, catching sight of the place, and her, might pester her in the night.

He had said no more. After all, they both knew that she had a more deep-seated reason for taking cover than that one. It was different for him. They were all used to his vices. They might not think sweetly of him, but they did not detest him either. He was too easy-going, too free-handed, too reckless to incur their absolute dislike.

'Muráid,' he called out for the second time. 'Are you there?'

Again, there was no human reply, only bird song: the buzzing trill of a redpoll; a reed bunting's thin 'tiu' and unremarkable jangling. Seconds later, a dark finch with a slim forked tail took flight out of a bush of haws.

Could she be in and sleeping? He secured the reins around a low branch without disturbing his horse's grazing and stepped forward into the imbroglio, circumventing a sly red naked offshoot that reached out in the hope of tripping him up. He ducked, straightened, arrived at his destination.

The house had been built more than a hundred years before, at a time when taxes had been levied on the number and sizes of windows. The two tiny openings, one on each side of the half-door, were nothing more than slits, grudgingly permitting the minimum of fresh air and light to pass through into the single room beyond.

There was no one inside. The only movement was the flicker of flames from the hearth, itself very narrow, with a recess just wide enough to accommodate the fire and its medley of fire-irons. Over the flames a neglected pot of water, already half boiled away, dangled from a swinging iron crane. In front of the fire a crusie-lamp patiently waited for evening, along with a three-legged stool with a hole in its centre. Against one wall was her bed, raised on truckles as a safeguard in case of unexpected flooding.

He sighed, contemplating the bed, thinking that after what he had gone through this last month he had much need of its owner. Who had to be found, and quickly. To provide the obvious palliative. To efface for a short while his desolation, the acuteness of his loss.

Retreating from the house, he set off along the boreen to Kylnamelly wood, attempting to concentrate his thoughts on his current quest rather than on the immediate past.

He was a man who in his youth had been called more beautiful than handsome: the description was still apt, although an enemy, suspecting that he had been cuckolded, had insisted that the fellow looked foreign. His eyes were deep-set and dark and the lashes were long and thick and curly. His nose was short and straight, perfectly formed, his mouth soft and luscious, his cheeks and jawbones rounded, womanly. He had a deep dimple in his chin.

And yet he was over six feet tall and his chest and shoulders were broad. The shooting coat he wore over the shawl-collared waistcoat emphasized his breadth. Both these garments were missing buttons and neither were perfectly clean. But his check trousers, which had a narrow band of contrast material sewn down on the outside seam, were jaunty enough, and so was his full flat bow tie, although it was carelessly tied.

Every so often as he strode along he bellowed out: 'Muráid!' until a black and white farm dog of indeterminate ancestry took pity upon his solitary state and linked up with him, stopping every few yards to mark out the perimeters of its territory by peeing against a tree.

She could be in the wood gathering faggots for the fire, he thought or, if she were wiser, in the bog helping herself to turf when the cutters' backs were turned.

But when was she ever wily?

'Come on now, fellow,' he said to the dog. 'We'll find her, the pair of us.'

He was fond of animals, talked to them as if they were capable of conversing. His father, he recalled, had been the same, and his grandfather, carrying their love to absurd lengths on occasions.

The evidence of it was there to this day. The famous inscription, positioned on a semi-circular gable under a window of mullion and transom cross in the old house, so visitors could see it:

This stone is erected to the memory of a much lamented animal who with a beauteous Form possessed those qualities which are esteemed most valuable in the Human Species, Fidelity and Gratitude. And Dying April 20th 1797 aged 11 Years was Interred near this Place.

Alas! poor Fury.

She was a Dog, take her for All in All. Eye shall not look upon her like again.

'What do you think of that then?' he asked the mongrel beside him. 'It's not *your* fate, I'd say, to be remembered with such excitation!'

9

The dog wagged its fan of a tail, shaking its hind quarters.

The trust in its eyes! He thought again of the girl.

It was almost at this point that he had first come across her. That Sunday afternoon, his head throbbing, his tongue apparently coated with fur, after a night in which much claret and whiskey had been consumed.

Then, all of a sudden, the girl stepping out from behind a silver column of birch trees. No sign of her there now. Perhaps the bog, screened from him by huge, shoulder-high, tan-turning ferns, had lured her?

He parted the monumental ferns and peered through at a sight so exquisite that even he, so used to this place, caught his breath in wonder. The soft peat-brown earth of the bog was striated with purple ling, dotted all over with a myriad of dark orange asphodels and tiny cross-leaved heaths, tubular and purple. Away to his right was Bounla Island and the land mass behind it, more blue than anything else, and the lake, gleaming silver.

Lough Derg. Not always either this shade or this serene. Eochy, king of south Connacht and Thomond – who had plucked out his eye to fulfil a promise made to a bard and, in washing the gaping socket, had turned the waters red – had named it Lake of the Bloody Eye. There were times when its waves rose seven feet high in fury.

Turning his attention back to the bog, he spotted her wandering. Wearing a gown he had given her months before, a flouncy garment more than ten years out of date, trimmed with buttons and ribbon bows and made for Harriet, who could never have imagined it being worn in such a setting . . .

'Muráid!' he called out one last time, raising a hand to attract her.

But she had finally caught sight of him and was hurrying in his direction, the wind whipping back the stuff of which her skirt was made against her calves and thighs.

Watching her approach, he remembered his first impression of her – that she was a woman out of her place and time.

Well, with her ash-blonde hair she was an aberration for these parts: a reminder that Vikings had once set up bases near Limerick and plundered these Shannon waters. And left their memory in this tall, strong, lean, blue-eyed girl running towards him through the heather.

A practical woman, you might think, looking at her. She was a dreamer, though. It was her feyness that set her apart as much as her flaxen hair.

But she gave great love.

Trying to push the thought of his dead son into the back of his mind, he whispered: 'Hurry to me, my girl.'

To Muráid Dillon it was as if the extraordinary hues of the wild flowers and the earth and the lake and the land beyond it had been drained away and used to make a luminous aura around the man.

She had convinced herself that she would never see him again, that after the funeral in Athenry Abbey he must have gone over to England for good: now the sight of him waving and calling to her seemed nothing short of miraculous.

'Thank you, thank you!' she said silently, not to God or the Virgin Mary either, since They must surely be displeased with her, but to an as yet unidentified Heavenly accomplice who must be on her side Up There.

Minutes earlier she too had been marvelling at the beauty of the heather. Now it seemed to her merely an irritant, slowing down her progress across the bog.

'What have you got in your hand? Let me see,' he said when, red-faced and panting, she stood before him.

'Red berries. For to put into the house.'

Talking to him after all this time she was aware of the harshness of her intonation in comparison to his. She bit her lip, wishing that she could emulate his own way of

11

speaking, its gentility. Amused, he had told her once that before his marriage he had been described as a man with only one defect, and that a fondness for low company, but the propensity was reflected neither in his vowels nor his choice of words.

In spite of this he had been her lover this last year without anyone in Rossmore or Cloonoon or Shragh or Portumna being aware of the fact.

(Only they were going to know. In the joy of seeing him, she had forgotten that.)

'Are you not going to kiss me?' he demanded, cupping her face in his hand and tilting it upwards.

She shut her eyes automatically, willing her mind to go blank. Instead, her thoughts continued to race obstinately on, the kiss only acting upon them like a whip.

What will he say?

Unlike her mind, her legs did not seem to be functioning, so that she held on to him for stability as well as for affection.

'What is it?'

'It's nothing.'

'You're frightened of our being seen together? There's only himself –' pointing at the dog, sniffing in the ferns. 'But we'll go back to the house anyway.'

'The berries have stained your coat.'

'Damn' dangerous things, berries. The more gaudy they are, the more poisonous. Like a woman.'

'*I* can't be much of a danger to you then!'

He laughed, throwing his head back, startling the dog so that it slunk away.

'It wasn't you I had in mind. Look where you're walking, will you? Cows have been down this way.'

'I was looking at the lake,' she said. 'Yesterday I saw a dead swan on it, and the cygnets swimming around, sorrowing. You must be feeling his loss.'

'Hold on to my hand,' he said. 'Stay close to me. I have great need of you now.'

In many ways Muráid Dillon identified with the community into which she had been born twenty-nine years before. Like everyone else she believed that cows would drink blood if swallows were interfered with, or that crows would bring death to an inhabitant if they flew directly over a house.

But the people who lived in the remnants of *clacháns*, small clusters of farmers' houses which were scattered around in the area close to the lake, thought of her as different; as seeing herself as a cut above them.

They were right for, gentle as she was, she was arrogant in her way, rating her own poeticism and sensitivity above her neighbours' practicality, which she told herself was coarse. She was alone less because her parents were dead and her three brothers long since emigrated to America than because she had elected to stay apart, to reject the advances of the local men who, because of her good looks, had been attracted to her. To realize her dreams – or to attempt to do so – she had looked beyond them as a matter of course.

Like many people who spend too much time on their own she took herself seriously, and the love she finally found even more so, believing it sacrosanct.

'It's nothing,' she had answered, when he had asked what troubled her, but this, of course, was a lie – a huge falsehood; for soon her down-to-earth neighbours would learn of her love, be in a position not only to condemn her behaviour but, much worse, to laugh at it as well.

At the prospect of her relationship being exposed, vilified – the men whose attentions she had scorned nudging each other as she passed, winking, exchanging ribald comments – the colour rose in her cheeks. Something as precious as this love should surely not be laid open to such debasement. She wanted to protect it, to erect a high wall around it, the way they would not be able to sneer.

At the same time she knew that she was powerless. She walked hand-in-hand with her lover knowing full well that the stones with which she had planned to build the wall had been taken from her hands and placed beyond her reach.

They were back at the house.

'You left water boiling.'

And I too distracted to think . . .

Nevertheless, he had been right: it *was* better, far better being inside the house. Here she could tell herself, and almost believe, that she had no need of walls. With him her imagination could soar, transforming the drab interior of the cottage into a much more splendid although somewhat hazy setting: so that she was not in a cottage at all but in a fine palace with blue silk walls and white flounced curtains, and carpets not on the floor but on the walls. There was gilt everywhere and ceilings painted in pastel from which mauve zinc and crystal chandeliers threw down light; and a white dining-room with Wedgwood plates; and portraits of girls in the hall.

She closed the top half of the door in order to further this illusion. In her dreams she was a grand lady with gold-coloured hair powder in her chignon and white stockings with the seams knitted in on her long pale legs.

As she turned from the door she saw herself wearing buckled mules on feet that, in fact, were bare.

She gazed adoringly at her companion. In the dim light he looked much younger than he actually was. It was possible – just – in that sense to envisage the two of them as equals.

'Come here to me,' he said to her.

As soon as she was beside him he began to unfasten the buttons on her gown, fumbling and muttering at his own incompetence when one of his fingers got caught in the ribbon bow on her shoulder.

'Ah, you're a lovely creature,' he said to her when she was naked.

'You love me still?'

These words, which she had always warned herself not to utter, nevertheless slipped out.

One of his hands cupped her breast. He licked the forefinger of the other, dampening her nipple with his spittle.

'I have love for you all right, Muráid.'

'*I* love *you*,' she said.

All the time she was watching his hands – willing herself not to cry out, although she knew she would do so later.

Reminding herself that she had said enough – too much – already.

She must not let him know how much she had missed him this last month because then he would understand that he had captured all of her, and lose interest and go away.

She must not plead: '*Don't leave me ever again.*'

In bed he was surprisingly gentle. She had discovered at the beginning that he was a man who responded to tenderness as well as to passion.

As he made love to her the complicated imagery of grandeur – of wealth and of power – faded out of her mind.

Instead she saw the silver lake and the rocky outcrop on the shore in front of the castle, and then an archway that had not been there before and, beyond that, a strange white city.

The lake was flooding, spilling on to the shore, bearing her through the archway towards the platinum city. As she reached it she realized that it was no longer pure white but tinged with rose-pink. All over its buildings flowers were falling, milky-cream and coral, and there was a gateway, old and fashioned out of a dark metal, and through that the lake, which had turned into a river, rushed.

Trees lined the banks of this river and in the distance ruined houses appeared on each side of a wide clearing.

Beyond the clearing was a hill and on its pinnacle a triangle containing two figures in silhouette.

Apogee . . .

She heard herself cry out.

Afterwards she said, 'I saw the city. Were you happy in St Petersburg?'

'The post was important. The Emperor knew that the serfs would have to be emancipated sooner or later. He was making plans for that . . .'

As usual he had evaded a personal question. Whenever she asked him about Russia he would either talk of politics, or of the landscape of the country in which he had once lived: describing the beauty of the countryside; saying that in winter the snow would have strange blue and yellow and grey tones to it, that these hues contrasted with the brilliant azure of the sky; that in spring the lilacs bloomed, and the cherry trees; or he told her of the splendours of the palaces which he had visited, providing the material for her sleeping and waking dreams.

But he seldom spoke of the people he had met then, or of his children, and he never referred at all to his wife except obliquely.

Today, however, he lapsed into silence. This was unusual. As a rule he could not resist the temptation to tell a good story. More than once she had heard how he and his friends had been quite unjustly accused of murder when the furious wife of a man who had collapsed under the table – appearing in the dining-room at 3 A.M. clad in her night-dress – had failed to realize that the fellow in question was only the worse for drink.

When he remained quiet, the thoughts that had been

16

troubling Muráid earlier came pounding back into her mind. She had no alternative but to tell him, she decided, and the sooner the better, in order to get it over. Even if he were angry after hearing – that cross he wouldn't say a word, but dress and go away . . .

Still, it had to be said.

They were lying side by side on the bed, and he seemed miles and miles away. Wanting but not daring to touch him now she said: 'Ulick . . .'

'What is it, my girl?'

Not looking at him but at the thatched roof over their heads, she said, 'I'm going to have a child.'

Only a month ago the thatching had been reinforced. The straw was slightly green.

It was ages before he answered.

But when at last he did, it was only to say: 'Of course it was bound to happen,' not, by the sound of him, put out in the least, reacting as if her pregnancy was the most predictable, most natural thing in the world.

Which, when you extracted the fear out of it, surely it was?

'You're not cross with me then?'

'How could I be cross with you?'

'I wasn't sure –' she said, faltering.

But he had caught ahold of her hand and he was saying: 'Listen to me, Muráid. This is what I will do . . .' The rich, warm, eloquent voice offered the necessary reassurance, laid down his terms. '. . . house will be yours for life. Money . . . yourself . . . The child . . .'

There was a part of her that rebelled against what he was saying, offended by the contrast between the protection he was offering and the aesthetic quality of her love for him.

Maybe, she thought – searching around in her mind for a more high-minded outcome – maybe this child that you are carrying inside you will grow up to replace the son who has died.

17

To gain the inheritance that had been destined for Dunkellin.

Who then would dare to laugh at her love?

'Are you listening to me, Muráid?'

Another son, she thought. To make up for the son he has lost.

A wondrous dream. She woke from it with the abrupt realization that of course he had a second son already.

She had forgotten all about Hubert.

That my sturdy, handsome son be taken, thought the man on the truckle bed – that *he* should die so prematurely.

Of a complication of disorders affecting the kidneys and the heart. The drink. (But I've drunk more and survived.)

Still, he was like me. A lover of life. Dunkellin. The name they had all given him.

But he was called after myself. The son of whom I was – I *am* – proud. Soldier and politician.

The man who should have been heir. Instead of which . . .

Laugh, not weep, at the irony . . .

When the woman beside him stirred and he looked across at her, momentarily diverted from his pain, he thought that in her after-love languor she looked a little like Harriet. Or like Harriet used to look in the early days of their marriage when they were still happy.

What would Harriet (remarkable Harriet, with fire in her beautiful eyes) say if she knew about Muráid? Something sarcastic? A smart jibe, well-calculated to hurt? Or would she – only daughter of Lord Canning, one-time Prime Minister of Great Britain; a woman who had been a leader of London society in her heyday and who still took her place in it – merely conclude that the *affaire* and its outcome were quite simply unworthy of recognition? To Harriet, Muráid Dillon was merely one of the hundreds of peasant tenants who were obliged to pay her husband rent.

'Ulick . . . ?'

His full title was Ulick John de Burgh, 14th Earl of Clanricarde, Baron Somerhill of Kent. He had been educated at Eton. Had acted as Secretary of State for Foreign Affairs; Captain of the Yeomen of the Guard; Privy Councillor; Lord Lieutenant of County Galway; and Ambassador to Russia.

'Muráid,' he said. 'About the arrangements – the house. Did you listen to what I said?'

1

In that part of East Galway which borders Clare and faces Tipperary across Lough Derg, Eva Dillon was held to be a *scubaide bheag leitheadach*: a conceited little hussy.

The women of the district went further than that, telling each other that Eva was a brazen thing who strutted around like a hen in stubbles, as if she had nothing in her background of which she should have been ashamed.

A few of the women who spoke of her in these terms were the sort that would lash anyone with their tongues, but most of them were kind enough souls and some of them had reached out the hand of friendship to Eva's mother nearly nineteen years ago when the news had got out that the poor creature was in the family way.

Those who had made a point of not turning their backs on Muráid at that time felt betrayed when her daughter grew up and snubbed their own daughters, making it plain that she would look well beyond their sons for a husband.

When their womenfolk were present the men agreed that Eva did indeed behave as if she knew full well the eyes that were upon her. But the minute the women were out of the way they cast sly glances at Eva and said that a man might let the weight of the world drop from his shoulders as he marvelled at her sweetness.

Eva was only of average height but she was slender and long-legged and gave the impression of being taller. Her hands and feet were small, her waist so tiny that she looked as if she were tightly laced into a corset – a garment she had never seen – and her breasts full and firm.

Her face was exceptionally pretty: the cheeks rounded, the nose straight and short and perfectly formed, the mouth rosy, the chin disarmingly dimpled; it had a distinctly thoroughbred air.

But it was her colouring above all that made Eva stand out from the crowd. The people of that place had very pale skin, almost as white as milk, but Eva's complexion was more of a *café-au-lait*. Still, you would expect a person whose eyes were as dark a brown as Eva's, whose eyelashes and eyebrows were nearly black, to have a darker skin.

The shock came when you looked at her hair and saw that it was flaxen. Nordic hair, quite out of keeping with the eyes and the complexion. The contrast made Eva appear somewhat ethereal: there were those who, simply because of her odd colouring, attributed strange powers to the girl.

She intimidated the local people, which was why they gave out about her, as if their words would destroy their fears.

What they could hardly be expected to understand was that Eva saw herself as their uncrowned queen, aloof from but concerned for her subjects; though perhaps it was as well they didn't know what was in her mind since they had one queen too many already, even if the other one was in England.

Eva thought of herself as another Grainne, another lively and wayward girl who had turned her back on many suitors.

Grainne, daughter of Cormac, grandson of Conn of the Hundred Battles, High King of Eriu; Eva, sired by Ulick John de Burgh, born therefore – albeit out of wedlock – into a family whose pedigree could be traced back to the early thirteenth century. From a young age Eva had been made to believe that she was superior because of her noble blood.

'You must always remember that you are a de Burgh,'

Muráid had said. 'The daughter of Lord Clanricarde himself. Isn't that nearly royalty!'

So, not surprisingly, Eva got it into her head that her kingdom spread out before her in Clanricarde country, the way Grainne's had from that ancient royal enclosure on the Hill of Temuir. Eva, though, had never so much as laid eyes on her castle. She had never been invited to picnic by the fabled Earl's Chair in Derry Crag, that elaborate stone seat, cut in the shape of a ship, on which the Earls of Clanricarde traditionally rested their illustrious backsides in the course of a hunt or a shoot. Others in the district – men like Mr Patrick McDermott the miller who had lent Ulick de Burgh a badly needed £1,000 – had been so honoured, but never the erstwhile queen.

At the beginning, when her father was still alive and playing a part in her life, Eva had hoped that he would take her with him to the Big House after one of his visits, but this had not happened. Her father had come and gone at irregular intervals, sometimes stopping for a night or two at the cottage before disappearing for several days or weeks at a stretch.

Even after his death – in that grim dark time when her mother had been so tormented – Eva had expected to be acknowledged by the de Burghs; had waited for her half-brother, Hubert, now 15th Earl of Clanricarde, to come and fetch her to live in the family house.

When he had failed to arrive at the cottage by the lake, Eva had enquired about him. Muráid had explained that Hubert resided in England and never came back to Portumna, not even to attend his own father's funeral.

She had considered writing to Hubert. She was going to school at Shragh and was well able to spell. But when she had suggested this to her mother Muráid had explained that Hubert de Burgh hated the Irish people.

'Aren't I his own sister?' argued Eva.

'Even so,' her mother reasoned. 'He has no interest in us.'

Eva found this hard to believe. She went on hoping that Hubert would materialize and take her off with him, the way she had planned.

Time went by without any word from Hubert. Far from issuing invitations to his half-sister to join him, either up at the house or over in London, he appeared to be oblivious of her existence.

It was a most unsatisfactory state of affairs for an uncrowned queen to live with – especially a sovereign reared as an only child. Eva, having been taught to take herself seriously, did not like being ignored. If Hubert would not come to fetch her into their ancient kingdom, she decided, she would have to get there herself.

The childish resolution turned gradually into a teenage ambition. As time went by Eva's dignity began to depend upon its realization. The truth was that there were those at school who reminded her, too frequently for her liking, that she was a bastard child, the daughter of Ulick, Lord Clanricarde, maybe, but still and all without much to be proud of on the other side.

'I'll be a fine lady yet,' she would vow, 'and then they'll think again.'

This manner of talking alarmed her mother, but then Muráid was a nervous woman.

On this March day, 1886, others too were beginning to lose their nerve. A ripple of fear was running through County Galway, through all of rural Ireland. And with good reason. Due to a series of disastrous farming years, many tenants were unable to pay their rents. Whole families were under threat of being evicted from their homes.

Only the month before in the little town of Woodford a large eviction party in the shape of 150 police accompanied by the Resident Magistrate and the County Inspector and other officials had arrived with the intention of throwing out some of the residents.

It was true that in the first house visited by the party,

that of Mr Stephen Walsh, one of the largest traders in the town, the officials had been disconcerted to find his shop door strongly barred and admittance being refused.

While Mrs Walsh and her children waved handkerchiefs from the drawing-room windows above the shop at the big crowd of sympathizers who had gathered below, crowbars and stones were used to gain entrance. Soon enough the front door gave way and the bailiffs went into the shop and started to clean it out, taking drapery and other goods out into the street.

Poor Mr Walsh had been forced to hand over to the sheriff the full amount of rent for a year, including the running half-gale and £4.4s. costs, all the while protesting about the illegality of the sheriff's proceedings amidst loud cheers of support from the crowd outside.

After that much more had happened, for Mr Francis O'Farrell of Allendara, the next tenant to be approached, decided not to give in to the demands of his landlord unless all tenants in the district got a reduction of five shillings in the pound in the rent due in November.

Again the house had been broken into and the furniture thrown out, with Mrs O'Farrell insisting that only she was entitled to touch her private altar and the religious belongings that went with it.

When the O'Farrells had been evicted the gang of housebreakers had gone on to the residence of Mr John McCabe to carry out similar work.

Sites for ten huts in which evicted people would be required to live had been traced and later on erected. It had been forecast then that there would be many more evictions yet in that district and others unless landlords gave compassionate thought to the plight of tenant farmers, forced to survive on poor land on which furze, heath, ling and bracken abounded. Some farmers did graze cattle on this land; but, thought Muráid, in reality it was only fit for goats.

And it was unrealistic to expect compassion from the

landlords. What did they care about their tenants' vicissitudes? Did they even know about the adverse circumstances in which the farmers were placed? The landlords so often were living over in London, far away from the south-west of Ireland, and perhaps they had forgotten about the kind of grazing there was in East Galway; had no inkling that their tenants' spirits were broken with the poor return they got for the work they put into the land and the small amount that land was capable of producing?

But unless the landlords took care of their tenants there might be massive bloodshed yet. So Muráid said that day to Eva. The topic of further violence emanating out of the rent problem was relevant: only the night before, James Finlay, process-server to the Burkes of Marble Hill and the Lewises of Ballingar, had been murdered.

'After that, who knows what might not happen?'

'We'll be all right down here anyway,' said Eva. 'No one will bring us into it.'

'You're right I'm sure,' Muráid murmured, not looking in the least bit reassured.

'We should only be worrying if my brother Hubert starts bothering us.'

Eva talked like that, as if she and her aristocratic half-brother were on visiting terms. Still, Hubert – Lord Clanricarde, to give him his correct title – was bothering others all right for rent: he an absentee landlord, living in London and never once coming over to see his Irish estates.

Not only bothering by all accounts, but persecuting, showing no mercy towards the recalcitrant, the tardy. Who would have thought that Ulick's son would have been so insensitive and cruel, Muráid asked herself, not daring to put such a question to Eva in case the interrogation fall back on herself.

Wasn't her father exactly the same, Eva would begin; what provision had *he* made for the two of them so that instead of existing in near penury they could have money of their own, no worries about the next meal, and decent clothes on their backs? How different was *he* from Hubert?

Muráid had been through all that before with Eva, not once but many times, and she always tried to explain to her daughter that Ulick, so far from being inconsiderate and callous, had actually been the most benign and tender of men, as well as the most attractive.

'We were well looked after when he was living.'

'He's been dead these last twelve years. And we're still wearing the hand-me-downs he got for you off his wife!'

No, there was no point in talking like that with Eva.

She was tormented over her father, Muráid knew. As a child she had worshipped him and he had shown powerful love for her. They had been close then – almost too close for her own liking. Sometimes Muráid had felt excluded by the strength of the relationship between father and daughter.

That game they had played, with the wooden sticks welded together to concoct a makeshift frame.

'There's a painting for you!' Ulick would say, and the child would peer through the frame at a boat drifting by on the lake, or flowers in the bog. It was from that amusement that Eva had derived her interest in drawing.

They had other interests in common, too – had shared other characteristics. And now Eva was finding it impossible to reconcile the memory of that time with what Ulick had subsequently done.

Or not done . . .

'Ma?'

Where had they got to in the conversation? Muráid groped for the threads. Hubert, that was it – the likelihood of his bothering them . . .

She said: 'We've never been asked for rent. Not like some. I was talking yesterday with Maria Tully and her two sons. They're worried sick in case they'll be thrown

27

out of their house at Kylenemelly. It seems they paid their rent all right but without the abatement that was asked for.'

'Haven't they got Father Coen and Father Egan to help them?'

The two clergymen, Father Patrick Coen, parish priest of nearby Woodford, and Reverend Patrick Egan, the curate, had been inspired by the patriotic Bishop Duggan of Clonfert and were both deeply committed to the cause of the tenantry.

'Yes, but you can't expect them to work miracles,' Muráid observed, hooking the filled kettle on to the idleback and taking advantage of her proximity to warm her hands at the fire.

'They should be praying for them so,' retorted Eva, and off with her out of the house.

At the back of the cottage the Dillon women kept hens. Eva could hear one cackling now, boasting about what she had laid.

There was another one, broody, clucking, when Eva went out of the back, ready, given half a chance, to sit on her eggs until chickens had been hatched.

'Come out of that and quit your chittering,' she said to the hen as she took her off the egg and found an upturned pot to put over her until the broodiness had worn off.

In spite of her words and her actions Eva's manner of acting was gentle – far more sympathetic than her behaviour inside the house – for she had a deep love for birds and animals. This sympathy even extended towards the cantankerous cockerel, despite the suggestive way he would strut towards a chosen hen, eager to copulate at any hour of the day or night with no regard for the sensibility of his owners.

Or the muck beneath his claws! It had been raining heavily earlier in the morning and the ground on which

Eva was stepping was sticky with runny mud and poultry droppings.

Still, she had thirteen eggs, a dozen to sell at the market and one for her mother and herself to fight over, each insisting that it was the other's turn for a treat.

She was bored and irritated by her mother and, at the same time, protective of Muráid. As she packed the eggs destined for the market into their basket she was thinking what a fool her mother was for idolizing the irresponsible man who had seduced and impregnated her and then failed to provide adequately for her and their child.

Muráid, she decided, was a born victim: the kind of woman who courted disaster. It was as well for her that she had a daughter who was by nature strong and invulnerable and immune to the philandering ways of men. Men like her father, who made love and gave false promises to one unfortunate woman while another – his wife – was waiting for him at home.

As always when she thought of her father her throat began to dry up and her eyes to prickle with tears. The antidote to this condition was anger – anger and reflection upon his style of living. She forced herself to consider the money he must have spent, the power he had wielded, the grand travelling he had done, to London and other places.

Even to Russia. She was rather vague about Russia's position on the map of the world and she knew even less about that country's domestic and foreign policies, but she imagined that it was a glamorous sort of a place where a tsar, which was another name for a king, presided over a nation covered in silver snow.

She dimly remembered her father telling her stories of his time there. Weren't all the people rich? Didn't the women wear beautiful clothes made out of satin and silk, with fur-lined cloaks thrown over their shoulders and jewels in their hair? And wasn't he going to take his darling daughter there one day to look at the wonderful paintings?

Except that he could not have done that even if he had lived, she being a bastard child born to a lowly tenant . . .

A few feet away from her the irrepressible cockerel had vacated his customary position on the dunghill and was making his confident way towards the hens.

'Oh, get on with you!' said Eva, momentarily forgetting her affection for him and infuriated by his aggressive male behaviour. 'You bold thing!'

In a rare impulsive gesture she hurled the thirteenth egg at his head.

By the time Eva had sold her eggs, her anger with her father was encompassing men in general. The insolent way they ogled you, as if you too were a commodity that could be bought or sold. Their intentions were so plain you would need to be blind in one eye and unable to see with the other in order to ignore them. Looking for notice. Muttering, 'The dotey little girleen', or 'My sweet contemptible', as you, with your head in the air, went past.

The market had been held at Cloonoon that day and as Eva walked back towards Shragh school she saw another suspect male holding the handle of the pump, bending to drink the water.

He straightened up as she approached and looked at her not so much boldly but as if he were surprised by what he saw.

He was a young man in his early twenties. His hair was dark brown with a tinge of auburn in it and his eyes were a very dark blue. A pale face, not handsome, but not ugly either, with a deep cleft in a rather prominent chin. He was on the tall side and well-built with a good pair of shoulders and a sturdy chest.

Not that any of this was of interest to her one way or the other . . .

Still, he was a stranger in the district and that alone was worthy of being noted. She took a look at his clothes – a thick jacket and breeches that buttoned at the knees, striped stockings and high-buttoned boots, none of it that new – and decided he was from Dublin. There was something in the cut of his garments that looked too stylish for Galway or Limerick or Clare.

But what would he be doing in these parts?

He was still gazing at her, and his expression now was more admiring than startled. He had no cap on his head but his hand went up there, all the same, and groped around as if to seek for one in order to raise it to her.

'Good afternoon,' he had the impertinence to say.

About to stalk past him and settle his hash by ignoring his overture, Eva was betrayed by her own curiosity. Strangers were rarely encountered on this road, especially strangers from Dublin.

She stopped and looked pointedly at the pump.

'Are you finished drinking?'

'Yes, I am,' said the strange young man and she swept past him and went to drink from the pump herself while he stood by and watched her.

At this point they reached a stalemate, both of them wondering what to say next in order to prolong the encounter.

Finally the newcomer said: 'Could I ask you a couple of questions? You should know that I am a reporter down from the *Irish Times* to report upon the evictions. I heard as soon as I got here that a murder had taken place.'

Now that he had spoken more than a few words Eva could tell that the young man did not have a Dublin accent but a Galway one, like her own but with more education in it.

A reporter down from the *Irish Times*? Nothing had

happened before in her lifetime in Shragh or Cloonoon or Rossmore to attract so unusual a visitor.

'There's trouble all right,' conceded Eva. 'But is it surprising, the way the people here are treated?'

'There aren't many signs of prosperity,' the reporter observed, and waited for her to take up his point.

When she had discussed the same subject with her mother earlier in the day Eva had shown less compassion for the plight of the tenants and their families than she actually felt.

'If there *were* signs of prosperity, the value of the farms would only be rated higher and the rents raised,' she said seriously. 'But most people can't afford to be making improvements. You must know that already.'

'Indeed I do,' said the reporter. 'Tell me, is your own family having troubles with rent?'

'*My* family?' echoed Eva, surprised. '*My* family wouldn't have troubles. We're not like everyone else.'

'You're not?'

'I was talking about the *tenants*. My mother and I don't have to pay rent.'

'Why not?'

'It's a long story,' Eva said, 'and I haven't got the time to tell it to you, or the inclination either. I don't even know your name.'

'It's Dan Fahy,' obliged the young man.

He has a nice, rich voice, Eva found herself thinking. And a strong kind of a face . . . The girls round here would go wild for a fellow like that.

But not me – not someone from *my* background.

'Is that so?' she said coolly. 'Well, I must be on my way. Good day to you!'

'Wait a minute –'

But that Eva was not prepared to do. Without another word she turned on her heel and went past the school with the two windows on each side of the porch, walking at a steady pace, turning right, heading down to the lake and home.

Dan Fahy gazed at her retreating back, thinking that he had never seen such a beautiful girl. Not even up in Dublin where gorgeous women paraded in Grafton Street on a Saturday morning, proudly showing off their smart hats and dresses.

This girl wasn't wearing a hat and her wool jersey and its flannel underskirt were not only years out of date but looked as if they had been made for another kind of a woman.

But what she wore was of no consequence. In rags, with dirt on her face, this girl would be any man's fancy.

Intelligent, too – and mysterious. What was that she had said about her family not being like everyone else?

You're a right eejit not to elicit more information out of her, he said to himself crossly.

But how, since she didn't have either the time or the inclination?

Still, isn't your job the gaining and compiling of information?

Meanwhile, your vision of loveliness – a fairy queen you would think, to look at her golden hair – has turned off the road and is gone out of your sight. While you – the great reporter from the *Irish Times* – failed to discover her name!

Eva was also annoyed with herself. Dan Fahy would have been pleased had he known the reason.

In spite of telling herself that he was of no consequence to her, she had felt a distinct pull towards him as they had been talking. Being a country girl she was not ignorant of the facts of life and, while she was able to attribute the sensation to mere carnality –the raw instinct that was in all animals and which human beings too had to accept as being in their nature – the realization that she should experience it at all was disquieting. Attraction to the opposite sex – unless the man in question was truly eligible – was a symptom of that deadly disease: the kind that had destroyed her poor mother.

When she got home, Muráid was not waiting at the door for her as she usually was.

'Ma?'

There was no answer, but Eva heard a low moan coming out of the house. She pushed the door open, calling out again: 'Ma, are you there?'

She was, and seemingly none too happy, although that was nothing new.

What's the matter with her now? thought Eva. Surely she's not still bawling over the loss of my father; and the hard advisory voice within her warned again: 'See where love can get you!'

'Ma?'

Instead of replying her mother only gave a sort of sniff.

'What ails you?' demanded Eva, more exasperated than concerned. 'What are you crying for?'

For now that her eyes had grown accustomed to the variation of light inside the cottage she could see that her mother was in floods of tears.

'Why are you moping like that?'

Confronted by her daughter's severity, Muráid sobbed again.

'Will you whist!' exclaimed Eva crossly. 'And tell me what's up?'

Muráid swallowed and blinked, groping for words.

'The worst thing that could happen! They're putting us out of the house!'

'*What?*'

The older woman nodded and her tears fell on to the dung-strewn floor.

'The rent-warner came while you were out. He said that no rent had been paid for the past twelve years . . .'

'Is it asleep and dreaming you are?' asked Eva,

assimilating what her mother had said. 'Does he not know who we are?'

'I told him that Ulick – that the late lord had given the place to me to live in without paying rent.'

'So then?'

'He said that had nothing to do with the present situation, that he had been ordered by Lord Hubert to collect all outstanding rent. Eva, he wants us to pay twelve years' rent today!'

'And how could we do that?'

'I asked him that myself and he said that if I did not he'd have us out of the house in no time.'

'I'll make him scratch where he doesn't itch yet!' said Eva furiously. 'The cheek of him, talking to you like that. So how did you end it with him?'

"Twasn't I that ended it, but him,' Muráid said sadly. 'He told me that we had until tomorrow to find the money. He's coming back again.'

'Well, then we'll tell him about you and my father and the promises he made. We'll tell him who I am,' Eva declared proudly.

She was quite sure that, properly explained, these assertions would impress the rent-warner and sort the matter out.

The man who came to the Dillons' door the next day did not look impressionable. He was a thin, parsimonious kind of fellow without a pick on him.

'Is your mother in?' he said, not even smiling at Eva.

And why not? she wondered. Weren't men always trying to charm her?

Until now . . .

'We're both in,' Eva said – meaning – I'm here to defend my Ma.

'Would you call her out?'

And then it began, the demand for back rent. A request

35

so preposterous, so unreasonable, that Eva could hardly credit that it was being made.

'Do you not know who we are?' she asked the rent-warner when he drew breath.

'Who are you?' replied the skinny man.

The impudence of him! And the foolishness, not to have found out about the Dillons before arriving at their door.

Eva, as she had stated her intention of doing, gave the rent-warner a full explanation of their relationship to Ulick de Burgh, and the promises he had made.

'So you can be off with you now since we're entitled to live in this house for the rest of our lives without paying rent,' she concluded triumphantly, expecting the man to cower and turn away.

To her amazement, he stood his ground, the expression on his face as inflexible as ever.

'Lord Clanricarde's mistress and her bastard child!' he said, not impressed but sneering. 'Well, I have news for the two of you, for there is no record of His Lordship having made any such provision.'

At this, Eva heard her mother gasp.

'Who says so?'

'I do, Miss Dillon, and before that Lord Hubert said the same. It's only come to his notice lately that two people have been living on his estate without paying rent since his father died. I am acting on his instructions to put you out of the house unless you can do as he asks.'

'And what does Lord Hubert know of our situation? And he spending the money he gets from his tenants in high living in London?'

'That's none of my business, Miss . . .'

'It's not? Well, you go back to Lord Hubert and tell him that my father issued his own instructions in connection with this house.'

And still the thin man did not go away. Instead he stood his ground and his watery blue eyes narrowed.

One of his large-veined hands reached out to the door-post as if to establish his power over the cottage itself.

Over the future of its occupants . . .

'It might interest you to know,' he said deliberately, seeming to take pleasure in his words, 'that the late Lord Clanricarde is reputed to have left other mistresses in these parts and, according to Lord Hubert, an apparently unlimited number of illegitimate children. They have also insisted that promises were made to them. Lord Hubert says that between them they have demanded more from himself than the whole rental he has received from his property in County Galway since his father's death.'

These words seemed to cast an evil spell over the cottage, rendering not only those inside it mute, but all living creatures in the vicinity, so that no dogs would bark or birds sing near that place again.

Then after what seemed like an eternity, somebody – Eva herself? her mother? – whispered: 'God between us and all harm!' and Muráid collapsed on the floor.

After she had got her mother on to the truckle bed and coaxed her out of her faint and into a proper sleep, after the rent-warner had finally gone, Eva thought again of her father. Wherever he was – in purgatory, if not in hell – his conscience must be pricking him about what was going on down below on earth.

It was to be hoped that he too was suffering. He deserved to be punished. But doubtless he had evaded reprisal. It would be like him to have used his charm on the saints so that they would intervene on his behalf and get him into heaven. The women saints would have listened to him, thought Eva angrily. They would have been taken in, just like Ma. Like myself, too, the way I listened to his stories when I was young and was bewitched by his beautiful voice.

Well, I'll not be beguiled again by any man. I'll be hard and strong instead of gentle and yielding. I'll close my heart and my ears to love-calls and *use* men, rather, to advance myself. And when I'm a great lady I'll be able to laugh at the lot of them. Especially my half-brother Hubert.

Still, this wasn't the time for dreaming about the future.

The fact was that she and her mother had to leave the house by the lake within the week. So the rent-warner had confirmed prior to his departure. It was tempting to muse how she might one day get even with people like him.

But in the meantime she had to find a place in which to live.

On the third day, after asking around all over the place, she got an offer to move into a barn at Cloonmoylan, not far from Clondaguav castle where the Burkes, connections of the de Burghs, lived.

The barn was part of a small property rented from the Clanricarde estate by a family called Halloran who were said to be well in with the policemen from the barracks nearby and thought themselves immune from persecution as a result.

'You're a good man,' Eva said to Paddy Halloran when he said that she and her mother could live in the place.

She hated being under obligation to him, or to anyone else. But what option do I have? she asked herself, unaware that Paddy Halloran, too, was in torment over the arrangement, having had opposition from his wife to the Dillons moving in.

'Ah, you're welcome,' Paddy Halloran assured her, knowing that he was not speaking for his wife who had observed the way he had glanced at Eva when the girl had come to the door to offer the eggs laid by her chickens in exchange for a place to live. 'Will you be all right, now, out here in the cold?'

He was a kind man, genuinely concerned about what had happened to the Dillons, and he had been nagged to death by his wife already for taking pity on them, but Eva suspected his motives.

He needn't think that he has any chance of keeping *me* warm himself, she thought, and Paddy Halloran, catching sight of the hardness in her face, retreated from her, puzzled.

A barn for a home! Instead of moving up in the world as she planned, she was actually moving down!

But only for a while. A short while.

Then she, Eva, daughter of Ulick John de Burgh, the 14th Earl of Clanricarde, Baron Somerhill of Kent, would take her rightful place in the world.

And when that happened, men like Paddy Halloran, with the offers of foolishness in their eyes, would discover how much she despised them.

2

The barn was cold and draughty and Muráid pined for her old home. But the spring was mild and the summer better and Father Coen found work for Eva in the house of a widowed lady at Woodford.

Mrs Reardon was 64 and her late husband had spoiled her. In her day, she had been a beautiful woman and she had turned into an elegant, selfish, manipulative lady who wanted a fuss made of her. To her a maid was not so much a hired person but a slave to be at her continual beck and call.

Mrs Reardon lived in a big house with large rooms which overflowed with gloomy mahogany furniture and too many ornaments and fiddly pieces of silver which went green unless frequently polished.

To this house came other elderly ladies who stayed for afternoon tea for which bread had to be cut into fine wisps and butter put on with great care lest a hole be made in the slice, and chocolate cake produced, and afterwards Mrs Reardon made a show of checking what was left over so that her staff would think twice before helping themselves.

'So how are you getting on at Woodford?' Paddy Halloran asked Eva when he met her coming along the road at night, her feet aching and her head throbbing after her day's work.

Eva shrugged.

So that's the way it is, thought Paddy.

'I'll have to get the matchmaker round here and he'll find you a good husband, Eva Dillon, and a home of your own as well,' he said to her teasingly.

Most country marriages were arranged in this manner,

a sensible collaboration between two sets of parents and an emotionally uninvolved middleman.

And what man would say no to Eva, thought Paddy, beaming at the girl.

Eva looked at him coldly.

'I'll have no one find a husband for me, Paddy Halloran,' she retorted. 'I'll arrange that matter myself.'

'What did I tell you about That One?' demanded Paddy's wife when he recounted this conversation to her. 'Mark my words, we'll see her keeping company, walking on these very roads with a man yet, and getting into trouble. You'll be waiting till the cows come home, Paddy Halloran, if you think that girl won't act the same as her mother. It isn't off the ground that Eva Dillon scrapes her loose-living ways!'

'Will you whist, woman!' Paddy said irritably.

It was strange that a man could not do a good turn for anyone without bringing trouble down on his head.

By August of that year trouble of a different kind was fermenting in East Galway. True Irish men and women were beginning to think that, after all, they were not inferior to the well-educated Protestant settlers whom the English regarded as 'Irish of the right sort'.

People were starting to declare that a system under which 10,000 landlords owned or laid claim to 90 per cent of the Irish land was unacceptable and unjust. Landlord–tenant relationships were growing visibly worse.

'There will be more aggrievation yet,' predicted Mrs Reardon to Eva.

Mrs Reardon was going away to the seaside, to Kilkee, for the month of August, and Eva was helping her pack.

Into the trunk went the clothes Mrs Reardon needed for her holiday: elaborate tea-gowns and evening finery and a stockinette bathing costume consisting of a long tunic over drawers which were gathered at the ankles, and a fur coat to ward off the wild Atlantic winds.

Eva took good note of what Mrs Reardon wore because although she was an old lady, as far as fashion was concerned she made sure she was up to date.

'Do you think so?' Eva asked, keeping the conversation going for the sake of her job, although at that stage she was more interested in the contents of Mrs Reardon's trunk than in what was in the minds of the local community.

'So Father Coen says,' Mrs Reardon confirmed, looking around the room to see what else she should take with her.

Her eyes fell on a high-waisted Princess made out of green knitted wool. Why did I have that dress made? she asked herself, for although Mrs Reardon had never had children and was about the same weight and height as Eva this weight, over the years, had repositioned itself around the waist and hips. I should never have ordered a jersey that clings to the figure down to mid-thigh . . .

'There,' she said to Eva, 'you can have this dress,' and thought herself very kind for giving it to the girl.

It more than compensated for the fact that Eva would not be paid for the month of August when the house was closed up. After all, the girl would not be required to do a stroke of work.

'Yes indeed, trouble,' added Mrs Reardon, returning to her earlier theme. 'Take care now, Eva, while I'm away, and don't you be mixing yourself up in what is going on.'

'Indeed I will not,' said Eva quite sincerely.

Queen or no queen, what could *she* do to assist her people's plight?

So when, in mid-August, Eva heard that Thomas Saunders, a member of the pro-tenant Land League, was intending to take a stand against his landlord, the Marquis of Clanricarde, she pricked up her ears.

'He's refusing to pay last year's rent on his holding at Drummin,' Muráid said, having heard the story from Paddy Halloran.

Drummin was two miles from Woodford and a stone's throw from Looscaun.

'Fourteen pounds he owes from last year and with the extra six months that was due this May, that's twenty-one pounds in all,' Muráid went on, even though she was getting no response from Eva.

But on Friday 20 August Paddy Halloran came into the barn with a story that attracted even Eva's attention. Thomas Saunders had barricaded himself into his slated house and now a mighty force of the Royal Irish Constabulary was going to force him out.

'Will you come over and see what's happening?' Paddy asked the women. 'He has the green flag flying over the door!'

'What good will that do him?' Eva wanted to know. 'He'll need more than that to drive off the RIC.'

'Ladles of boiling water mixed with lime to toss out at the assailants!' exclaimed the excited Paddy. 'And there's stores of fuel in the house.'

It was only later, when a triumphant cheer rang out and the story was told that Thomas Saunders and his allies had flung hives of bees down at the RIC, that Eva felt that maybe there *was* a chance for them. If not to win over the authorities, at least to register a valid protest against the way they and others were treated.

At the end of the next day the slated house remained impregnable and people were calling it Saunders' Fort.

'He has the Marquis bate!' Paddy maintained.

Hubert vanquished! Although of course her brother did not yet know about his defeat, being still over in London.

But as the following week went by it began to dawn on

the people of Woodford and Portumna and the districts around that neither the Marquis of Clanricarde nor his agents nor the Royal Irish Constabulary were going to give in.

The authorities it seemed had come to the conclusion that a much larger force and extra materials were going to be needed in order to oust Thomas Saunders and make him pay up.

By the end of that week what amounted to a small army had been assembled in Portumna. Five hundred members of the Royal Irish Constabulary armed with rifles and sword-bayonets, two companies of Her Majesty's Somerset Light Infantry, several score of civilian 'Emergency Men' armed with revolvers, and a fleet of jaunting-cars, brakes, carts and jarveys brought down from Dublin by train to the railhead at Birr.

'Nearly a thousand of them – and only twenty inside the fort!' Paddy Halloran marvelled.

In retaliation the Birr branch of the Land League had issued a manifest forbidding tradesmen to supply provisions or modes of conveyance to the military and police.

Battle, it was understood, would recommence at crack of dawn on 27 August. On that day the Dillons and Mrs Halloran declared their own unspoken armistice and the two families set off for Drummin to see what would happen next.

It was only five A.M., but as they approached the gateway to Thomas Saunders' house Eva saw that a large crowd had already assembled.

In the forefront of it was a vaguely familiar figure. A man – a well-built young man with dark brown hair with a reddish tint to it.

The reporter from the *Irish Times*, Dan Fahy, with a notebook and pencil in his hand and a serious look to his face.

Finding that she was glad to see him again she hastily

reminded herself that there were more exciting things going on this day than the reappearance of a young man who had no position in society, or money either.

He had seen her too, and his expression was grave no more but merry. The hand with the notebook and pencil went up in a gesture of recognition.

Eva did not return the greeting. What was the point? A girl like herself would be foolish to encourage the likes of *him*.

When the news editor told him to go back to East Galway to follow up the evictions story, Dan could hardly believe his luck. The news editor was an irascible man who discouraged rather than fostered the ambitions of aspirant young reporters, judging them, as a breed, to be too clever by half. The more enthusiasm you showed, it was agreed in the newsroom, the more likely you were to get the duller assignments.

Not knowing that the editor himself had been impressed by his earlier reports and had made his views known to the desk, Dan hotfooted it out of the building lest the news editor change his mind.

Word had spread about the unrest in East Galway, not only in Ireland but across the seas. The foreign Press – representatives from France as well as from *The Times* of London – were reputed to have arrived in the country with their sights fixed on the area.

As well as wanting to cover the story, Dan also hoped that he might make contact with the journalists from overseas. Particularly with the representative from *The Times* of London. Ever since he could remember Dan had wanted to work on a big daily newspaper which employed foreign correspondents. The thought of it! Being posted to India! Or to China, or Japan!

He knew well that *The Times* of London was not that sympathetic to the Irish cause, but he was young enough to believe that if he got the chance to work on it then he could ultimately influence its policy for the good of his own land.

He did not confide these ambitions to anyone, least of all the news editor who would have snorted, wanting to know why his own newspaper wasn't enough to satisfy a nonentity like Dan Fahy.

As if a desire for knowledge about foreign places and people should be quashed instead of being satisfied and satisfied quickly, before he, Dan, became an old man of fifty like his derider and lost his inquisitive zest!

Dan was already twenty-two, which seemed to him quite an advanced age, and although part of him understood only too well that he was not yet experienced enough to be hired even as a junior reporter by an institution like *The Times* of London, let alone get an overseas posting, the other part of him was straining to be gone.

Thinking of his assignment in East Galway as one step along the road he was planning to travel, he arrived there in a fair old state of euphoria, thrilled to be in the thick of things.

When he caught sight of the beautiful girl he had encountered on his original visit he was elated. She had not observed him yet but since she, like everyone else, would be bound to be stopping by Thomas Saunders' gate for some time yet, he would make his presence known to her in due course, and familiarize himself not only with her story but with the lady's name!

The crowd at the gate was swelling by the minute as men, women and children of the district turned up, gesticulating and surmising and waiting impatiently for signs of the evicting party.

Several trees had been felled and dragged across the road to inhibit the party's progress. The rumour that a battering ram was to be used in the operation was augmented by information that the bridge of

Kilmanahan had been destroyed to prevent access at that point.

And then something happened that made more than one of those present think that God Himself had intervened on behalf of the men inside the fort.

Bells rang out – the bells of nearby Looscaun church, and Mrs Halloran muttered: 'Jesus, Mary and Joseph!' and immediately afterwards crossed herself lest the Almighty be angry at the indiscriminate use she had made of these sacred names.

The Land League must have look-outs posted all over the place and the priests must be helping them, Eva thought, and the ringing of the bells be intended to warn Thomas Saunders and the others that the evicting party has started out from Portumna. As everyone else came to the same conclusion the crowd cheered lustily.

'There's Father Coen now,' said Paddy Halloran, 'and Father Egan beside him.'

Hot on the heels of the two clerics came a man, panting and gasping for breath but bringing the news that the authorities had brought planks along with them, with which they had erected a temporary bridge to replace the one found broken. There was much conjecture about the real size of the army which was advancing. A Captain Hamilton was said to be leading forty emergency men to boost the numbers of police and infantry.

It was at that stage that Eva found herself standing next to Dan Fahy who was conducting an interview with Father Coen.

'. . . calling it the Land War,' the priest was saying to Dan, frowning as he spoke and looking as concerned as he had done when he had called on the Dillons after their own eviction.

'Ah, Eva girl,' Father Coen greeted her when he became aware of her presence. 'And how is Mrs Reardon? Mr Fahy, this is someone you should be speaking to while you're here. A young girl and her mother thrown out of their home!'

Dan Fahy started, though Eva wasn't sure whether this was due to Father Coen's account of the Dillons' plight, or to the sight of herself so close to him.

Either way, Eva was none too pleased that as a result of Father Coen's revelation the young man beside her would see her in the role of victim rather than victor. She drew herself up to indicate to Dan Fahy that even if she had no control over her rights of residence she could cope with this encounter; wishing that she could maintain a dignified silence rather than, out of respect for his cloth, being obliged to talk back to the priest.

'Mrs Reardon is fine,' she said, 'and my mother and I are doing well.'

'Living in that cold barn!' said the good priest, drawing further unwanted attention to the Dillons' situation, to Dan Fahy's obvious interest.

Any minute now he'll be writing it all down in his book and making eejits out of us by putting our names in the *Irish Times*, thought Eva, furious at this prospect.

Such a thing must not be allowed to happen. She would have to talk to Dan Fahy privately to ensure that it did not.

'A barn, did you say?' queried Dan, as Eva might have expected. But that was as far as he got.

'Will you look at that!' someone shouted from the crowd and people began to roar in anger as the evicting party appeared along the road.

It was a strange phenomenon, they all agreed, for the small army – carrying, as rumoured, a battering ram – was proceeding under the protection of a shelter shed.

The crowd began to press back, turning itself into a gargantuan human wall in front of Saunders' gate.

Squeezed between fat Mrs Halloran on the one hand, and a group of oratorical youths on the other, Eva lost sight of Muráid.

We'll be squashed to death for sure, she thought, and stumbled, catching her foot in a clump of the dark green reedy grasses that grew on the side of the road.

'You're all right,' a voice reassured her, and a strong hand was under her elbow yanking her out of the crowd. 'You're all right now . . .'

'I was always all right,' Eva said to Dan Fahy, lest he get any other ideas. But he had got her out of the worst of it, and even as she spoke she was retreating with him from the human wall and the advancing party.

With all the yelling that was going on from the crowd it was pointless even attempting to speak again. Dan mouthed: 'Up there,' and gestured towards a stone wall-stile.

Perched on the wooden crossbar, Eva had a perfect view of the evicting party – carriage-loads of armed police, military and civilian supporters, officers on horseback darting hither and thither, with their red coats making a blaze of colour and, at the procession's end, carts loaded with baulks, planks, pickaxes, crossbars and sledgehammers. In one cart was a strange object which she presumed was the battering ram.

The din was now tremendous. As well as the noise from the crowd the church bells were ringing again and horns were blowing.

It was not the moment to talk to Dan Fahy about keeping her name out of his paper.

By midday it was all over. Stones, sticks, boat-hooks, gaffs and yet more bees had been hurled from the roof by Thomas Saunders and his supporters, along with another load of boiling water and lime.

But finally, after three ineffective efforts to gain entrance, police with drawn swords climbed ladders and got into the house, and the men inside it were arrested and taken to Galway Jail.

All the while Dan Fahy had been scribbling away in his

notebook. Eva concluded that he had gathered enough information not for just one but for several articles and would hardly need more from herself.

But she was wrong: Dan was still interested in the Dillons' eviction. The minute he closed his notebook he asked her if they could have a quiet chat.

'We can, but maybe not along the lines you're thinking of,' she said to him. 'Come down the road with me.'

Mrs Halloran, overhearing this remark, nodded knowingly to her husband. Still, Dan found Eva's attitude more aggressive than seductive. Beautiful she might be, and interesting, but he was not altogether sure that he liked her.

It was the journalist in him who said: 'I will,' and with Mrs Halloran's eyes burning into their backs they moved away from the crowd.

'Listen to me, I don't want you putting my name into your paper,' Eva began as they walked along the road.

'But I don't even *know* your name, not your full name anyway,' Dan protested, thinking, like a lot of other people, that this was a conceited type of a girl.

Had someone told him that Eva was known in the district not so frequently by her name as by The Leitheadach, he would have wholeheartedly agreed with the general consensus.

'But now that you mention it I could easily find it out. Father Coen would tell me.'

She glared at him. When she was angry a film seemed to form over her eyes as if the fury in them was so fierce that a curtain had to be drawn over it.

'He won't tell you.'

'He would. And you'd make a right fool of yourself if you tried to warn him off.'

On one side of them was an open wooden field-gate. She swung away from him into the field beyond.

Determined not to let her evade him he followed doggedly.

'You can be off with yourself,' she shouted over her shoulder at him, and quickened her pace until she was almost running.

Dan came after her until they reached a haggard and dilapidated farmhouse where nobody seemed to live. She stopped there and turned to him.

'I don't know why you're moping after me like a stray ass, but 'twill do you no good,' Eva said, rudely. 'You'll get nothing for it.'

'Look,' Dan said, 'I'm not going to write unsympathetically about you – and if you feel that strongly about it, I won't mention you at all. It may surprise you to know that the events at Saunders' Fort this day have been more important as far as the *Irish Times* is concerned than any other eviction – including your own!'

Then what are you doing chasing after me? he expected her to ask. He was somewhat confused himself about his motives and was relieved when, instead of speaking, she sat on the grass and distanced herself from him, gazing at a brown stream meandering a few feet away, and the little tuft of an island that was on it, with a couple of scrawny trees.

And then he spotted the cat. A black cat . . . It was known that if you ground down the liver of a black cat into a powder you would end up with an aphrodisiac so powerful it would make the most timid lover wild!

He had a mad thought. What would happen, he speculated, if he were to kill the cat and feed such a meal to the girl sitting over there on the grass . . . ? What kind of a personality would she turn into? And how easy would it be to actually catch the cat . . . ?

Then he noticed that the cat was limping badly. It had probably been abandoned by its owners when they had moved on, as was the custom under such circumstances.

Having no serious intention of molesting the creature –

51

black cats, anyway, were lucky – he drew Eva's attention to it by raising his arm and pointing.

'You've frightened it!' she said furiously before he had a chance to speak. 'It's running away . . .'

And to his amazement she was up on her feet again and rushing after the cat.

The creature, in turn, was limping in the direction of the river. It won't let her near it, Dan thought. He had his countryman's distrust of cats. Everyone knew how intelligent they were, the way they possessed reason and understood human conversation, but if you looked at a cat that had wiped its face with its paws you would see the first person in the household destined to die.

No wonder visitors denied them a blessing, calling out: 'God save all here but the cat.'

But this cat, having fled from himself, seemed to be well-disposed towards his companion who had picked it up in her arms and was carrying it back across the field as tenderly as if it were a baby.

'It's starving,' she said when she reached where Dan had slumped down in the grass.

As if the cat's hunger was his fault!

'Have you not got any bread with you?'

Does she think I'm a baker by profession or what? Dan asked himself.

Either that or she had eyes that could bore through into your pocket where, by sheer coincidence, he had several pieces of bread with butter on them and thick wedges of ham to make them into a suitable meal for lunch.

Not to mention a hunk of cheese.

Much too good for a cat!

Nevertheless, he found himself rooting in his pocket and laying his lunch on the grass.

And as he might have expected, the girl reached out and extracted the ham out of the sandwich and fed it to her charge.

The cat ate ravenously, which was hardly surprising.

What was much more noteworthy, he thought, was the change that had taken place in beautiful Eva.

Her anger was gone. For the first time he saw the softness in her. When, holding out her hand for another bit of ham, she glanced up and their eyes met, he saw that she was crying.

What kind of a girl was she that could care so deeply about the fate of a cat and not seem to give one jot for anything else?

'Don't cry,' he said to her gently and, producing a crumpled and rather grubby handkerchief from his pocket, he gave it to her, so she could wipe her eyes.

To allow her privacy in which to recover her composure he got up and walked a few paces away. In the distance he could see the slated roof of Saunders' Fort. In which, he thought, if fate had dictated otherwise, I might be living now. Because that was the irony which he had chosen not to reveal to the news editor when he had been selected for this job. The fact that in the 1860s his own family had lived in a cottage on that same land now occupied by Thomas Saunders. And had themselves been evicted under less dramatic circumstances for failing to pay their rent.

He had heard the details many a time from his parents. The girl and he had more in common than she realized, he thought. Not only had both their families suffered eviction, but both their fathers were dead.

It occurred to him again that he still did not know the name of the girl's father. Maybe she would trust him enough now to tell it to him?

What harm was there in asking?

Half expecting her to snap at him again he ventured: 'You never did tell me your full name.'

But again she surprised him. When he turned round to look at her he saw that there was pride, not anger, on her face.

'I am the daughter of Ulick de Burgh,' she said haughtily. 'I am Lord Clanricarde's child.'

Was she mad, Dan wondered, lost in dreams; so pretentious in her fantasies that she was making up this story?

Or was she really the daughter of the very man who had thrown his parents out of their house?

'Are you indeed?'

'I am.'

'So your name is Eva de Burgh?'

She paused only for a couple of seconds. Then – 'They call me Eva Dillon,' she said reluctantly. 'My parents were not wed.'

That makes more sense of it, thought Dan. The old fellow was said to have been a womanizer. But he must have been well on in his life when he fathered this girl.

'Eva Dillon,' he repeated.

But daughter of the very man who had put his own parents out of their home.

He wouldn't tell her that – not now, not yet.

Still clutching the black cat in her arms – itself a revelation, the way the creature trusted her and was making no struggle to escape – Eva got to her feet, ready, it was obvious, to leave.

'Don't go.'

Ignoring him, she began to make her way back to the road.

Following her again, Dan suggested: 'You should come up to Dublin and find work there. It might be better for you.'

'I have my mother here.'

'Bring her too,' he said. 'I could help you find work.'

'You?' she said, derisively. 'And what power do you have to be finding anyone work?'

'I could get you a job in the Gresham Hotel. One of the

Board of Directors is a Cork man who knew my father well . . .'

'Hm!' she said, sniffing, but more interested than before. 'And what is the Cork man's name?'

'Never mind his name!' said Dan, reaching the end of his patience with her arrogance. 'It's *my* name you should keep in your head, along with my address.'

He tore off a piece of paper from his notebook and scribbled on it.

'Here. Keep this. You may need it yet.'

She took the paper from him and, without looking at it, stuffed it into the neck of her dress, infuriating him even more, edging him towards cruelty.

'If you're down on your luck as you seem to be,' he said, 'what will you do with that cat?'

She stopped and looked up at him, holding the cat into her, stroking its black head.

'I'll have Mrs Reardon, the widow I work for, take the creature in,' she told him. 'She's due back in a couple of days.'

'Won't she mind?'

Eva only laughed. Was she putting a good face on things, Dan wondered, pretending to have more influence with her employer than she really had, or could she in fact dictate the terms?

It was hard to tell. She was an exasperating piece of goods altogether, full of nonsense and yet able to invoke pity in you.

And he was wasting valuable time with her when he could be back in Portumna, making contacts with journalists there.

'You can rest assured that I *won't* be putting your name in the paper,' he said to her as they parted.

A normal girl would have thanked him, he thought. Eva Dillon merely nodded, as if that was the least he could do.

3

Having put Dan's address away in a box on the premise that you never knew when it or he might be useful, Eva told herself to forget him otherwise.

The black cat, conversely, remained in the forefront of her mind and, after Eva had extracted a large thorn from one of its back pads, was duly installed at her insistence at Mrs Reardon's house.

August turned into September and there were black sloes on the bushes, and red haws, but the blackberries were still too small and too bitter to eat.

October was rainy. The barn in which the Dillons lived leaked and Eva became aware of her mother's persistent cough.

What would they do when winter came and they couldn't light a fire? Eva wondered. As it was the two women huddled in bed, shivering, when Eva got home from work.

To complicate matters further Mrs Reardon wanted Eva to live in, and offered as enticement a warm room up at the top of her house.

'How could I leave my ma?' was Eva's reply to that, although the room was very tempting.

But she only had to look at Muráid to know that she could not desert her. Her mother had visibly declined since being put out of her home. She would go to pieces entirely, Eva decided, if she were left to live on her own.

'I can't live in,' she told Mrs Reardon, and the widow woman sulked.

This was a pity because lately Eva had been doing well out of Mrs Reardon. The latter had fattened out during her holiday at Kilkee and as a result had given Eva several more of her dresses, the ones that did not fit.

She had six altogether now, including an evening dress with a large bustle and a heart-shaped neckline caught with flowers on one side. These cast-off gowns made up a wardrobe which, although it hung from a peg in a barn wall, would form the basis of what she would need when she went into society.

So Eva fantasized, looking at her clothes, imagining herself making an entrance, descending a stairway that opened out into a great hall where elegantly dressed men and women were assembling to greet her at a ball.

More often than not this ball took place at Portumna castle house, she having been received with acclaim into her own family. She could not be specific about the setting, having not yet been inside this house, or even glimpsed it, for it was well hidden by trees. She glossed over what the rooms would be like and concentrated instead on the men and women who would be present.

They were all handsome people, as a matter of course, and exquisitely costumed. Amongst them was her brother Hubert who, for the purpose of her fantasy, had undergone a change in personality and was less sinister than benevolent and certainly delighted to welcome her.

Sometimes she arrived at the ball on the arm of the most eligible of all the men. But other times, far gone into dreamland, she envisaged being escorted by her father, he being back from the grave and thrilled to have his gorgeous daughter present to show off and boast about.

While she thought of such things, another part of her mind was storing away pieces of information about Mrs Reardon and her household which would assist her own transition into a Great Lady. The fact that obvious use of rouge or scent was incorrect. That hair should be dressed very simply and close to the head. Points of etiquette: amongst them the necessity for a gentlewoman to sit straight-backed at the table and to leave it hungry rather than, as Eva had hitherto imagined, satisfactorily replete. Mrs Reardon herself emphasized this criterion, while appearing to exempt herself from it altogether, eating three or four baked potatoes with her roast beef and large helpings of blackberry pudding sprinkled with sugar and nutmeg while her staff in the kitchen dined off boiling oatenmeal and shredded cabbage cooked with butter and salt.

Let her eat till she bursts, thought Eva – I'll have even more dresses then.

But in the meantime winter was coming, and she had only a thin shawl to put over her everyday clothes in order to keep her warm. November, which could surprise you with its mildness, came in that year in a truculent state, spitting rain and wheezing bitter winds. In East Galway and in other parts of Ireland where resistance to rent-demands, now known as the Plan of Campaign, had resulted in eviction, former tenants were having to depend on the charity of friends or of relations at home or abroad to supplement the small amount of money the Land League could afford to let them have. Some people were resorting to using the roadside, or 'the long acre', as it came to be called, for grazing for their stock; others, in a worse situation, were sleeping rough. When Eva walked home from Mrs Reardon's house in the evening there were cows and sheep straggling over the road and, once, a whole family huddled together under a leafless tree.

It was at this time that Paddy Halloran, too, got into trouble. Earlier in the year the Hallorans had built a two-storey house at a cost of £150, a third of which Paddy had been able to raise as a loan from the Board of Works.

But then the Board had refused to let him have the last £10 instalment. Compelled by his wife to have the slated roof put on before winter really set in, Paddy had sold one cow, bought his materials, and got the work finished.

As he said to Eva, all would have been well had the two other cows not taken sick from a strange complaint and died within the month, leaving their owner without milk and cheese and buttermilk to sell from which to pay the rent.

'Any minute now Mr Frank Joyce himself will be after me,' he said gloomily, referring to Lord Clanricarde's agent who had set up an office in Portumna to deal with low-rent tenants.

'What will my mother say if she hears this, and she looking so poorly?' mused Eva aloud.

'The flesh has walked off her lately,' agreed Paddy. 'Ah sure, listen to me, maybe we'll get away with it yet.'

But Paddy was proved wrong in his optimism. Summoned to Portumna, he returned from the Low-Rent Office ashen-faced and disturbed.

I wouldn't take a lease of *his* life, Eva thought when he came to the barn to seek her out.

'What happened in Portumna?' she whispered, not wanting Muráid, who was dozing in a corner, to hear what she and Paddy said.

'I'm destroyed with talking,' he said in an equally low voice. 'And they not listening to half the words I said, except for one time . . .'

'When was that?'

He swallowed, putting his head down and gazing at his feet.

'What *is* it?' she demanded, thinking, what story of his caught their attention in Portumna?

And he muttered, so softly she was only just able to hear: 'I said I'd given you shelter. I got an extension of two months to pay the rent. But –'

'Yes?'

'There was a condition attached to the offer. Eva – *I have to put you out.*'

* * *

Even her attempt to be quiet failed. When she turned from Paddy, Muráid was standing in front of her, having heard precisely what he had said.

'We'd better go,' she said dully.

'We will not go!' Eva almost shouted. 'Now listen to me, Ma. Tomorrow you and I will go to Portumna and talk to the agent ourselves. We'll tell him the whole story. They say that Mr Frank Joyce wouldn't say boo to a goose if he didn't have to, so maybe we'll talk him round. Come in from the wind, will you? You'll get your death in the cold.'

It was nine miles from Looscaun to Portumna. Paddy had been persuaded to tell Mrs Reardon what had happened, and Eva and Muráid set off on their mission on foot.

Rain belted down on their bare heads and a strong wind lashed at their faces, but after four miles a woman gave them a ride in her carriage and dropped them outside the Catholic church where she stopped to say a prayer.

Although Eva had been reared in this area, it was the first time she had actually been into Portumna itself. Here was the castle-home of her ancestors – and the remains of their original castle which had been partly burnt, as well as her father's burial ground in the nearby Augustinian Priory.

But there was no time to dwell on any of that – or to wonder what it would be like to be a Great Lady breakfasting in Taylor's smart hotel either. She had other more pressing matters on her mind.

'Come *on*,' she said to her mother who was standing with an empty look on her face as if she were thinking of long ago things. 'We must hurry.'

A long queue had already formed outside the Low-Rent Office, men and women shivering in the winter blast, apprehension written all over their pale faces.

'We'll be here all night,' Muráid said in the beaten, resigned voice that always infuriated her daughter.

'We will not so!' said Eva decisively. 'I'll see we get in,' and marching ahead of her mother she walked up to the front of the queue.

A mutter went up from the line.

'Will you look at that one?'

'Did you ever see the like?'

But these murmurs of protestation came from the women not the men. The three men at the head of the queue remained silent, their faces reddening as Dan Fahy's had when Eva came purposefully up.

'Ma?'

'I'm coming,' Muráid said, blushing too at the temerity of her daughter and looking in Eva's opinion for all the world like a dog in expectation of a blow.

And indeed at times like these she did want to hit her mother and make her stand up for herself and go and take what she wanted out of life instead of waiting for it to strike her.

'Squeeze in here beside me,' she ordered Muráid, and the three acquiescent men moved back from their position outside the agent's door to let the newcomers in.

After a short time the door opened and a woman in a black shawl came out weeping.

'The poor creature – 'Muráid was beginning, but Eva had taken her by the arm and was marching her into the agent's office.

There were two people inside the room: a young man wrapped in a long, loose Inverness cape, who was sitting in front of a table, and another, older, more familiar figure looming up behind him.

Mr Frank Joyce, doubtless, and certainly his odious rent-warner friend, Eva concluded. The rent-warner looked far more menacing than the agent, but the latter had a revolver by his right hand which surprised even Eva.

Could it be loaded? Conscious that her mother was trembling, Eva stuck her chin up and transferred her eyes

61

from the gun to the two men, whose own eyes were already fixed on her.

'*Dia daoibh*,' said Eva, out to take the initiative not only by greeting the pair of them first, but also by doing so in Irish. Most people these days didn't even speak their own language, let alone dare to utter a few words in it to representatives of their enemies and, as she had anticipated, Mr Frank Joyce looked gratifyingly surprised.

He nodded, and drew himself up in the manner of a rather young man who is trying to look older than his years.

'Your names?' he asked in a voice that was attempting to be stern.

Before Eva could answer, the rent-warner stepped forward and whispered in Mr Joyce's ear. Whatever he said seemed to surprise the agent even more than her greeting. His eyes widened and his eyebrows shot upwards as if in search of his receding hairline.

'I see. I see,' said Mr Joyce, and he fiddled with the pile of papers in front of him on the table, looking neither at them nor at the two women but at a spot to the right of the pair of them. Only the space there was bare . . .

The rent-warner's told him who we are, thought Eva, watching the agent's reaction. Now I will confirm it.

'Mr Joyce, I am the daughter of the late Lord Clanricarde, Ulick de Burgh's child,' she said, and her young, clear voice rang out proudly with the declaration. 'And this is my mother, Muráid Dillon, for whom my father promised to provide for the rest of her life.'

Still the agent avoided looking at her. She got the impression of a hunted man casting around him in urgent search of a refuge.

'So I understand,' he said finally. 'So I have been informed.'

'Then you should also have been told that we were wrongly evicted from our own home earlier in this year and are now threatened with eviction again, having been housed by Mr Halloran.'

Why wouldn't he look up at her, the way she could mesmerize him with her beauty? And why did she have no such effect on the rent-warner himself, leering behind the agent?

'It was not a wrongful eviction,' said Mr Frank Joyce, in an odd voice from which all emotion had been drained. 'Orders had been given. My predecessor had no alternative but to carry them out.'

'And you have no alternative but to see justice done,' Eva said, forgetting the loaded gun and stepping close up to the table, willing the agent to face her. 'Instead of threatening to put us out of Mr Halloran's barn you should take steps now to reinstate us in our original house.'

Then, at last, Mr Joyce raised his eyes and looked into her large brown ones. His own eyes were laden with embarrassment and grief.

'I can't reinstate you,' he said miserably. 'And I can't allow you to stay in Mr Halloran's barn either. I am only an employee of Lord Hubert's, like my predecessor, and I have no power of my own in your case or in anyone else's. I am acting under orders. I am very sorry – more sorry than I can ever say – but you will have to leave the barn. I will take it upon myself to let you stay there for another few weeks, during which time you may be able to make other arrangements for yourselves out of this estate. But you have to be out by Christmas.'

As these words sank in, the rent-warner moved as if to eject the women out of the room. That was the impression Eva got, and Mr Frank Joyce must have had the same feeling, for he raised his right hand and shook his head at the other man. Whose triumphant expression was more than Eva could bear. She wanted to tear at his face, to scrape off the hateful mask of success, to draw blood, to see humiliation in the place of victory.

But the rent-warner had been arrested in his tracks and was still too far out of her range, on the other side of the table.

Far closer to her was Mr Frank Joyce.

'To hell with you then!' Eva hissed at him, and he shrank before her anger. 'For that is all you deserve. God blast you!'

'Eva!' protested Muráid weakly.

But Eva had stepped right up to the table and had her two hands on the edge of it. As Mr Joyce gazed up at her, seemingly hypnotized, she spat into his face.

'My God, I'll settle your hash for you!'

The furious exclamation emanated not from Mr Joyce but from the rent-warner who was reaching out to take a hold of Eva and would have manhandled her had the agent not intervened.

'That's enough,' he said. 'Let them go,' wiping the spittle from his face and adding, more to himself than to his companion as the two women retreated: 'This damn' position! I'll not be in it for long.'

The encounter, which put his untenable position into perspective for Mr Joyce, also enabled Eva to think more clearly.

Under her rage and concern for their immediate welfare, her mind was ticking away, detecting in the orders issued to Mr Frank Joyce and the rent-warner the direct involvement of Hubert.

Until then she had thought of her half-brother as a landlord who strove to extort from his tenants the maximum possible rent. She had realized he was ruthless in this pursuit: inflexible, conveniently closing his eyes to the fact that, in the past, it had been traditional for landlords with any claim to humanity to permit rent abatement in bad times.

But these days other absentee landlords were being equally heartless: he was not alone in that. All the same, other landlords did occasionally visit their Irish estates, whilst Hubert never did so. He had not even attended his own father's funeral when the older man's body had been taken home to Portumna after his death in London. That was very odd.

But maybe even odder was the way her half-brother was involving himself in Muráid and her own evictions. Orders had been given to this end. So Mr Frank Joyce had said: 'I am only acting under orders.'

Yet in the case of other tenants, Mr Joyce – as Eva knew well – had more discretionary powers. Paddy Halloran had been given two whole months in which to find his overdue rent.

On one condition: that he threw Eva and Muráid out.

But why should such vindictive measures be taken against Ma and myself? Eva wondered.

Because Hubert loved his own mother so much that he could not bear his father to have taken another mistress and so he sought revenge upon this woman and her child? Was that the reason?

But if the rent-warner is to be believed, my father was a notorious womanizer, with many other bastard children.

So why focus on us?

This was the time for action, though, not for speculation. Eva's next move was to attempt to find them another substitute home.

Demand for Land League-funded eviction huts was growing daily. The League could not promise shelter in a hurry – only a coupon which Eva was able to exchange for goods in certain shops. Still the Poor Law Union too provided Outdoor Relief in proportion to the size of evicted tenants' families, and Eva applied for that.

But they had no immediate prospect of a roof over their heads. Those who would have helped in the past had already assisted others and had no more room for Eva and Muráid.

The week before they were due to leave the Hallorans' barn, Eva asked Mrs Reardon if she could take both of them in.

'Both of you?' queried Mrs Reardon somewhat vaguely.

Mrs Reardon's mind was elsewhere. A man of her own age – a Mr Danaher, whom she had met in Kilkee – had been out to Woodford to visit her. Although it would have seemed improbable to Eva, Mrs Reardon had fallen in love. She had every reason to believe that Mr Danaher – a lonely man who enjoyed female company and card-games, at which she herself excelled – was going to propose.

'Your mother as well?' she asked Eva, without very much interest. 'Oh, no, I don't think so.'

'But we have nowhere else to go,' the girl persisted.

'Not both of you,' said Mrs Reardon, getting up. 'I think that's Mr Danaher. No Eva, not your mother – I couldn't have her here.'

And so – until they could move into an eviction hut – they were ready for the road: as people in that place said, they would have to stick their heads up wherever they could. Paddy Halloran, stricken with guilt, put up a shelter for them out of a rail and an old gate with bags on it, and the truckle bed from their old home tucked in under it along with a table and stool.

They were not alone in their misery. Others on the road spoke of the frustration they felt at the throwing down of the good houses they had occupied and the wanton destruction of property and agricultural imple-ments: the way crops of turnips and mangels had been eaten and trampled on by cattle turned into the fields; now furze and ling were beginning to encroach upon fences and water-courses.

There were others who were cold, like them, and damp.

There were other evicted tenants who expressed their hatred for Hubert, Lord Clanricarde, that winter of 1886.

But no other woman on the road confessed that she too had been Lord Ulick's mistress. No boy or girl, man or woman, professed to be his child.

Meanwhile Eva continued to work for Mrs Reardon, leaving Muráid alone in the shelter during the day. Her mother was coughing more frequently now and was thinner than ever, although Eva was trying to fatten her with left-over food which, with increasing recklessness, she stole without a qualm from her employer's pantry when the cook was out of the way.

Christmas was almost upon them and still there was no news from the Land League about a vacant hut. Still, Mrs Reardon, who would herself be dining off spiced roast beef on the following day, presented Eva with a gift of corned beef and told her to take one item of her choice from the cakes, puddings and pies which were being made ready on Christmas Eve.

That night as she walked to the shelter she saw that candles fixed in a sconce made out of a turnip or a piggin filled with bran or flour had been placed by the man of the house in the principal windows – one for himself, one for his wife and one for each of the grandparents who lived alongside them. Some families had lit three candles in honour of the Holy Family to indicate that those who had found no room in the inn at Bethlehem would be welcome in this house.

'I brought us some food home,' said Eva to Muráid, thinking she would be hungry.

Christmas Eve was a fast day and most people did not eat at all until the main meal.

Muráid shook her head.

'Ah, Ma!' said Eva. 'What ails you?'

Instead of answering Muráid coughed, gasped and, to Eva's horror, retched and brought up blood.

'Have you the 'flu?' cried Eva.

Two years before there had been a severe epidemic of influenza and everyone was conscious of the dangers of this illness.

'I'll run over to the Hallorans,' Eva went on, 'and see if I can get some flax seed off them.'

All the authorities maintained that flax seed contained a mucilaginous principle which, when added to boiling water, would soothe irritation.

But the Hallorans could not help in this respect, although Paddy insisted that stout mulled with a red hot poker or *poitín* sweetened with honey was a more palatable form of treatment for 'flu.

'Is there stout or *poitín* in the house?' asked Eva promptly.

Paddy shook his head. 'I was only suggesting –' he was beginning to say, but Eva, with a muttered exclamation, had turned on her heel and was off.

It was getting on for eleven o'clock, but she half-ran, half-walked back to Mrs Reardon's, coughing herself as she went with the cold air that was getting into her throat.

That Old One will be in bed by now, she thought as she went, and I'll have to get her out.

As luck would have it Mrs Reardon was not in bed, but was preparing to go to Midnight Mass with her new suitor.

'Well, Eva, what is it?' said Mrs Reardon, not looking too pleased to see the girl at the house.

'My mother is coughing blood,' said Eva bluntly. 'I'm looking for *poitín* or stout.'

'*Poitín!*' exclaimed Mrs Reardon, raising her eyes to Heaven at the mere mention of the illegal brew. 'What next, I ask you!'

'Coughing blood?' enquired Mr Danaher, far more gently. 'That is a serious matter. Where is your mother at this moment?'

And the Dillons' story came out. When it was told, Mr Danaher looked sad and serious.

'Did you not know about this situation, Mrs Reardon?' he asked and, when the widow did not reply, he gave Eva a pitying glance and said he would go with her this minute in his carriage to fetch her mother up to the house.

'*Here?*' demanded Mrs Reardon, as if she could not believe what she had heard. 'But we'll be late for Midnight Mass, Mr Danaher!'

'I daresay the Lord would get over it if we didn't get to Mass at all this Christmas, under the circumstances,' Mr Danaher said drily.

And forgetting to put his overcoat on, he ushered Eva out of the house.

And that was how Muráid and Eva ended up spending Christmas not in the shelter but at Mrs Reardon's.

Mrs Reardon herself was put out by the whole business and she let Eva know it when Mr Danaher's back was turned.

But Mr Danaher was even more sympathetic when he took a look at Muráid. So determined was he to assist the Dillons that he persuaded a Protestant doctor to come out from Limerick on Christmas Day to treat the sick woman.

'Come in here, girl, I want to talk to you,' Dr Gilbert said to Eva after he had completed his examination of her mother.

He beckoned Eva into the drawing-room and, to Mrs Reardon's indignation, shut the door in her face.

'Now, let me tell you this without any beating about the bush,' said the doctor before Eva herself could say a word. 'It isn't influenza your mother has, but consumption, and –'

'Consumption,' Eva repeated dully.

It was a word that most people did not like to use. 'The poor girl is not strong,' most would say instead.

But Dr Gilbert was not like most people.

'– as if that wasn't bad enough,' he said angrily, 'she has pneumonia on top of it. She won't last for long. It was a criminal act putting her out on to the roadside. No wonder she caught her death.'

My own brother has done this to her, Eva thought that Christmas night as she sat up by her mother's bed.

Until Dr Gilbert had diagnosed Muráid's condition, Eva had not hated Hubert de Burgh.

She had not really shared her mother's regret at leaving their old home because to Eva that home had been only a temporary abode. In her mind, her true home was the castle-house of the de Burghs, and she had been convinced that one day she would be received into it.

The barn had been considerably less comfortable than the cottage, but that too had been to her merely another transient dwelling, as had been the shelter.

All the time, even when she had perceived herself to be thinking with utter clarity, she had retained the irrational belief that Hubert would repent and alter his attitude to her mother and herself; that justice would be done.

I was only dreaming, she told herself now. For some reason that I do not understand my own brother – who has never laid eyes on us – hates us and wishes us ill.

Muráid's condition rapidly worsened. St Stephen's day came and the Wren-Boys called to the door carrying the dead body of a bird tied into a holly-bush; after that came the ill-omened Holy Innocents' day, *La Crosta na Bliana*, commemorating King Herod's murder of the children. All the time a cranky Mrs Reardon kept out of the Dillons' way.

On New Year's Eve, *Oíce na Coda Móire*, the night of the big portion, other girls were putting holly and ivy leaves under their pillows so they would dream of their future husbands, and they whispered:

> *Oh, ivy green and holly red,*
> *Tell me, tell me whom I shall wed!*

before they fell asleep.

A foolish incantation, Eva had always thought. She had no intention of relying upon fate to find her a husband. She would select one for herself. But that year she did not pay any heed to the foolishness of other girls or to anyone or anything but Muráid.

Her mother was coughing incessantly, and although Eva had put a poultice of mustard powder mixed with honey on to her chest, it did not seem to help. It was obvious that death would soon take her.

When it came, Eva was startled at the way her mother's expression changed. Muráid smiled and her eyes, which had been glazed with sickness, seemed to be sparkling not with fever but with delight.

'Ma?' Eva whispered uneasily, because her mother was trying to sit up. 'Ma, lie back, will you? I'm here.'

Only Muráid was not looking at Eva but past her, as if at somebody else, though no one else was present.

'Ma?'

'It's Ulick I see,' her mother said clearly, as if she were patiently trying to explain her pleasure to a *leath-dhuinne*, a half-person, instead of her own daughter. 'Ulick's come for me.'

After that she was content to lie back as Eva wanted, but she did not speak again.

Eva was left alone with her thoughts, berating herself for the times she had chafed at her mother, not taking the trouble to hold her temper.

Is she really with my father? she wondered. If she is, I hope he's behaving better to her than he did when she was down here on earth. All the same, she looks happy.

71

'You look after her,' she said aloud, in case her father was listening. 'Or I'll be after you yet! As for that son of yours, I'll see that *he* pays on earth.'

4

Two weeks passed before Eva became aware of Mrs Reardon's feelings towards her. In that time she had gone on living in her employer's house, occupying a servant's room on the ground floor. She was still in shock after losing her mother, and in a dazed kind of way she took it for granted that Mrs Reardon, having once asked her to live in, would still want her to do so now that she was alone and unencumbered.

'We'd better settle something between us,' the widow stated one January afternoon, coming into the kitchen.

Mrs Reardon was put out by the amount of attention Mr Danaher was paying to Eva of late; the way it was deflected from herself. With him in Limerick for the day she had decided to take action.

'What is it you want to settle?' asked Eva, showing none of the deference for which Mrs Reardon would have wished.

Her attitude was a red rag to a bull. I'll bring her down off her high horse, thought Mrs Reardon.

'I won't be needing you any more in the house when this month is out,' she said to Eva. 'But you can stay on till the 31st.'

That would give me good time to find a replacement, thought Mrs Reardon sagely. Not that it's hard to find staff, with them walking the roads for jobs. But an efficient maid is another matter altogether. It will take me a couple of weeks.

'If that's your attitude I'll be off now,' said Eva loudly.

As bold as brass. Mrs Reardon could hardly believe it.

'What did you say?'

'I said I'll be leaving now.'

Realizing that, after all, power was once again being taken out of her hands, Mrs Reardon erupted.

'Get out of the house this very minute,' she hissed. 'Before I box your ears.'

It was a beautiful evening, one of those that occasionally occur in mid-winter, as if to confirm that there is hope for a dreary world. The sun – it had been shining most of the day – slashed red into the darkening sky, presaging another fine day to come.

Still, when Eva went out of Mrs Reardon's house there was a cold tingle in the air, indicative of frost. She was still somewhat dazed by what had occurred, although not in the least repentant for having stood up to her former employer.

She was about to make her way back to the shelter when she spotted the black cat which she had made Mrs Reardon look after, sitting on a wall and looking for all the world like a coffee-pot, with its paws tucked in and its head tipped up like a spout.

The minute it saw her the cat emitted a welcoming sound, a sort of chirrup of joy, and as Eva approached it tilted its head to one side to coax her into stroking it.

'She won't put you out, anyway,' said Eva to the cat. 'She knows full well if she did she'd have mice around the house. Isn't it a pity you can't come with me? But you're better off back here.'

Come *where* with me? she asked herself at that minute. She would be hard put to it, she knew, to find another job in the Woodford area.

So what then should she do? Go into Nenagh and look for one – or even to Limerick?

Purring ecstatically, the black cat leapt down from its perch on the wall and began to walk around her, rubbing its head against her legs as it went.

Nenagh or Limerick?

74

'What do *you* think I should be doing?' asked Eva of the cat.

But there was a third alternative. She squatted down on her haunches, rubbing the black cat's back, scratching its spine so its tail stuck up straight and taut with pleasure.

A third alternative. With more risk to it but maybe more opportunity in it at the same time. Weighing up the advantages and disadvantages, she narrowed her dark brown eyes.

'I think that's what I'll do,' she said to the cat.

The more thought she gave to it, the more obvious it all seemed to her. It would be the first step on the road to becoming a Great Lady.

One thing remained to be done. Before leaving the area she would visit Portumna and see her ancestral home.

And why not now – this very evening? That too was a better alternative – more attractive by far than staying alone in the shelter with the ghost of her mother beside her.

With a lump in her throat she said goodbye to the cat and turned to walk away from it, intending not to look back. But when she had gone a dozen or so paces she peeped over her shoulder. The black cat was standing in the road, gazing after her.

'I'll take a bit of your luck with me,' Eva called back. 'But the rest of it you'll need yourself, to live alongside that Old One!'

The first bit of luck she had was in getting a lift from a man with a horse and cart who had been delivering turf to Woodford. Even so it was late enough when she got in to Portumna.

'Where will I put you down?' the man asked.

Eva put up her chin.

'As near as possible to the castle-house,' she told him.

'Do you mean the old place that was after being burnt down, or the new house?'

'I'd like to look at them both,' said Eva.

The man's eyebrows went up.

'Well, if that's the way it is, I'll leave you down the road by the lake and you can make your way to either of them from there.'

After she had been dropped off Eva stood for a while with her back to the lake contemplating the ruins of the original castle. Even in its derelict state it was still majestic, with a distinct air of classicism about it: a rectangular block with four flanking towers, standing three storeys high above a basement. The beautifully crenellated parapet was embellished with semi-circular gables flanked by balls on pedestals, and from where she was standing Eva could see the bay with two flights of steps leading up to the front entrance which her mother had told her had been built to mark her father's coming of age.

'Carriages used to come in by a round-about,' she remembered Muráid recounting. 'And stop on a cobbled area outside the Tuscan gate. And the ladies would be handed down and the gentlemen would all take off their hats and not put them on again, although it might hail, rain or snow, because Lord Clanricarde always set that example to his company. And when you went in, Eva, there was a huge big hall with half an ornamented screen of carved wood to separate the doorway and keep off wind from the fireplace . . .'

'*Half* a screen?' Eva had interrupted when she had first been told this story, and Muráid had said seriously: 'The lord fell into it in a bad state of health one time and work on it had to stop. Oh, and there was a chimney-piece of black marble and a piece of sculpture nearly as large as life representing Faith, Hope and Charity, and other emblems and family banners there.'

Dark red wainscoting. A wide oak staircase. A ceiling

76

extremely rich with a very deep frieze. Window panes fitted with painted glass. A room intended for a library up on the third floor.

Her mother's voice had droned on, savouring these words which had been spoken once by her lover, and Eva had seen the castle through her parents' eyes.

'And there was a courtyard called the Grianán, which was the ladies' pleasure ground; and a shrubbery and stables and an orchard and the Castle Green . . .'

Ah, Ma, thought Eva, and you never got the chance to see any of it.

But then she thought, how could you have, since it was burnt before you and my father met!

But in this place her father had spent his youth. And perhaps even to this day something of him lingered on with which his daughter could make contact.

Without stopping to think that it could be a bit illogical to search so nostalgically for the spirit of a man of whom you totally disapproved and even purported to hate, Eva crept towards the ruined castle. It was moonlight now, a clear crisp night; and the castle and the remains of the old friary down to the side of it were all plainly visible.

So that when she reached the steps that led up to the front entrance it was perfectly possible for her to read the inscription on the gable.

This stone is erected to the memory of a much lamented animal . . .

Her eyes ran over the old words:

She was a Dog, take her for All in All. Eye shall not look upon her like again.

A dog! A memorial to an animal in the front of a castle wall!

She laughed aloud, enchanted by the madness of it.

What ancestor of hers could have done so capricious and marvellous a thing?

Whoever the person was she would have got on with him fine, even if everyone else thought he was not the full shilling.

The incident satisfied her, making her feel that in an odd kind of a way she had established a relationship with at least one of her ancestors. Although she prowled around for some time afterwards, peering in through windows long since bereft of painted glass, attempting to catch a glimpse of the remnants of red wainscoting and rich ceilings, all she could spot were dirt and cobwebs and broken pieces of wood.

When she tried to work out where the stables and orchard and paddock had been, her father's spirit did not call out to her, or any other ancestral voice; and eventually she gave up on the old castle and decided to walk over to the new castle-house – the black castle as it was termed in the area – which she had been told was about a mile away.

It was tingly cold and frost was forming on grass and bushes and trees. Shivering, she reached the new gates and pushed them open, making her way up an avenue lined with a rhododendron hedge.

What she found at the end of it was much less of a castle and far more of a big house. It was in darkness apart from a light burning in one downstairs window.

Who could be in residence? Eva wondered. Hubert himself, over on a secret visit from London? Maybe he came all the time, and had done so for years, and no one but the staff, whom he had sworn to secrecy, knew of his presence in Portumna!

It was an intriguing idea and she toyed with it as she went round the side of the house away from the illuminated window. Imagine Hubert's face if he learned that his own sister, whom he loathed, was even now tiptoeing around his grounds, spying upon the property!

Not for the first time she wondered what that face would be like. Their father had been a marvellously handsome man, so her mother had said. And even if you took that with a pinch of salt, remembering how love had deluded Muráid in other respects, she, Eva, had got her good looks from him to a great extent.

Did Hubert too take after their father? Resemble herself? It was a queer thought to consider that she might this very night walk into a room and confront the masculine equivalent of her own self.

She reached the back of the house without a confrontation of any sort and paused, wondering how to proceed from there. There were no lights in any of the rear windows and it was generally much more gloomy.

But when out of sheer devilment she tried the back door, she found that it was unlocked.

Better to be born lucky than rich, she said to herself, not believing a word of it, and went through a scullery into a cavernous kitchen. Moonlight showed up two long stretcher-based tables with spare legs and four-planked tops, five settle-chairs, two dressers and a high-positioned cupboard painted a bright green.

On one dresser were a couple of salt-and-candle boxes and a large jug which, when she peeked into it, turned out to be full of milk.

And what would Hubert have to say if he caught her drinking out of his jug? It was almost a disappointment when he did not appear at the other door – the one that must lead into the back hall, and onwards!

But Hubert failed to appear not only in the servants' part of the house but elsewhere: when Eva walked boldly into the front hall there was no sign of life. On either side of her were closed doors without any light creeping through under them.

So where in relation to the hall was the room in which a lamp had been burning earlier on? Presumably it would open off the room on her left.

Half tempted to go in there and beard Hubert in his den – for she was quite carried away with the concept that Hubert *was* in the house – she hesitated.

It would be a wondrous thing to walk in upon such a devil, state who she was and stand up to him; berate him for the evil he had done to her poor mother.

But if Hubert was as bad as he must be, what good would it do her in the end, since he would only summon his minions and have her put out?

Maybe she *would* ultimately accost him. But before that she would enjoy herself for a little longer, walking around in his – in their father's house: where, when you came to think about it, she, as well as he, had every right to be.

With the feeling that she was merely inspecting her ancestral home, conferring something of a favour upon it, she went into the room on the right-hand side of the hall, which turned out to be a dining-room dominated by an enormous mahogany table. With its webbed claws and ball feet it might have been a large clumsy animal rather than a piece of furniture. It was stiff and awkward, but Eva thought it remarkably fine: as splendid as the sideboard with its low-relief foliated details incorporating oak-leaved festoons and tassels on grotesque lions' masks; and the elaborate rococo mirror surrounded by squirrels and winged birds.

The sideboard was loaded with silver tableware and candelabra and a peculiar, unfamiliar object. She picked it up and contemplated it, noticing that it had a stopper at one end which she was able to screw off.

The pungent smell of Irish whiskey wafted up to her nostrils. Out of curiosity she raised the flask to her lips and drank from it, recoiling at once from shock.

By the time she had recovered she had registered other details of this, her father's dining-room. The big, cut-glass chandelier above the table. The white marble fireplace. The pictures and portraits in ornate frames which hung on the crimson walls.

One particular portrait . . .

It depicted a young man in his early twenties. A beautiful young man with dark, deep-set eyes, a soft and sensual mouth and a straight and perfectly formed nose.

She gazed up at the young man. In spite of the fact that the young man had dark, not fair hair, she knew that she was looking at a portrait of her father, for he was the image of herself. He seemed to her also to be as alive as herself, so well had the unknown artist painted. Alive and well able to see his daughter enter her true home.

Without any shame, either.

On the contrary.

'So you see,' said Eva aloud, addressing the portrait, 'that in spite of all your neglect I got here all the same. It's you that should be ashamed of yourself, for what you did to my ma.'

The man in the portrait however looked neither ashamed nor penitent. On the other hand he did not appear unsympathetic. That was the peculiar thing about him – the fact that, instead of having the face of the Devil, he seemed a compassionate man.

But before it scrapes the cat purrs . . .

'You needn't think you'll cod me with your soft soaping,' said Eva to her father's portrait.

It was not the only portrait in the room. There was another of a proud-looking lady with flashing eyes and a third of a young man.

It was the picture of the young man that interested her. Doesn't he too look like our father? thought Eva, marvelling at the likeness. Surely it must be Hubert, she reasoned. But if it was, then where was the portrait of the elder son, Lord Dunkellin, who had died before she was born?

'Your father was that proud of Dunkellin,' she remembered Muráid saying. 'He was never the same after burying him.'

So he would hardly not have his portrait up on the wall alongside his own.

In which case, why not a picture of Hubert?

'Well I'm damned, the Dillon girl!' exclaimed a man's voice and, gasping, Eva swung round to confront the agent Frank Joyce. 'What are *you* doing here, miss?'

Shocked as she was she managed to answer him back.

'This is my father's house,' said Eva. 'And I have more right than you to be here.'

'That's as maybe. But neither of us has the right to steal from it.'

Pointless trying to explain that she had had no such intention for there was the flask in her hand. Futile, anyway, attempting to talk to this man, who must have been standing in the doorway for some time spying upon her. Listening to what she had been saying to a portrait of her father . . .

And all the while, pleased with himself, having apparently caught her red-handed.

At that point Mr Frank Joyce made a move in Eva's direction. She tensed, her eyes fixed upon him, but conscious of the vacated doorway and simply awaiting the chance to escape.

'*Was* that why you came?' enquired Mr Joyce, not sounding as severe as one might have expected.

But from Eva's point of view he presented a menacing enough façade.

'Put back the flask,' he said.

It was all he said before she was past him, as nimble and fleet as a cat, through the doorway and into the hall and back the way she had come.

Fleeing, she heard him shout – heard his footsteps come after her.

But she was out of the back door and around the side of the house, belting for her life, with her ash-blonde hair streaming out behind her, making her much too easy to spot.

She ran fast, much faster than her pursuer, but she ran without knowing where she was going, motivated only by the instinctive need to make her getaway.

Through the grounds of the black castle she ran and beyond them, past the old castle, gasping and panting, holding her skirt up in one hand and the silver flask in the other.

All the way down to where a small door in a wall led into the ruins of an abbey.

She was in the old Dominican priory, or rather in the priory graveyard, and all around her tombstones talked of the dead in the night.

She crouched down behind one of them, biting her fingernails, wondering how far away her pursuer could be, how likely he was to find her.

Her shoulder against a headstone, her face close to the coldness of it, expecting to hear a shout.

But no shout came and after a while she fidgeted, edging herself into a more comfortable position and eventually half standing up, holding on to the stone.

In that position, in the moonlight, she could see the words engraved on it.

To the memory of Ulick John de Burgh, 14th Earl of Clanricarde. Died April 1874.

She was standing on her own father's grave.

'Jesus, Mary and Joseph!' she whispered, crossing herself.

And then she heard the shout.

After he had dropped Eva off the man who had been delivering turf turned his cart and headed back towards Portumna town. But he only went a few yards before the need for sleep caught up with him. It had been a long day, he decided, and he had far enough still to go before he could join his wife in bed.

The same wife wouldn't miss him if he was another few hours yet, so he concluded as he pulled into the side of the road and tethered his horse. That done, he went into the priory ruins, looking for a good spot out of the cold where he could settle down for a nap.

He did sleep for quite a long while; was still dreaming as Eva was heading in his direction. But when she too reached the priory the turf man began to stir.

He woke properly at the precise moment that Eva realized the significance of where she was positioned. From the turf man's point of view it was all very different. To him Eva seemed, quite simply, to be rising out of the earth, a ghostly apparition, made all the more eerie because of the moonlight shining on her flaxen hair.

'Be the holy –!' exclaimed a voice inside his head.

At the same time another voice which he hardly recognized as his own emitted a frightened shout.

After that he had one thought in his mind – to get away as quickly as possible out of that haunted place. He scrambled to his feet, made blindly for the Portumna road and, forgetting all about his horse and cart for the time being, rushed out of Eva's life.

To Eva his precipitous exit had one superb advantage. As soon as he was well out of her way, she stole his horse and cart.

She was sure that Frank Joyce would be after her. Even if he had given up tracking her down for now, he would be hot on her heels in the morning and if he was allowed to catch up with her she was equally convinced that he would have her put in jail.

So having initially set off for the shelter, she came to the conclusion well before she reached it that she should go a lot further than that this night.

When she had crossed the little bridge over the Woodford river and passed the turn to Looscaun and Saunders' Fort, she drove on into Gurteeny, going straight on over a crossroad, conscious that the lake must be somewhere away to her left.

Sure enough, after she had traversed another couple of miles she saw Coose Bay in the moonlight, with humps of land behind it.

In due course she came to Derrainy, that spot which is at the corner of three parishes without being in any of them. It was only for the sake of the horse that she stopped, so he could drink from the stream that ran under the four-arched bridge, because the place put the fear of God into her, and into everyone.

Under the ancient oak tree, said to be nearly 2,000 years old, which was towering above her, were literally dozens of unmarked graves where the bodies of unbaptized children, who could not be buried in Christian cemeteries, had been interred over many centuries. Their souls were in limbo, another void, and would never go to heaven.

It was wholly appropriate that on her journey into her new life she should pass through Derrainy and remember that many of these children must have been born to unmarried girls. Since those sinners who had resorted to suicide and were in the same position as the babies were also buried in this place, it stood to reason that some young mothers must be laid here. What love stories had ended in tragedy under this tree?

Take a lesson from it now, Eva said to herself. Don't *you* ever be giving in to love. Let no man bed you out of marriage.

'Are you finished drinking yet?' she asked the horse. 'You're taking your time.'

'Will you stop your shivering, Eva Dillon, and remember that Saint Caimin himself slept here a night and is sure to have blessed the spot. Didn't Patrick Sarsfield stay here on his way to the Siege of Limerick? *He* wasn't afraid!'

All the same, she was immensely relieved when the

85

horse had quenched his thirst and they could be away, past more newly erected eviction huts, out of that eerie place.

It was not quite dawn when she reached Williamstown in the parish of Whitegate. A scattering of skinny trees, denuded of their leaves, seemed to be making mock of the departing night, their branches like lean, many-fingered hands gesticulating up at the sky.

Nearer to the harbour was a more substantial line of trees and, at last, the lake and the outline of land on the other side of it.

And in the harbour, exactly as she had hoped, was a barge, loaded with turf, presumably destined for Limerick. Mercifully there was no sign of life – the crew must be sleeping aboard.

'I'll be leaving you here,' said Eva to the turf-man's horse, turning the creature loose from the cart and ushering it into a nearby field. 'I hope the grazing is good.'

Minutes later she was on board the barge herself.

Burrowed in under a pile of turf she had left herself a peep-hole. Except that there was hardly anything, now, to see. A mist had come up on the lake, swirling, and as the barge edged its way through the water she only had sight of the rippling grey water for a couple of yards. Beyond that was a whiteness and, where the sky had to be, a canescent circle that must be the sun, with a cloud moving fast across it.

Then the circle too was lost in the white totality. She stared at where it had been, having nothing better on which to focus, and the sun reappeared all of a sudden as an icy, pale yellow beam, pointing down at her as if to draw her pursuer's attention to her presence on the barge.

It was as if nature, as well as Mr Frank Joyce and her

brother Hubert, had ranged itself against her. She clutched her father's silver flask so that it might have been a weapon.

As quickly as it had materialized the yellow beam receded into the canescence. But then it came forward again, and retreated again, and returned, altering radically, or so it appeared, in size and in brightness.

You're stupid, said Eva to herself. It's the same size all the time. It's not really picking out the boat.

And three black crows flew out of the mist and vanished overhead.

She must have dozed then: when she came to her senses the fog had mostly lifted. A white sun had taken control of the day. There was no wind and the serene waters were silvery-grey. Two white swans swimming past were dipping their heads in search of fish. What she could see of the land was yellowed, grasses by the water's edge bleached.

A man said thankfully: 'Jaysus, Mick, but I thought the fog had done for us; and not a marker visible. Wasn't it a miracle we didn't end up on the rocks!'

'Ah sure, the foolish have luck!' said someone else in jest.

And I, Eva thought. *I've* had luck. They'll not catch up with me now. I've been told these barges go to Killaloe and along the canal to Limerick.

As soon as this boat docks I'll be off in search of Limerick station. And there I'll look for a Dublin train. And when I'm in Dublin I'll soon see if Mr Dan Fahy keeps the promise he made about the Gresham.

If I get a job there'll be no stopping me. In no time at all I'll turn myself into a Great Lady.

So plotted Eva, lying hidden in the turf. It was only when the barge docked that she realised, with rage, that she had left Mrs Reardon's six dresses behind, hooked to a nail in the shelter.

5

In the *Irish Times* newsroom in Dublin Dan Fahy was sitting at one of the long tables which acted as communal desks for reporters and sub-editors, scowling out of the window into Westmoreland Street.

Although his own work for the day was almost completed, Dan was reflecting on its subject matter. A divorce case! The petition presented by one Bridget Devlin, otherwise Hill, of 104 Rathgar Road, fruiterer, for a divorce, *a mensa et toro*, from her husband, George, on grounds of alleged cruelty. A whole day spent in the Probate and Matrimonial Division of the Dublin courts reporting on George's alleged addiction to drink, his supposed habit of beating and assaulting his wife, mother of nine: this was no work for a man who wanted to be around the country, writing in depth on the progress of The Plan of Campaign as it fought for the rights of tenant-farmers in Ireland.

There were plans afoot to beat down the prices of estates so that tenants could purchase their holdings at a fair and reasonable rent. To win the country inch by inch for the people.

And here was he writing about people's matrimonial problems! And all because an irascible and unreasonable news editor wanted to keep him in his place.

'There's a woman downstairs that wants you,' one of the copy boys, a cheeky twelve-year-old with a freckled face, broke into Dan's reflections.

'What kind of a woman?'

'As sure as there's a bill on a crow I can't for the life of me remember!' said the copy boy, his smirk giving the lie to his words.

'I'll give it to you, hot and heavy, one of these days!' Dan said to him.

It was probably the woman who had turned up at the front desk the week before demanding to see a reporter, holding in her dirty hands a bunch of leaves on each of which, she had insisted, the face of Jesus had been mysteriously etched. She must have found out his name.

He stumped downstairs crossly, telling himself that this time, instead of showing compassion to the woman, he would tell her that Christ's connection with the leaves was a figment of her imagination and that she must not bother him again.

But the woman at the front desk had no leaves in her hands . . .

'Eva Dillon!'

Or was *he* suffering from delusions? Only –

'You said you'd get me a job if I came to Dublin,' said Eva Dillon. 'What are you going to do about it? And where can I sleep for the night? And don't be looking at me as if you're ashamed because my clothes are destroyed with turf and travel! I can tell you now, Dan Fahy – now I'm here I'll never look dirty again!'

Finally, he got a word in. 'I'm not ashamed of you,' said Dan truthfully. 'Your eyes are playing tricks.'

With a promise not to be long, Dan sat Eva down in a corner, gave her a copy of yesterday's paper to read and disappeared upstairs to finish his report.

She was glad to see the back of him for a while. In spite of all her admonitions to herself on the subject of young men in general, and Dan in particular, she had felt another twinge of attraction in his presence.

She was overtired, that was the trouble, and consequently more susceptible than usual. Still, it was amazing the way these sensations could creep up on you. No wonder that there were women – weaker and more vulnerable than herself – who succumbed to them.

Ignoring the other young man at the front desk who was staring at her with ill-concealed admiration she began to read the *Irish Times*. Its two front pages were given over to advertisements.

Exhibitions of Dissolving Views. New effects. Views from Egypt, Pompeii, Paris, Killarney, etc, etc.

Magic Lanterns. Conjuring Tricks.

Wanted. Left-Off Clothes. The only Export House in the City. Mr and Mrs Finn, 9 Bedford Row, Aston's Quay, Dublin, will buy for Cash Ladies and Gentlemen's Left-Off Clothes, Officers' Old Uniforms, Old Gold or Silver Jewellery, Oriental Goods, Old Artificial Teeth . . .

But she had left Mrs Reardon's dresses behind in Looscaun and her teeth were all her own, and in her pocket were her monthly wages of one shilling and sixpence.

How far would that go in Dublin? Dan had better get her a job quickly so she could start equipping herself with more good clothes. M'Birney & Co, which must be a shop, were advertising a winter sale.

'Ladies' ribbed merino hose, 4½d,' she read. 'Ladies' Thread Lined gloves, 6d. Ladies' Corsets, strong and durable, 1/6d.'

A whole month's wages to buy one corset! It would take longer than she had expected to stock a wardrobe up!

The Fahys were living in York Street. As Dan and Eva walked in that direction Dan was wondering what his mother was going to say when she laid eyes on the girl.

Still, whatever she said or thought he knew that he would be able to override it. His mother always came round to agreeing with him in the end, especially now that he was the only one of her children still living at home. She was inordinately proud of his achievement in having been employed at the *Irish Times*, where most of the staff were Protestant.

But would she and Eva get on . . . ?

'You told me that you could find me a job at the Gresham Hotel as if that was the best hotel in Dublin,' said Eva out of the blue. 'But I notice from the *Irish Times* that all the lords and ladies seem to be staying at the Shelbourne Hotel, while the Gresham has to call on people to stay there, telling them that the place has all the comforts of home. But who would be wanting that if you could have luxury at the Shelbourne!'

'You don't know anything about the two hotels,' Dan told her, thinking it was just like her to have studied the latest arrivals and departures at the Shelbourne Hotel, and to have taken notice of the Gresham's advertisement. 'The Shelbourne *is* very smart. But so is the Gresham and it's much nearer to Capel Street, where there are lots of good shops. And it's near Arnotts' Department Store, which belongs to Sir John Arnott, who owns the *Irish Times*.'

'Is he rich?'

'Of course he's rich. He earns £30,000 alone out of our newspaper!'

As soon as he said this Dan regretted it. The next thing she will want from me is an introduction to Sir John, he thought.

But as they walked through College Green, past Trinity College and into Grafton Street, Eva seemed preoccupied. The street lamps had been lit. Students with no thoughts of study in their heads mingled with others, like Dan, coming late out of work.

'One of these times I'll show you round Dublin,' said Dan to Eva. 'But I think we should go home first. The poet Clarence Mangan used to live in the same house as ourselves. Do you know that he fell in love with a woman who let him propose to her and even buy her a ring before she confessed to him she was married. It was then that he took to the drink.'

'More fool he!' Eva said. 'If the gentry stay at the Shelbourne Hotel, that's where I want to work!'

After three days Dan faced the fact that his existence had been turned topsy-turvy by his unexpected guest.

For one thing, knowing that Eva was in the house sleeping only two rooms away from him, he lay awake half the night lusting after her.

For another, although, predictably, his mother had acquiesced to his request that Eva stay in the house until he could find her employment, the more the two women saw of each other, the less his mother seemed to like it. His uncle Dominic, who was stopping with them, could not understand what had got into his sister over Eva, and said so privately to Dan. Whatever it was it elicited remarks like, 'There's a fool born every minute and every one of them lives' and, 'Experience is a hard school but a fool will learn in no other way' from his mother in the presence of the two men, her eyes squinting in Eva's direction.

And as if that weren't enough to contend with, Eva herself had the life plagued out of him, urging him to get her an introduction to the manager of the Shelbourne, whom he had never met.

Eventually, worn down by Eva's insistence and his mother's hostility towards her, he went to the hotel and asked for the manager, wondering what card he could play next if this one proved not to be an ace.

To his immense relief the man who came into the foyer was an equable enough fellow, whose interest in Dan intensified when he heard that he was an *Irish Times* reporter.

'Is that so?' he said. 'I was saying only the other day that Sir John should consider putting a report about this hotel into the paper. You could suggest that to him, perhaps?'

'Indeed I could,' agreed Dan, although his

acquaintance with Sir John was limited to occasional glimpses of the great man as he strode through the newsroom.

Conscious that he was risking his career and hoping devoutly that Sir John and the manager's paths would not cross in the immediate future, he brought up the subject of Eva.

'A young girl from the country, looking for a job . . .'

'Send her in. Send her in,' said the manager. 'I'm not promising anything but we'll consider her. Would you write the report yourself?'

'Possibly,' said Dan, putting a brave face on it. 'When would you want her to call?'

It was quite easy to get a job in Dublin, Eva concluded when she was installed in the maids' quarters of the Shelbourne. The reference that she had made Dan write for her, purporting to come from Mrs Reardon, had probably helped, as had Dan's introduction to the manager. And it had been of assistance, too, that Dan's mother was more or less her own build and that Dan had purloined one of her dresses for Eva when Mrs Fahy was out. Being stylish, or at least neatly attired, always gave a positive impression.

And once she was in the presence of the manager he had been all over her, the way she had expected, offering her four times the wages Mrs Reardon used to pay, adding up to four corsets a month, or several pairs of French hand-sewn kid gloves, and most of a black silk bonnet.

She had persuaded herself that she had got Dan Fahy and his so-called attraction under control, and that she saw their relationship merely as one of convenience.

The possibilities of what she could buy from her money interested her far more than anything else, although she had accepted Dan's invitation to spend her day off in his company if it coincided with his own. She needed an escort round Dublin, even if she had reservations about Dan's ability to take her to the right places, where lords and ladies went.

But that was for the future. Before she could even consider mixing with such people much thought and care would have to go into her own appearance. She would study the gowns and the outdoor garments and the hairstyles worn by the ladies who came to stay at the Shelbourne and emulate them herself. She would save money to buy evening satins and rich Brioche silks from M'Birney's silk department and make beautiful gowns and bonnets, and maybe even velvet pockets and, when she had truly conquered sewing, embroidered handbags to carry over her arm. Then, at least, she would *look* like the lady she was.

Sounding like a lady presented another small but hardly insurmountable problem. After a week in Dublin she had become acutely conscious of her Galway accent. By contrast to herself, Dan's mother – not someone she would describe as a Great Lady – sounded more cultured, as did Dan, and his uncle, and the manager of the hotel.

Real ladies and gentlemen, not to mention lords and ladies, would speak in an even more genteel fashion. She would have to listen to them carefully as she went about her work, studying their pronunciation and their mannerisms so that she could copy them. Behave as they did when she and Dan went out, rehearsing until she was quite confident that she could not only play the Great Lady but had metamorphosed into one. In that sense, at least, Dan could be very useful to her yet.

How exciting it was making all these plans! Soon, very soon, everyone who mattered would know her as Eva, daughter of Ulick John de Burgh, 14th Earl of Clanricarde, Baron Somerhill of Kent.

* * *

In the meantime, however, to everyone who mattered – or those amongst them who came to stay at the Shelbourne – she was only a maid in a black dress who made their beds and picked up their abandoned finery and cleaned out their rooms. If it were true that men were nonetheless aware of her presence in the hotel, it was equally true that their wives, having taken heed of their husbands' covetous glances, never left them alone in their rooms for long: Eva was far from being taken up.

All the same, she began to learn, just as she had planned. Where style was concerned she soon found out as much about what ladies wore under their gowns as what they wore over them. Skirts stuck out at the back, she discovered, because of a *balayeuse*, a pleated frill of stiff muslin liberally trimmed with lace. Stockings might never be seen in public but they were changed several times a day, cotton and ribbed cashmere and plain lisle with coloured clocks being worn in the morning, silk stockings with designs embroidered on the front during the afternoon, and black silk in the evening. And as for corsets, they were the foundation on which all finery rested, even that of little girls. For sometimes children came to stay with their parents at the Shelbourne, girls in smocked dresses and straw hats with bows in front and boys in tight-fitting tweed knee breeches and Norfolk jackets or Little Lord Fauntleroy velvet suits. Eva watched their antics without enthusiasm.

I will never have a child, she vowed. No one will ever depend upon me. Unlike the mothers of these children, my life is going to belong to me. When I am a Lady I will continue to be free . . .

But she was beginning to learn that becoming a lady could be a more costly business than she had imagined. It was one thing to emulate accents and manners, quite another to accumulate the essential wardrobe.

There seemed to be no end to what was required in order to go out into society, from fur coats – currently all the fashion – to parasols the handles of which had crystal or china knobs.

At first her rudimentary efforts at sewing, trying to fashion lengths of material bought cheaply at M'Birney's, proved unsatisfactory. It was difficult, she found, to make a mantlet or a Dolman-pelisse which looked anything like those garments being worn by lady guests, even if she could have afforded the lace and the jet and the ruching with which they should be trimmed.

But after several attempts during which she worked by bad light late into the night, Eva began to get the knack. She made a gown in the Empire style with a rounded yoke and sash and decided that she could wear it without any fear of shame.

What a pity that she could not make her own jewellery! The ladies who came to the Shelbourne wore cabochon garnets and cameos and heart-shaped lockets and brooches and earrings fashioned out of filigree gold and turquoise which made all the difference to an ensemble's overall effect.

If only she had a single piece of jewellery, a locket or a brooch, thought Eva, angry that, no matter how hard she worked, these treasures remained out of her reach. It did not help that some of the guests were careless, leaving their jewellery strewn around, tempting her to take it . . . But if she did she risked the likelihood of being caught and dismissed from the hotel, at least. Only recently, another maid had been discharged for stealing silk stockings.

Then, that summer, an elderly lady moved into the hotel whom Eva learned was something of an eccentric.

'Always forgetting things,' said the hall-porter. 'Last time she was here she arrived without any luggage, having left her trunk on the train. Didn't she lose her husband in an accident, the poor creature, and a bit of her mind along with him?'

All the same, Mrs Browning turned out to be an amicable and chatty soul.

'My husband was an English Protestant,' she informed Eva, sitting up to receive her breakfast in bed. 'The English are nice people. Of course we all know that they did terrible things in Ireland during the famine. Throwing all that tea into the harbour. The waste, you know. When people were starving here.'

In spite of her absent-mindedness, Mrs Browning seemed to have many friends in Dublin. On a couple of occasions they called for her at the hotel, apparently by arrangement, only to find her out.

'Didn't surprise them a bit,' reported the hall-porter. 'Take my word for it, one of these days she'll forget her own name.'

Mrs Browning did not forget her name, but when she booked out of the Shelbourne Eva found that she had left a jet brooch set in gold and studded with eleven pearls on her bedside table.

She picked it up and, going to the mirror, held it against her breast. How pretty it was. How elegant it would look, worn on her Empire dress. She could even pin it on to a piece of velvet ribbon and wear it round her neck.

If it were hers . . .

She's always forgetting things, the hall-porter had said of Mrs Browning, and her subsequent behaviour had testified to the truth of what he had said.

But, afterwards, does she remember what she has forgotten? wondered Eva pensively. Will she make enquiries about this brooch, insist that a search be instigated? Or will she never recall having left it behind?

In any case it would be some time yet before she could even write a letter, since at that moment she was on the mail-boat, off to England on holidays.

I'll wear the brooch tonight, Eva decided, when I go out with Dan. Then he can take it home and keep it for me for the next six months. After which, I should think, I can safely call it mine.

* * *

Having met Eva in Baggot Street, Dan explained that he had to go back home first of all, to fetch a book to drop in at the *Irish Times*.

As they walked back towards Merrion Row and the Green he wondered idly if his mother and uncle would still be in by the time he and Eva got there, or whether they would already have left to spend the evening with his cousins in Clontarf. Perhaps it would be better to have his mother and Eva kept apart.

'Well, it's a nice night for a walk,' said Eva.

'It is. All the same, if we live influenced by wind and sun and tree, and not by the passions and deeds of the past we are a thriftless and hopeless people. Do you know who said that?'

'I do not.'

'Thomas Davis, in *Young Ireland*. He died in that house over there.'

'You're always telling me these things. What is Thomas Davis to me?'

But Dan refused to be provoked.

'It's a pity not to be interested in the history of your own country,' he said mildly. 'And even great ladies – if they have good minds like you – like to know about other things than clothes and manners. It's time you read some books.'

'Because I'm not educated enough?'

'Because, sooner or later, and probably sooner, you'll become bored if you don't. At the moment you're obsessed with learning only one subject. When you've mastered that – and I'd say you've almost done so already – you'll begin to crave the knowledge that counts.'

Eva did not reply but she did not seem to be annoyed. She's certainly beginning to look like a lady, thought Dan, all dressed up in her fancy gown. As usual, he noticed, other men were feasting their eyes upon her, not that you could blame them for it.

Even two urchins, hanging about on the corner, were staring at her, neither of them a day older than fourteen.

'What books?' demanded Eva suddenly, stopping dead in her tracks. 'What do you think I ought to be reading? Political treatises, I suppose?'

Her command of English has certainly improved, thought Dan, stopping himself and looking down at her. And as for her grand accent . . .

'Not necessarily. I could lend you books.'

'Books written here in Ireland?'

'Do you object to Irish writers?'

'All the people who come to the Shelbourne talk about English writers. There's a person called Brontë, I heard that name mentioned. And Charles Dickens. He's controversial, they say.'

'Because he dares to write about that disturbing crowd called The Poor,' said Dan drily. 'All right. You shall read Dickens and the Brontës. And Thackeray and George Eliot and Sir Walter Scott as well. If you can find time for reading with all the sewing that's going on.'

'I'll find time,' said Eva, walking on.

And no doubt she will, said Dan to himself, falling into step beside her. Once her mind is made up there's no stopping her. That recognition did not get in the way of his renewed compassion for Eva. He had gradually come to understand that beneath her harsh bravado there was a vulnerability, a naïvety in her. Some quality that would inspire pity in you . . .

'You're very quiet all of a sudden,' observed Eva. 'What are you thinking?'

'Never you mind,' Dan said.

She would be wild with rage if she knew what was in his head.

Dan's home had not struck Eva as being in any way remarkable. She looked around at the parlour as if she were seeing it for the first time, through the eyes of a lady, taking in the mantelpiece over the neat iron fireplace, the clock placed in the dead centre of it; the mirror above; the tea table with turned legs standing against the wall, its two dropped leaves down; the rush-seated chairs; the oil lamp with its engraved glass shade; the brass coal scuttle. In one corner stood a sturdy Singer sewing machine. It was the only object in the room that excited her interest.

'Are your mother and uncle out?'

As she spoke Dan noticed the jet and gold brooch studded with pearls which she was wearing, fixed to a piece of ribbon around her neck.

Some man has given it to her, he thought. At the implications of such a gift, he was the one who was wild – engulfed by a wave of fury.

Up until that moment he had felt more of a boy than a man with Eva, a boy who – no matter how he might disguise it – felt disadvantaged in her presence.

But it was as if his anger were a blaze of fire which, in an instant, had consumed his boyhood, and with it his uncertainty. He was no longer secretly in awe of Eva, nor would he ever be so again.

But he remained furious, with the man whom he believed had given her this magnificent present which he himself could not afford to buy, and with Eva for having accepted it.

Under what conditions?

In his anger he considered the possibilities, trying to assess how far her ambition might have taken her.

'Where the hell did you get that bloody brooch?' he snapped.

Then they were facing each other.

'A woman left it at the hotel,' answered Eva, startled by his anger and what she sensed as a new authority in him.

About to explain about Mrs Browning, she lost the thread of what she had been going to say. One of her hands went up to the brooch as if to ascertain that it was still attached to the piece of ribbon, then opened out, palm upwards, in a curious gesture that conveyed either bewilderment or supplication, he was not sure which.

'It's a mourning brooch, didn't you know that – a mourning brooch,' repeated Dan, who had only just realized this himself. 'Women wear such things when their husbands die. It must have been precious to her – to this woman. Why didn't you hand it over to the porter at the desk?'

He sounded no less furious than he had been a few minutes before and Eva had no way of knowing that he was mightily relieved.

The clock on the mantelpiece went on ticking, but Eva might have been stone deaf, so quiet did the room seem to have become. She and Dan were still staring at each other and she noticed that his eyes were neither blue nor green but a kind of turquoise, the colour the sea was sometimes, and she kept thinking of the sea and its habit of tempting you to rush, fully clad, into its waves. His eyes like the sea and he calling to her . . .

She did not run, only took a step forward towards him. And then they were kissing, not tentatively or gently, but both of them with a kind of fury, as if they were annoyed at having waited so long. Dan's one hand was around her waist, drawing her in to him, but the other was tearing at the pins that bound her hair until it was free of them and he could pull the heavy strands around her face, and his.

Seaweed binding them as they swam together in the sea. Kissing – no more than that – kissing and floating together; until the terror seized her that she might be dragged down by him and drowned unless she saved herself now.

She wrenched savagely out of his arms and stepped backwards, panting, eyes wide and troubled, tangled hair tumbling around her shoulders.

'Leave me alone!'

'Ah, come on now,' he coaxed, reaching out for her.

'Don't touch me!'

She swung around – in search of a would-be weapon, he soon realized, for she made a grab for the oil lamp, holding it as if she would smash it into his face, looking less like a young girl who had just been kissed than a wild and dangerous animal whose very existence was threatened.

Dan was profoundly disturbed. He did not fully comprehend the extent to which she was entrenched in fantasy but he knew that, for a brief respite, she had responded to his reality and then become terrorized by it; that she had re-erected the barriers that protected her from love; that he was, for the time being, the enemy.

And yet he was truly noble, did she but appreciate it. In those few moments he had truly grown up. He kept his distance, waited for her to put down the lamp and regain her composure, frowning and trying to make sense of what had happened, and although he was frustrated, his concern was all for her.

6

After that bizarre incident the forces that were driving Eva's life lost momentum for a while. But almost a year before, on an estate outside Saint Petersburg, plans had been made which would clamp spurs on them again.

Since her husband's death, Alexandrovna Pavlovna Pobedonostsev, the mother of four children, had continued to live with her unmarried son, Sasha. Now Alexandra was determined to take a holiday in the spring of the next year, 1889, and she had long since made up her mind that Sasha would act as her escort on this trip.

'You can't expect me to travel alone to London,' she said, helping herself to salted cucumber and marinated fruit. 'You must come with me.'

She spoke in the assured manner of one who knows that the matter is already settled. And with absolute confidence in her power over men, thought Sasha, who was often unsure himself.

He was twenty-eight and looked older. His brown eyes were sad and the complete absence of laughter lines at the side of his mouth had a perversely ageing effect. He and his mother were similar in build – tall, long-legged, angular people with high cheekbones, and thin lips, and thick straight dark hair – he the male version of her.

Yet while Alexandra appeared svelte and graceful, Sasha gave the impression of being gaunt and haunted, a man who expects life to be hard.

In material terms, however, Sasha Pobedonostsev had known nothing but affluence, born into an old and wealthy family, his father's only son and heir. His inheritance consisted of the estate itself, Klyonovo, which was situated about two miles from the Catherine

Palace; two apartments, one in Saint Petersburg, the other in Moscow; and a considerable sum of money in the Gunzburg Bank.

Alexandra resumed her attack, employing an alternative strategy: 'In any case, you take Klyonovo far too seriously. For the last year, ever since your father's death, you have immersed yourself in this estate.'

'Somebody has to do so.'

'Not all the time! Most of our contemporaries stay away from their estates for three quarters of the year. *Sasha*, our climate is such that one can only stay in the country for the summer months. You will become dull here. You are dull already! At Varya's party you spent the entire evening discussing music with the most serious and unattractive girl in the room!'

'Olga Brodsky is charming,' said Sasha defensively. 'And she plays the piano exquisitely. She says that if she were a man she would like nothing better than to be appointed professor at the Conservatoire.'

'Since you're not in the least in love with her it doesn't matter one way or the other what she would like,' said his mother. 'Sasha, I am *longing* to go abroad. I need a little frivolity in my life – a little exploration! After all, I was so young when I married, only seventeen – a child! And now that Varya, too, is engaged, so all three of the girls will soon be settled, I shall be free. Imagine that! Free to do whatever I want at last. But I need you to escort me.'

'In London you will have our English cousins.'

Alexandra grimaced, wrinkling her nose without losing a shred of her dignity. She is still beautiful, acknowledged Sasha. No doubt she will marry again. Although she talks so incessantly of freedom . . .

'Our English cousins,' reflected Alexandra. 'I am sure *you* will get on very well with them. You are very alike, they being in reality as old as you are in heart.'

As the servants replaced the fish dishes with roast

goose and apples, Sasha wondered if his mother knew how deeply she could hurt. In the same way she had in the past made fun of his father's serious inclinations, dismissing them as melancholic.

Not for the first time, he wondered if his mother had returned his father's love. Probably not. Or not with equal passion.

If she had really loved him she would still be in mourning, Sasha thought. Or am I being unfair? But when he looked back on the period immediately following the funeral he could not recall his mother's tears.

And still he knew himself to be as much in thrall to his mother as his father had obviously been in his lifetime. He thought: In comparison to us, she is so alive – and so cruel. At least with Olga I do not feel constantly challenged, required to prove my manhood by being amused and amusing whenever it suits Maman. The only pity is that Maman is right about my affections for Olga. She *is* a charming companion, she loves me, but she does not incite desire!

Over tea, Alexandra introduced another dimension to her argument.

'You know you've always been as intrigued as I by Ireland. We will also travel there!'

Sasha's stern mouth relaxed into the semblance of a smile.

'Maman – *you* are the one who's fascinated by Ireland. Papa would be most distressed if he knew you had read Grandmaman's diaries and found out about Clanricarde and herself!'

'Then why didn't he burn them before he died? No, he *intended* me to discover them!'

'He did not!' said Sasha categorically. 'Grandmaman herself should have burned them, I suppose – would have done had she come back here before her death. But she had locked them up and Papa did not open them. It was you, I'm afraid, who did that!'

'But what I found out! Sasha – no woman could resist such reading! She was so deeply in love.'

'And Clanricarde was a married man.'

'But so romantic, so tragic. Your poor grandmother! How she would have loved doing what I propose, travelling to Ireland, visiting Ulick's estate. She never had the chance to go further than Kiev!'

'You're not thinking of visiting the estate?'

'For your grandmother's sake,' said Alexandra piously. 'A pilgrimage. But also to Dublin first: I believe one catches the mailboat to Kingstown, which is the port, so before we go to County Galway we will enjoy ourselves in the Irish capital. I have been making some enquiries on your behalf. We will stay at the Shelbourne Hotel.'

By June, 1889, Eva was anxious *not* to stay at the Shelbourne – or at least not to remain on its staff. She was heartily sick of her lowly position. More than anything, far more than general cleaning and sweeping floors, she hated polishing brass bedsteads. Why could people not sleep in beds made out of wood, she wondered sullenly – like the big truckle bed which she and her mother used to share and in which she must have been conceived?

What could have happened to the truckle bed? But it was pointless puzzling over questions to which you stood no chance of finding an answer, or being sentimental over a piece of wood either: as irrelevant to your life as making friends with people who could not help you to Get On in the world.

Into the category of insignificant people fell the rest of the Shelbourne staff. Eva behaved as if she were scarcely aware of their existence and they, in turn, were put out by her hoity-toity attitude.

'She's no time for any of us,' observed one of the

chambermaids to the hall-porter, as they watched Eva walk past. 'She's that mean with conversation, she's afraid to sneeze in case she'd give something away.'

'She has a wee thin mouth on her all right,' said the hall-porter, a man down from Antrim. 'And she's right full of herself. But –'

He hesitated, thinking of Eva's beauty.

'But what?'

'Ah, nothing,' said the hall-porter hastily.

He and the chambermaid were walking out: his thoughts, if expressed in words, could only lead to trouble.

But the chambermaid had her suspicions.

'She's well able to look after herself, anyway,' she said sourly. 'Where would you say the likes of her would go on her day off – and who would she be with?'

When she was on her own, Eva wandered around the shops, keeping up with the fashions, or along the quays, looking at antiquarian books, but quite often she sneaked off to the National Gallery in Kildare Street, pretending to herself that her father was still alive and with her, playing their old game with the frames.

She peered up at Lanfranco's Baroque works, or at Charles Jarvis's portrait of Jonathan Swift, and the artists concerned would have been insulted to learn how their paintings disappeared under Eva's scrutiny, to be replaced in their frames by recollections of lake and furze, of a swan or maybe a baby hare which a man had once pointed out in picturesque terms to his child.

Sometimes she was genuinely interested in a real painting – like Daniel MacLise's *Marriage of Aoife and Strongbow*, with the dead and dying Celts in it and the harp with the broken strings – but mostly these secret excursions were to do with her fantasy world. They were a drug of which she was ashamed and of which she spoke to no one, least of all to Dan.

Her friendship with Dan had survived, but he had never again attempted to kiss her. Perversely, Eva was not altogether pleased that Dan should be content to take a step backwards in this connection. It made her feel that she had no hold over him. And then, too, hadn't kissing him been – ? But that was a dangerous thought.

It surfaced again this particular day as Eva set off to meet Dan at Greene's Bookshop in Clare Street, about the time she was walking past Leinster House, once the residence of the Fitzgerald family, the Earls of Kildare. She banished it quickly, concentrating instead on her dream of self-improvement.

How much longer would she have to wait before she would be received into society? She, Eva Dillon – Eva de Burgh by rights – could not remain a chambermaid for ever!

'Miss, miss, mind the thread!' boys' voices shouted, and she looked up to see two urchins sitting on the ground ahead, apparently holding a piece of string between them. Hoping to see her making an eejit of herself, jumping and dancing and hopping to avoid being entangled in it.

'You needn't think you can fool *me*,' she said to them coldly and crossed over the road with her head in the air, practising being a lady.

Dan was in Greene's already with his nose stuck in a book.

This turned out to be a copy of Gladstone's *Measures for the Pacification of Ireland*: The Full Text of the Premier's Speeches and the Bills.

'I needed some information from this for an article I'm writing,' he said.

That was another development that did not altogether please Eva – the fact that Dan, having been hitherto kept in his place in the *Irish Times* newsroom, was now being recognized by his superiors as having his share of talent.

108

Lately he had been given far more scope for his work, and it had attracted the attention of Sir John Arnott himself. He had been invited to dinner at Sir John's house, and was going to go there again, thus getting himself in a position where he might meet all sorts of important people.

While she – But that was going to change . . .

'I've found an old book you might like to have as a present,' Dan was going on. 'It's a diary kept by Amhlaoibh Ó Súilleabháin, a school master and scribe who lived in the last century.'

'But it's in Irish,' protested Eva, looking down at the text. 'I can't read that.'

'It's your language. You should try to learn a bit of it.'

'It won't be any good to me when I'm out in society. No one speaks Irish out there.'

'What did Thomas Davis say: "To lose your native tongue and learn that of an alien is the worst badge of conquest." There's a new nationalism emerging in Ireland, one that will make us proud of our language and our ancient civilization.'

'Maybe,' said Eva, 'but you're the one who talks about leaving Ireland and going off to work on *The Times* of London.'

'I can do that and still be proud of my own culture. Anyway, you and Amhlaoibh would get on together, he being a lover of birds and animals and a man who deplored cruel sport.'

'Well, I haven't time to find out what he's saying,' said Eva pertly. 'Not with my ambitions. You'd better keep the book.'

Later that day they sat in Bewley's Coffee Shop in Grafton Street, eating cherry buns.

'The trouble with you,' Dan said, 'is that you live in the past.'

'I do not!' said Eva angrily.

Although she did not know it, she had sugar on her chin.

'You do,' insisted Dan. 'You live in your father's world – or you try to. You may even succeed in getting into society. Just don't expect to be happy when you get there. Being a great lady may not be enough for someone like you.'

'You're jealous because you're not capable of entering society,' Eva said, leaning forward across the table. 'Your father didn't have a title. The Fahys were nobodies.'

With the residue of a cherry bun on your chin you almost look human, Dan thought, smiling inwardly. And you're talking nonsense, as you always do when we speak about the de Burghs.

Aloud he proclaimed: 'Eva, the Fahys are an old Gaelic clan. Our family history can be traced back 1,500 years. We were the last of the County Galway clans to yield up our land to the de Burghs. What difference does it make any more? This is 1889. We are living in the age of electricity! In England telephones are being installed! I am going to learn to use a camera.'

But Eva's attention was gone. At a table diagonally across the restaurant from their table a man and a woman were also taking coffee.

The woman was slender and elegant and very, very attractive with large expressive eyes and high cheekbones, and she was dressed in what Eva recognized as the very height of *chic*.

Her companion looked very like her, but whereas she was vivacious, talking and gesturing and looking around to see what was going on in the restaurant, the man was restrained, listening to the woman and silently sipping his coffee.

He must be her younger brother, concluded Eva, although his mannerism indicated that he was far from young. Isn't it strange, she thought, how some people are born old, or become so very rapidly!

110

How animated his sister was – and how confident. Eva hoped *she* appeared like that to the outside world.

Dan said resignedly: 'You haven't listened to a word I've said. Still, I suppose I should be used to your insults by now. Come, we must be going.'

But he did not sound in the least offended and he made a more or less diagonal pathway for them, threading between the tables.

Sasha Pobedonostsev's reservations about travelling with his mother had turned into gloomy misgivings long before the pair of them even left Russian shores.

The logical, the sensible decision would have been for the two of them to have sailed from St Petersburg where the snows had already melted and cleared for the spring.

At the last minute, Alexandra had blithely announced that she had made arrangements for them to take a trip north first, in order to visit relations on her father's side.

'But you *promised* to come with me,' she insisted when Sasha tried to talk her out of it. 'And I, in turn, made a promise to them.'

The further north they travelled the more they seemed to journey back into winter.

And it was even worse on the return trip. The melted snows had turned into rivers of mud. The six horses drawing the coach plodded along tracks so agglutinated that Sasha feared for their safety.

Peering out of the coach window at the brown slush he observed that their small front wheel was submerged right up to its axle.

There was no alternative but to stay overnight at the nearest inn, unless they actually wanted either to over-turn or become embedded in the ditch.

He said as much to his mother.

Alexandra was unmoved. 'It does not worry me if we stay overnight at an inn,' she said maddeningly. '*Why* are you not more adventurous, Sasha? What is happening to us now is all part of our journey. I would hate it if we had no excitement.'

'I would hardly call trudging through mud exciting,' said Sasha, but Alexandra was looking bored.

Really, he thought, Mother is a mature widow, not a girl. And yet to hear her – to look at her (for there is no doubt that she looks absurdly young for her age) one would imagine that her own daughters are much older than herself.

What, he wondered, would Juliet and Varya and Tassya have to say about their mother's attitude to adventure? Not much. But then honesty forced him to admit that his three sisters were noticeably jealous of their mother's appearance and verve.

'There is an inn about two miles from here. I insist that we stop there,' he said after a couple of minutes.

'Just as you please,' said Alexandra, with the manner of one forced to give in to the rantings of a fool.

To Sasha's relief the two miles were traversed without incident and they booked into the inn.

'I'm sure you're tired,' he said. 'We must go to bed at once.'

'Tired?' his mother seemed shocked. 'On the contrary . . . What a handsome man the innkeeper is. I shall talk to him after dinner.'

God in Heaven, Sasha thought. She has taken leave of her senses.

Out of the corner of his mouth he hissed: 'The man is a Jew!'

'A Jew with beautiful eyes! Oh, why don't you go to bed, Sasha, and I will dine alone?'

'I wouldn't dream of leaving you on your own,' Sasha said, wondering where all this was going to end.

A Jew! His mother was surely mad.

He thought – he hoped – that all would be well when they were on board ship, but on the ten-day voyage her behaviour, at least in her son's eyes, went from bad to worse. It was as if she had set out to make every man fall in love with her, regardless of their age or size or rank. Even more disconcerting was the apparent success of her strategy.

To add to his discomfiture, while Alexandra flirted and dallied, staying up until all hours and emerging, fresh-faced, in perfect time for breakfast, he himself was seasick for most of the voyage.

He took comfort from the thought that, once they finally reached London, his mother would have to behave more circumspectly. Surely the English did? It was his first visit to England, but his preconception of its people, formed by a passing acquaintance with his English cousins, was that they were decorous and well-disciplined. In London, surely, Alexandra would be good.

He could not have been more wrong, at least about his mother's reactions. And while it was true, he thought, that the English as a group were admirable and well-regulated, Alexandra seemed to select and mix with a small clique who could only be called outrageous.

Sasha, having originally been hesitant about including Ireland in their itinerary, could hardly wait to get there. Perhaps in what he knew had once been known as the Land of Saints and Scholars, Alexandra would behave more like a mother and less like a seductress.

Having endured a rough crossing to Kingstown and booked into the Shelbourne Hotel as planned, he was pleased to note that his mother's thoughts appeared to have moved from men to shopping.

Dublin had many pleasant shops. As soon as they arrived Alexandra, dismissing the suggestion that they should take a nap before going out to explore the city insisted that they walk all the way to Capel Street and then back again to Grafton Street where she consented to stop for coffee in Bewley's before buying any more.

'Isn't this fun?' she said to Sasha. 'Oh, I am having such a wonderful time. I don't think I'll ever go home!'

'That was what I have been intending to talk to you about – our return to Klyonovo,' Sasha said, seizing the opportunity to pin his mother down. 'I can't stay away indefinitely, Mama.'

'Other men in your position take occasional holidays.'

'Many other men in my position in Russia are irresponsible!' Sasha said hotly, for this was an issue on which he held strong, if unpopular, views. 'They live decadently on the easy credit given them by the Nobles Land Bank, whereas I –'

'Agree with them in saying that the Tsar is right to reverse his father's reforms. *All* of you believe that it is enough to be noble to succeed in the army, in local administration, in the courts –'

'You sound like a member of the intellectual community, Mama. You have been reading Count Tolstoy's books – admit that you have! The man is completely unrealistic; some people say he is mad.'

'Not as mad as the rest of you,' said his mother drily. 'Particularly you, for quibbling with me and failing to look around you and observe the beautiful girls!'

'What beautiful girls?'

At the two tables nearest to them Sasha could see only a group of plump matrons and four middle-aged men.

'Beyond that! Over there! That one is really lovely. You see – opposite the young man. Oh, look, she's getting up!'

She was indeed lovely, Sasha thought, as Eva approached their table. More than lovely – she was the most exquisite and unusual woman that he had ever seen.

Did many Irish women have such colouring – the eyes so dark in contrast to the almost silver hair?

Or was she a foreigner, this girl: a stranger like himself on holidays in Ireland?

This alternative pleased him. We have something in

common, he thought, raising his own dark eyes to examine Eva more closely.

For the briefest of moments their eyes met. Then Eva, without smiling, looked away. And was gone.

'Was I not right?' Alexandra demanded. 'She *is* lovely, isn't she? Will you agree with me about that at least?'

Sasha nodded his head. He felt suddenly cold all over, as if he were at home in Russia in the middle of winter, instead of drinking hot coffee in Dublin on a warm summer's day.

'I agree. She is lovely. Quite extraordinarily so.'

The next day his mother wished to go shopping again. Sasha went with her as far as Capel Street bridge, wondering what excuse he could give her to slip away. From where he stood he could see the elegant city hall, the site of public whippings and garrottings not so very long ago. And there was Dublin castle itself which, although reputed not to look like a castle at all, was nevertheless the seat of British power.

'You'd be all right, wouldn't you, if I went off and met you later at the Shelbourne?' he asked his mother.

'Of course,' Alexandra said, mercifully. 'To be quite honest I'd be far happier shopping on my own!'

Then why didn't you say so yesterday? thought Sasha, exasperated. But it was futile saying so aloud. Forcing himself for the sake of peace to smile and raise his hand in a gesture of farewell, he parted from his mother.

He spent a far more satisfying day on his own, visiting not only the castle but also the ancient church of St Werburgh, Trinity College and Stephen's Green park where he studied the old bylaws and took note that he was not allowed to smoke, curse, pursue women or bring along a dog.

But at the back of his mind all the time was the memory of the girl he had seen in Bewley's. No woman had ever made such an impression upon him before. How

115

amazingly lovely she had been – and so graceful. To think that he might never see her again!

Although why not . . . ? She was obviously from a good family. One only had to look at her, observe the way she walked, to know that.

So surely his mother, with all her connections, would be able to find her again. Dublin society was not that extensive – certainly not as far-reaching as London's – so it should not prove too gargantuan a task.

Of course they could find her! He would speak to his mother about doing so as soon as they met again. She would laugh, of course, and tease him, but he would put up with her nonsense to track down such a wonderful girl!

Feeling so positive about his conclusions that he might have found the lady already, Sasha strolled back to the Shelbourne.

There was no sign of his mother downstairs and her keys had not been handed in at the desk. So she was still out. In which case he would go to his room and relax until she came back.

Leaving a message for her to confirm that he had returned, he made his way upstairs and inserted his key in the lock. But the door was open already. There was someone else – a member of staff presumably – inside his room, doubtless turning the covers down.

He pushed the door open and went in. As he had expected, a chambermaid in a black dress and white apron was attending to his bed.

'Good evening,' he said, for he was a courteous man who was always polite to servants. 'I hope I am not disturbing your work?'

This routine question, addressed to the chambermaid's back, was hardly deserving of anything more than a grunt. That was certainly all he expected.

Instead, the chambermaid straightened and turned around to face him. 'Not at all,' she said, equally politely. 'I have just finished . . .'

Her words trailed away.

As for Sasha, he could find no words, so dumb-founded was he, although a voice inside him was shouting out loudly. Marvelling on the one hand, and protesting on the other. Exclaiming: 'You are the girl from Bewley's! *My* girl! But what are you doing here?'

Except that it was perfectly obvious what the girl had been doing.

But if he was not, as he suspected, hallucinating; if she was indeed performing a chambermaid's role, why – why – why . . . ?

Sasha swallowed and, finally, was able to speak again. 'Who are you?' he whispered.

The chambermaid drew herself up. 'I am Eva,' she said, 'daughter of Ulick John de Burgh, 14th Earl of Clanricarde, Baron Somerhill of Kent.'

7

'Did you do anything interesting today?' asked Alexandra, when she had finished recounting her own tiny adventures.

'I have certainly got something extraordinary to tell you,' Sasha said.

But he was already coming to the conclusion that his encounters with Eva, her astonishing claim to be Lord Clanricarde's daughter, even the conversation he was having with his mother, were all part of a very enjoyable dream.

In reality, a beautiful young woman in a fashionable gown did not drift past your table in a coffee shop on a Wednesday afternoon in Dublin only to reappear on Thursday evening in the guise of a chambermaid – and in your bedroom at that! Even more improbable, to manifest as a chambermaid claiming to be of noble birth.

It is absurd and delightful, thought Sasha. In this dream I am reverting back into my childhood. Any minute now Mama will turn into my grandmother – acquiring a few wrinkles and grey hair as the transformation takes place – and she will continue the fairy story, just as she used to do when I was a young child.

'Yes – well, what *is* this extraordinary tale?' demanded Alexandra impatiently, sounding – and looking – like her contemporary self.

'It concerns Ulick de Burgh. I spoke today to his daughter!'

'To his daughter?' echoed Alexandra. 'My dear, how fascinating! Where did you meet her? The diaries never spoke of a daughter: they were concerned with love – and the boys, as we know. But how superb that she is in

Dublin. Is she at the hotel? Did you ask her to join us for dinner?'

'She *is* at the hotel, but I didn't ask her to dinner,' said Sasha. 'I think if I had done so I might have incurred the manager's wrath!'

His mother looked mystified. He plunged into a detailed explanation, still keeping an open mind as to whether he could be dreaming.

'Where is she now?' Alexandra wanted to know.

Where indeed? Where did chambermaids go when they were not dusting and cleaning?

'In her room, I suppose.' Or out with her young man . . .

Enough! said Sasha to himself. Since it seems that I am not after all asleep, I must stop lusting after this girl. This servant girl. Her assertions cannot be true. How could a chambermaid in a hotel be the daughter of Lord Clanricarde?

'You say she speaks with a cultured accent?'

'It seemed so to me, certainly. But perhaps my ear for spoken English is not as good as I thought.'

'You speak perfect English and can recognize whether or not others do so,' said his mother. 'What is more amazing about this story is that the girl is so young. But perhaps not so amazing . . . She must be a bastard child.'

'I suppose so.'

'Still, you would think he would have provided for her. According to Mama, he had a reputation for generosity. I must speak to this girl. You say that she is our chambermaid. Why have I not come across her before?'

'You might have done,' said Sasha wryly, 'if you had spent less time in the shops and more in the hotel.'

'From Russia,' said Eva thoughtfully, having elicited this information from the hall-porter.

119

'The other side of the world altogether. Wouldn't you be wondering what brings the likes of them to Ireland?'

The hall-porter could have speculated endlessly about the Pobedonostsevs' mission but, to his disappointment, Eva had no such inclination.

She said to herself: 'Russia, where Papa lived,' or he thought she did. But when he mulled over it, that did not make sense. Chambermaids at the Shelbourne did not have parents who lived in exotic locales!

Before he got a chance to clarify exactly what Eva had muttered, the self-same Russian lady they had been discussing a minute before appeared in the foyer and carted Eva off.

'My son has been telling me all about you,' said the Russian lady.

And Eva was as cool as sleet on a winter's day, as if she was that one's equal.

'What did she say to you?' Sasha asked when he and his mother were alone. 'What do you make of her story?'

'I think it's true,' said Alexandra thoughtfully. 'She knows so much about Ulick de Burgh – little things that no imposter could invent. Snippets of information about Russia, too, that he must have given her when she was a child. What Irish girl from such a background could have acquired such knowledge unless someone close to her passed it on?'

'Did you tell her about Grandmaman's friendship with her father?'

'I couldn't resist it!' admitted Alexandra, for once looking slightly sheepish. 'I went further than that – I told her that Maman adored him.'

'And?'

'Well, she was enchanted, naturally. Actually, more than that. She was – mesmerized. Quite odd, in fact. She stood there looking at me with those large eyes, so

120

excited. As if I had given her a gift. It must be fate, she said – fate that brought you here.'

It was a very warm evening, but for the second time Sasha might have been in the midst of a Slavic winter, so cold did his blood become.

Fate . . .

He must be getting a chill.

'At that stage I realized that something must be done,' Alexandra continued, unaware of Sasha's state. 'You're much too charming to remain in your present situation, I said to her. Even if you were not the daughter of Ulick de Burgh . . . As it is, it is quite unacceptable. What can I do? she said. In Ireland there are so few opportunities for girls in my position. The poor child. I kept thinking of Tassya and Varya and Juliet, comparing them to her.'

'They could hardly be less similar,' agreed Sasha, switching his mind to consider his sturdy sisters. All three of them took after his father, conspicuously lacking their mother's grace and good looks. And it is another enigma, he thought, that I who most resemble my mother in features, who like her is slender in build, should have inherited my father's outlook on life.

Alexandra refocused his mind again. 'So – she cannot help herself. It is obviously up to us to assist her. As you know, it is vital these days that Russian children learn to speak fluent English and German from an early age if they are to become cosmopolitan adults. I have told Tassya on a number of occasions that she should hire a governess now rather than later. This girl Eva would be perfect for the position.'

'Did you say that to her?'

To himself he sounded inconsequential, unmanly – like a puny youngster in the first throes of love.

'Yes, I told her that she should travel to Russia with us when we return,' said his mother.

His mother's expression was sardonic. He tried to

suppress his rising excitement, to enquire with only casual interest: '*Is* she going to do that?'

She made him wait. She sounded amused when she finally answered: 'Oh yes – indeed she is.'

Eva was fully convinced that the Pobedonostsevs had been directed to the Shelbourne by supernatural means. What other explanation could there be for this most splendid encounter?

The more she thought about it the more she felt that their lives – and those of previous generations on both sides – were silk threads in a tapestry designed aeons back in time. Her father's appointment to Russia, Sasha's grandmother's affection for him (Alexandra had said, regretfully, but to Eva's relief, that the two had not been lovers); the way she and the Pobedonostsevs had seen each other in Bewley's; the meeting at the Shelbourne; all were simply interwoven strands.

Hadn't she sensed it all along – known that she was destined for better things? And now here she was about to set off on her travels with a couple who were going to take her into her father's world, into the very city in which he had lived in Russia.

Certainly she was going to become a governess, which was not the same thing as being accepted into society, but Alexandra had explained that it was almost as good. In Russia, governesses were treated as one of the family for whom they worked, not as servants. Young girls in such positions were taken to parties and concerts and balls where they could meet well-connected men.

Alexandra's daughter Tassya – Eva's future employer – was married to a man called Lev Melikov and they had four children, three boys and a girl. The family lived on a splendid estate called Uspenskoye, which had been named after the Church of the Assumption. This estate – about twenty-five miles out of St Petersburg – had its own chapel and bakery, and it was in a delightful position overlooking the Gulf of Finland.

As Alexandra talked of this place, memories began to stir in Eva's mind of stories her father had told her, reiterated by her mother over the years – dreamlike images of the glitter of Russia, of gilt-spired Baroque palaces, with portraits of ladies in them, and elaborately patterned rugs, and chandeliers with ruby red cores and white silk curtains, flounced.

Men and women alike were dressed from head to toe in furs and they were all rich. And the houses were painted in gay colours and the yellow-white, blue-white, grey-white snow fell on the silvery land.

A suitable setting, indeed, for a princess. As she made her plans, Eva and Grainne, daughter of Cormac, were synonymous once again.

Lost in reverie, it was some days before she realized that she had not yet told Dan that she was going to Russia.

Dan often worked on Sundays, when Eva too was on duty, but sometimes their free days coincided. They had arranged to meet the following Wednesday to go to Harold's Cross at the foot of the Kilmashogue Mountains which, because of its invigorating breezes, was regarded as a rural sanatorium.

Once a maypole had stood in the green there, decorated with ribbons and streamers, and May sports had been held; these days, horses, donkeys and goats wandered in its precincts, eking out a precarious existence.

All that appealed to Eva, so she was annoyed when Dan announced that he would rather go to Bray.

'We can walk up to Kilruddery. It's a beautiful day for that and there'll be few people around, being a Wednesday.'

'Harold's Cross is better.'

123

'I'll take you there next time,' wheedled Dan. 'Or, if it's animals you want to see, we can go to the zoo instead.'

'I don't like seeing them in cages.'

'All right so, Harold's Cross next week. Come to Bray today.'

Why not so? thought Eva, relenting. With all that's working out so well for me I may as well give in about today.

'We could go all the way to Greystones and Bray,' Dan was arguing. 'You're the one who likes walking.'

But he was still surprised when Eva acquiesced. He sat beside her on the tram, talking of this and that, with no premonition that she might be about to make an astonishing announcement.

She had still said nothing about their plans by the time they reached Bray main street. On foot now, keeping to the left at the market place, they made their way upwards until they saw the entrance gate to Kilruddery, with the motto *Vota vita mea* in high relief surmounted by the arms of the Meath family. Directly opposite this was the entrance to the walk.

He signed their names at the gate lodge and they went through the gate, on to the track that led to the mountain, between a host of evergreen trees with soft, new, pale green needles. The sky was brilliant blue, Eva's draped dress the colour of honey. For the first and last time in his life Dan wished he could paint instead of write.

Or even have access to a camera. But the impression needed to be recorded in colour, not in black and white.

I must tell Eva my good news, he thought – and drowsed by the landscape, added to himself – when we stop for a rest near the top.

They reached the open countryside. The gorse was out in all its ostentatious golden splendour, and bright purple heather, and when they dared to look over the wall they could see, frighteningly far below, the railway and the path that hung over the sky-blue sea, and the white surf dashing on black rocks.

'Would that be Dalkey over there, Dan, and Killiney – there's Dublin itself.'

'And Ringsend. That used to be a nice village with high-gabled houses in it. Eva, I must tell you –'

'And I you.'

'In a minute,' he said. 'You can listen for once. Something grand has happened. I can't believe it myself, although I knew I was getting a good bit of attention over the feature I did on the effects of the Papal Rescript.'

This reportage on Pope Leo's condemnation of the Plan of Campaign and the practice of boycotting as immoral, unprofitable, and incompatible with the laws of Christian charity had been one of his best and most analytical articles.

And I was right in predicting that the pronouncement would produce little effect, Dan thought triumphantly. Just as they did in O'Connell's time, the Catholic people of Ireland took the view that Vatican dictates should only be accepted in spiritual affairs.

And to think that my work impressed the editor of *The Times* of London, made him think that maybe after all there is something to be said for a journalist who can interpret the Irish view.

'What grand thing has happened?' demanded Eva.

'Sit down,' he said. 'No, not on the wall. Down here beside me. Now listen –'

'Go on.'

The irrational fear came to him that, if he did not make haste to put the grandness into words, a mighty hand might reach out of the sky and take away the letter.

'I've been offered a job on *The Times* in London,' he said. 'And a well-paid job at that. Not that senior, but more important than I have now and with the chance of promotion if I prove myself. I could be waiting for years here before I get anywhere, there are too many talented men and not enough scope for them. So what do you think about that?'

'When would you be leaving?'

Not congratulating him, or even saying how pleased she was, how clever he must be!

Just like Eva.

'I start on the first of August. I have to tell my mother yet. Anyway, it started me thinking about yourself. *You* should get away as well, and try to improve your position. If you came to London as well –'

Eva's eyes widened. They were amazing eyes, he thought, animal's eyes – but those of a wild one, always at bay. Why would she look so wary at this minute?

She stared at him, not saying anything, and in the silence he read a danger signal. Other men under threat must have waited in this place, he thought. Smuggling vessels would have plied in that sea under cover of night. There were many places of concealment, like the Brandy Hole, where the road crosses the railway on the Head. Many's the time those who chose to ply a risky trade must have hidden around this coast.

Why doesn't she say something?

But then suddenly she did. 'I'm going to London anyway.'

'You *are*?'

There was no end to the good things that were happening to him. For months, for over a year, he had been struggling against his need to make love to Eva, constantly reminding himself that if he tried to kiss her again she would panic, the way she had in his mother's house.

All the while he had been waiting for a breakthrough in their relationship – a sign that she felt safe with him. It had not come. But perhaps in London all that would change.

'To London and then to Russia,' said Eva, as if the transition from one to the other was the most natural thing in the world.

126

What nonsense was this? What game was she attempting to play with him? Along with his irritation came an almost overpowering desire to make love to her. He fought against it, frightened that he might actually rape her. What would that do to them?

'What do you mean, Russia?'

When, without cunning, she had explained herself, the words tumbled out of him.

'You can't,' he said. 'You can't go away. Have you any idea how much I love you?'

The minute the words were out of his mouth he regretted having uttered them.

'Love?' echoed Eva, as if she were repeating an ugly word. 'I don't want love from you!'

'Why not?'

He might have known she would not spare him, and sure enough she did not.

Selecting her words carefully, calculating their effectiveness as weapons, she said cruelly: 'What good would your love do me? Anyway, you were fine for helping me to learn this while, but I've got all I want from you now. You're not rich and powerful – and it's money and power I'm after.'

She stood up and moved away from him as if to indicate that she was indeed finished with him and intended to continue the walk on her own.

He said to the back of her: 'I don't think you do.'

'*Yes!*' she said, swinging around.

'All right then – but not just like any other woman, any trollop might want them. You want money and power so you can become Eva de Burgh, instead of Eva Dillon; so you can spend the rest of your life being your father's daughter.'

'What of it?'

She was as angry as he by then, both of them with lumps of rage in their throats. Her voice was higher and shriller than usual. It was as if there were two Evas trying to speak and only one succeeding, drowning out the first.

'What of it?' she shouted at him. 'I *am* Ulick de Burgh's child. And I'm going away from here, going to St Petersburg where my father used to live, where he was an ambassador, and where I will be known for what I really am. It's written in my fate – don't you understand that?'

They were only a few yards apart, but there might already have been miles between them. When she goes for good, will I ever see her again? Dan wondered.

And when will I stop worrying about her? Even angry, part of him knew that she, rather than he, was choosing the dangerous path.

Far ahead of them, if they continued their walk, they would find the ruins that had once been the church of St Crispin. And in the graveyard the body of a sailor who had been washed ashore a hundred years before. The last interment in that place.

Dan's head was swimming with thoughts of death and destruction.

He said to Eva: 'Written in your fate is it? What can I say to you? We might as well walk on.'

8

Packing. Putting her father's silver flask carefully into her newly acquired trunk. Waiting for Sasha and Alexandra to return from an excursion to the west.

Would they come back to collect her? worried Eva. Alexandra appeared a creature of impulse. Her sincerity was anyone's guess. Yet they did turn up, Alexandra announcing that they had visited Portumna and later gone to Cork.

Eva was much too excited to listen to the strangely mixed impressions which Cork had produced in the visitors. Her new life was beckoning and she could hardly sleep for thinking about it.

And then, finally, they were due to depart from the Shelbourne. Eva joined the Pobedonostsevs in the foyer and the hall-porter, watching on, was heard to mutter 'Be Jaysus!'

Eva nodded coolly at him, the way other lady guests did as they departed from the hotel, thinking that it was a crying shame no other de Burghs saw her triumphant exit.

'I shall miss Ireland,' Alexandra said when they got to Kingstown. 'What a pity we haven't got time to make an excursion to Bray. I hear there is a delightful esplanade there, extending right along the water's edge, and that the place is well supplied with baths and pleasure gardens and spacious villas.'

'You would like Killiney as well,' replied Eva. 'The hill there rises to the height of 480 feet and the view from the top is said to be one of the finest in Europe.'

And suddenly, when she least expected, she found herself feeling sad, remembering her last day with Dan.

'Have you any idea how much I love you?' he seemed to be asking again.

She had no choice but to ignore him, put the memory of that day out of her head for ever. Hadn't they parted good friends, promised to write to each other? What more did he want? And why should she feel sad?

Throughout all this, Eva had given very little thought to Sasha, who had made no effort at the kind of light-hearted conversation in which Alexandra specialized.

On board ship he was not to be seen. As soon as the mail boat pulled out of Kingstown he disappeared into his cabin and did not re-emerge. Eva had rather expected Alexandra to do likewise, leaving the newly engaged governess to her own devices. Instead the older woman suggested they walk around the deck.

As they set out she linked her arm into Eva's and began to tell her about St Petersburg.

'It has been our capital city since 1712,' she said proudly. 'Great architects famed for their brilliance in other countries, as well as Russia, helped to create it. Many were specially invited to do so. It is the first city in the entire world that was built from the onset according to a plan. That is why everything about it – the thorough-fares and the imperial residences and the palaces and the churches – look as if God's hand had positioned each of them in exactly the right place!'

'My father told me there was a golden palace with 144 fountains.'

Alexandra looked at her curiously. 'In the Lower Park. He was talking of Petrodvorets. It is very near Lev and Tassya's estate. Which reminds me, I must explain that my daughter is not the most placid of women. On the contrary – but I am sure you will be able to cope.'

'I'm sure I will,' said Eva confidently.

The warning note in Alexandra's voice passed over her head. To Eva, Tassya and the children were merely characters in another transient phase of her life. Eva de Burgh was not destined to look after children for long

On the contrary, she would soon receive a summons from fate to move up in the world again.

They had already reached London when Alexandra announced that they would be staying at the Savoy Hotel which had opened the year before.

'The best hotel in the world!'

'We have not travelled the whole world, Maman. We cannot be sure of that,' objected Sasha.

Alexandra shook her head, tut-tutting. 'Always with Sasha the necessity for facts! But in this case I and not he can testify to the truth of what I say, having been to the Savoy with my friends on our previous visit to London. The view alone, of St Paul's Cathedral and the Tower of London on the one hand, and the Houses of Parliament at Westminster on the other, with Cleopatra's Needle in the foreground . . .'

Cleopatra's *Needle*, pondered Eva, bewildered, but she decided against making enquiries lest she reveal her ignorance about integrally English affairs.

'. . . each floor, a terraced balcony, supported by pillars of cream, and red and white striped blinds. Red, white, cream and gold are a most attractive combination. . . .'

I am going to stay in a hotel, thought Eva, exultant.

As Alexandra went on describing the glories of the Savoy she could see herself quite clearly sweeping up the grand staircase in the direction of her room – or, better still, her suite of rooms, all upholstered and arranged on the scale of a grand mansion, with pile carpets and brass bedsteads and inlaid cabinets.

'Put it down there, please,' she imagined herself saying to the porter who had carried up her trunk and, as he obeyed, Eva would observe with satisfaction a girl of her own age making up her bed . . .

The reality was even better than she had expected. Their carriage stopped in front of a palatial edifice, eight floors high, built of glazed white brick. In the middle of a rectangular courtyard a fountain played from within a bower of flowers.

And instead of walking up the staircase to her room, Eva was ushered into what Alexandra said was an American elevator, a strange but exhilarating experience.

As if all this was not luxury enough, the hotel boasted tasteful electric lighting, seventeen bathrooms on each floor, and unlimited hot water.

'The food also is superb. The restaurant is already extremely fashionable. Even the French speak of it with awe. We will dine there tonight.'

Eva bit her lip. Downstairs she had taken note of the finery worn by some of the other guests and she knew perfectly well that her home-made clothes, into which so much effort had gone, would not meet the standards of other lady diners.

The same thought must have occurred to Alexandra. She said in a down-to-earth voice: 'You will need an evening gown, naturally. We are more or less the same size. I will lend you one of mine.'

The dress which Alexandra picked out for Eva was fashioned from rose silk. It fitted snugly around the bosom and waist and spread out into pleated flounces at the hemline. On the inside of the skirt a *balayeuse* ensured that the back stuck out.

'You look beautiful,' Sasha said to her, unable to help himself.

When she simply raised an eyebrow in response he cursed himself, realizing that she must have heard this remark far too many times.

Walking to their table in the restaurant he was conscious of other men gazing at her, wondering who she was. Alexandra, meanwhile, was acknowledging smiles from adjacent tables.

'Comte de Gallifet and Lady de Grey,' she said when they were seated. 'And, I think – yes, I'm sure that is Mr Cecil Rhodes.'

Now that they were seated Eva realized that not every diner was conversing in English.

'. . . *la nuit tous les repas sont gris, et trop souvent les convives aussi. Mais ici, c'est différent . . .*'

French? Sasha confirmed it, and said that he could snatch traces of German as well. I am finally in society, Eva thought, enthralled.

She looked around at the restaurant, taking in the white tiled backing, the flowers on the tables, the elegant women, the nimble waiters in their short jackets and white aprons.

Perhaps Hubert was amongst the diners, looking at her, making enquiries as to the identity of the beautiful girl in rose?

'I am your sister,' she would say proudly when and if he came up to their table. 'Really, didn't you know?'

Delectable dishes arrived but Hubert did not. Eva had to content herself with the adulation in the eyes of other men.

Still, it was a good start. On this first visit to London she would simply enjoy herself. But one day – when she was accepted by society – she would come back to London and find Hubert de Burgh and take her revenge upon him. That, too, should be done.

After such a beginning it was an anti-climax when Alexandra, in a *volte-face*, virtually abandoned Eva and Sasha for friends of her own age, whirling off on excursions that lasted most of the day and night.

'Don't you want to be with them?' Eva asked Sasha.

He shook his head. 'Not at all. Their lives are much too frenetic for me. So many parties – and then dashing off to somebody's country house! And all in this one week! No, I prefer to be quiet, to walk around the city and look at the new buildings. London is growing dramatically. There are some splendid examples of Gothic architecture. The British Museum to see, the Houses of Parliament, the new Law Courts in the Strand. And a new bridge under construction over the Thames. Perhaps –' he hesitated, then plunged ahead: 'Would you care to accompany me this morning?'

'Thank you,' Eva said, although she would far prefer to have been with Alexandra and her exciting friends.

'Are you content to walk? Otherwise we can go by omnibus – or by tram.'

'I'll walk,' Eva said.

But afterwards she was sorry not to have travelled on one of the many differently coloured buses, covered with lively advertisements. Instead she walked beside Sasha who, to cover his confusion at being alone with her, was taking refuge in delivering little lectures about what was going on. Never a great orator, his shyness made him dull. Eva thought him exceedingly boring. Facts about the use of iron frameworks, the numbers of new churches which had been provided for the ever-growing metropolis, instances of restated English Baroque on several river front buildings, all went over her head.

But, by way of compensation, there was the charm of St James's Park, the view from it of the splendidly ornate pavilion roofs of a block of apartments, recently built, known as Whitehall Court. The alabaster and marble delights of the Café Royal, with its gilded Corinthian capitals and Venetian mirrors and wondrous stained glass windows. The palatial Criterion restaurant, with a theatre in the basement, and the Savoy Theatre where the operas of Gilbert and Sullivan were staged.

Sasha, however, was not enthusiastic about Gilbert and Sullivan. 'In Russia we have the operas of Rimsky-Korsakov. *He* is a master . . . You are fond of Handel? I had intended to go to the Albert Hall while I was in London. I hear that his later oratorios are to be produced.'

'I –'

It was difficult to know what to say. Eva had never heard of either the Russian or German composer. There was still so much to learn, and not only about music. In languages, too, she felt horribly limited. It occurred to her that she did not know a single word of Russian.

'Is Russian a very difficult language?'

Instead of being put out by the sudden switch in conversation, Sasha only said: 'For a start it has a different alphabet.'

That did not help very much.

'Speak a few words for me,' Eva urged. 'We are going on a journey. How would you say that in Russian?'

Sasha said: 'I don't think you should worry about trying to speak Russian.'

'Why not?'

'Because in Russia well-educated people – that is, not the peasants – converse in French, which is the language of the salon and ballroom. We speak English, too, naturally, and German, which is the language of commerce. But Russian is really only used when you are addressing social inferiors. It is, however, very important for *you* to learn French.'

'Would you help me to do that – now, and when we are in Russia?'

'Yes!' Sasha said at once. 'Yes – we could start this afternoon!'

'In that case, shall we go back to the hotel now?'

Eva was only too pleased to bring their walk to an end, Sasha delighted to spend any time legitimately with Eva.

At the Savoy – to their surprise – Alexandra was sitting, waiting.

'I must talk to you privately,' Alexandra said, taking her son's arm. 'Will you excuse us, Eva?'

'What is it?' Sasha asked as soon as they were alone.

He was trying to read the expression on Alexandra's face. She was elated – that was perfectly obvious. But hers was the excitement of a small child who knows that its next words will shock and distress its elders.

'What is it?' he repeated, this time more anxiously.

Alexandra reached out for his hand, a delaying tactic, he recognized, enabling her to go over in her mind the lines she was about to deliver.

'My darling,' she said, 'I know this will come as a surprise to you, but I've decided to stay on in London.'

She really cannot be serious, thought Sasha. She must be making a joke.

But although she was smiling at him most endearingly – as if they were young lovers, rather than mother and son – she did not actually laugh.

'Stay on?' he echoed, conscious of sounding weak. 'How can you stay on?'

'Quite easily,' Alexandra insisted. 'I have so many marvellous friends and I'm having the most wonderful time. They all want me to stay. I have had so many invitations. I will rent a little house in London and go to the country when asked.'

'But – what about the girls?' demanded Sasha, thinking of his sisters. 'They need you – their children need you.'

'No doubt!'

His mother sounded unimpressed, as if the exigencies of Tassya and Juliet and Varya and their children fell under the heading of Dull Duties.

'*I* need you!'

How absurd an exclamation, he thought, wincing as he spoke. But it was true – he did need Alexandra, particularly on the long sea voyage back to St Petersburg. Then, more than any other time.

'I can't travel alone with –' His voice trailed off.

'With Eva?' Alexandra finished for him. 'Why ever

not? It is not as though you will be required to share a cabin with her!'

'Maman!'

'How prudish you are. Exactly the same as your father! But it is true what I say. You will be amongst dozens of other passengers. All you will have to do is be civil to her on board ship and hand her over to Tassya on arrival in St Petersburg.'

'You make it sound so simple.'

'It can be simple – if you don't complicate it with your inhibitions. You mustn't be so frightened of life, Sasha. From a woman's point of view, fear in a man is most unattractive.'

'What an objectionable comment!'

But what was the use of denying his fear? He was terrified, alarmed by the strength of his developing feeling for Eva. It was not only a matter of lust. He was beginning to wish that his emotion was that straightforward.

'But truthful, nonetheless,' said Alexandra.

When their eyes met he did not like what he saw in hers. It seemed to him that his mother was taunting him, challenging his masculinity.

'I will hand her over as planned,' he said, and left the matter there.

The vessel on which they were due to sail – the *Vyatka* – was loading in London. Alexandra had said goodbye to them the evening before, promising that it would not be long before she followed them to Russia, and now, their packed trunks beside them, they were preparing to go on board.

Sasha, apprehensive about the voyage, had no idea that Eva was also put out. More enforced time in Sasha's company, she thought. Whereas his mother is much more fun.

She tossed her head in the air as leather-faced sailors

137

glanced at her with obvious interest. How dirty they were, and probably foul-smelling too.

'Shall we be able to bath on board ship?' she asked Sasha with concern.

Daily bathing, although possibly unhealthy, was a delicious new luxury.

'I'm afraid not,' Sasha said, to her chagrin. 'This is not what you would call a palatial passenger steamer. Still, it will serve its purpose and the voyage itself is not really very long.'

'I suppose not.'

Not long. Less than two weeks. And at the end of that time she would be in Russia. Sasha would have been astonished to know that Eva thought of his country as her father's land.

Dull or not, she had counted on having Sasha as escort and translator on board ship and she was indignant when, as soon as the *Vyatka* got out to sea, he made excuses, explaining that he suffered from seasickness.

'Does the rolling of the ship not worry you?'

'Not in the least,' said Eva truthfully.

She despised him for his weakness. The sea was relatively calm. What a ridiculous fuss!

To demonstrate her own resilience she took a turn around the deck. Most of the passengers seemed to be Russian and they were conversing in French. Important people, for all she knew, and there was Sasha down in his cabin instead of fulfilling his role!

On the second day at sea she was leaning against the taff-rail gazing down into the ocean, when she was joined by a tall figure who said suddenly and without preliminary: 'Were you wondering what treasures are hidden down there? On my journey over a mother gave one of her rings to her baby daughter to play with. The child threw it over the rail at once!'

Eva laughed. 'Poor mother!'

'Not at all!' said the stranger. 'She was a horrible woman. Rich and spoiled, like too many of her ilk in Russia.'

'You are Russian?'

But of course he was: the accent, in spite of the perfect English, had told her that already.

He was a man of about thirty, thick-set, his jet-black hair already striated with grey although his beard showed none of the signs of age. He was about the age her father had been, she thought, when he went out to Russia.

'Yes, I am Russian,' he said to Eva. 'Of course –' as if no other nationality was of importance.

But then he added, to her surprise: 'And you, I would say, are Irish. I have just come from Ireland.'

First the Pobedonostsevs and now this stranger visiting her land!

'What were you doing there?'

A silly question since he, too, must have been taking a holiday.

Even more surprising, the stranger said: 'I was a witness at a number of evictions. I spoke to the local people,' as if travelling around the world in order to witness evictions was an everyday occupation.

'Did you go to County Galway?' Eva asked eagerly.

'I did.'

'To Woodford and Portumna maybe?'

'Yes. You come from that part of Ireland?'

'I do,' admitted Eva.

'Wreckage,' the stranger said. 'It will lead yet to bloodshed and revolution. It is as inevitable in Ireland as it is in Russia.'

'A terrible thought,' agreed Eva, keeping the conversation going while she tried to size him up. Was he a member of the Russian diplomatic service?

'It is not so terrible,' said her companion. 'From that wreckage new societies will emerge. Therefore it is essential that havoc be wrought, blood shed, in the first place. Remember the story of the phoenix. Nothing but ashes and yet –'

Eva shifted her position to enable her to get a better view of this mysterious man. He wore spectacles which gave him a scholarly air but behind the glass his eyes – darker even than Sasha's – were sardonic and worldly-wise.

These eyes were summing her up, boldly scrutinizing and evaluating. Well, wasn't she used to men looking at her? Except that other men's eyes sought out the shape of your body under your clothes while this one's bore through your flesh into your very bones!

'What kind of a person are you to have been going around the place looking at evictions in Ireland?' she demanded.

'I am an artist,' said the man, 'and an artist has to go out and look at life on many levels.'

'You drew pictures of people being turned out of their homes?'

'I don't draw pictures of *people* at all,' he said. 'I am a landscape painter. But in order to paint well you must understand life.'

'You never paint people?'

Just when she had been thinking that maybe he would like to depict her.

'Sometimes I draw funny pictures of the characters I come across, but it *is* just for amusement. Like that man over there. You see – the one who is looking seasick!'

There was Sasha further along the deck, hunched into his clothes, the epitome of despondency. Eva could not but laugh.

Meanwhile the Russian had taken a small drawing pad and a pencil out of his pocket and was busy sketching away.

'There!' he said, tearing the sheet off the page and handing it to her. 'A man of misery!'

'But how did you know?' exclaimed Eva. 'He's just like that: serious and –'

'Pedantic and earnest? It is obvious from observing him that, as well as suffering from seasickness, he is a victim of other malaises! Is he an acquaintance of yours? There is more agony in his face since he has seen us together. I would say the man is in love! You see, in spite of the condition of his stomach, he is coming to take you away!'

A man of misery! Sasha did live up to that description, as well as looking cross. Without acknowledging the artist he said to Eva: 'I was – feeling better. I thought that we should resume our French lessons. It is so important that you master the language as soon as possible.'

Do you have to let my companion here know I cannot speak French? said the expression on Eva's face.

'Shall we begin at once?' Sasha, intent on removing her from the other man's clutches, was insensitive of her rage. 'I have found a quiet spot further along the deck where the two of us could sit.'

To resist would be to lose dignity, which was unthinkable, especially as the artist was amused by Sasha's insistence.

A victim of other malaises . . .

'Very well,' said Eva resignedly.

'Who was that fellow?' asked Sasha as they moved away.

'An artist, he says.'

'An artist!'

Sasha was deeply suspicious of all intellectuals. In his view these were the very people who were threatening the stability of Russia, putting ideas into the innocent heads of peasants, doling out the same kind of insane potion that had once, with such appalling repercussions, been force-fed to the French.

'You must be more careful who you talk to,' he said

141

quickly to Eva. 'It is one thing to appreciate artistic work: to look at beautiful paintings, listen to great operas – or to our Russian folk-melodies for that matter. But to actually befriend painters and musicians and writers is another thing altogether. You know very little about Russia yet but you will soon learn of the dangerous influences which are currently permeating from certain intellectual quarters.'

'What do you mean?'

Sasha sighed. 'Our writers are largely responsible – Gogol, Turgenev, more recently the demented Count Tolstoy. Their work is all part of a destructive campaign to undermine the Tsar's power. Until the 1870s, artists were guided by the dictates of the Academy of Fine Art and concentrated on historical and biblical paintings, but then a rebel movement was formed – said to be inspired by the writers – which urged painters, too, to describe so-called Russian realities. The church was attacked by the decadent paintings of Perov. Zhuravlev made a mockery of our custom of arranged marriages, depicting weeping brides and aged bridegrooms. They called themselves the Itinerants – people who go from one place to another: because, of course, this sort of work cannot be accepted at official exhibitions, the artists in question had to separate themselves from the Academy.'

Indignation reddened his cheeks. When Eva did not say anything in response to this diatribe he thought that she was impressed. It was vital, he thought, that Eva conform to his own, conservative view. After all, his cousin, the highly reactionary Constantine Pobedon-ostsev, procurator of the Holy Synod, had once been tutor to the Tsarevich.

Before they began their French lesson he reinforced what he had said about threats to Russian stability with comments about Ireland.

'Some of these destructive influences have spread into your country, too, remember. It is an epidemic! Dillon and O'Brien and their cohorts in Ireland have caught the disease and have persuaded the tenant farmers not to pay their rents. The outcome for the common people is always tragic under such circumstances. It is they who inevitably suffer in the end.'

It was by far the longest speech Eva had ever heard Sasha make, and she was immensely relieved when he came to the end of it and they returned to the study of French. Yet, for once, Eva's mind was not concentrated on improving herself. Again and again it wandered back to the intriguing and exotic man she had encountered further along the deck.

Imagine him having been at an eviction – at a number of evictions, he had said, and in her own home place! Because in order to paint well you have to understand life. To understand the sadness of it – and then be able to draw, with only a few strokes, its screamingly funny side. The gift the man had for seeing into the heart of a person!

She was still marvelling about it when she went to bed that night. But in the morning she began to see her encounter with the artist in quite a different light. He was an attractive, a charismatic man with whom she had been stupid enough to relax her own defences. And to Eva this was a step on the road to doom.

I haven't a titter of wit, she admitted to herself. Although in everyday speech she made sure she spoke the Queen's English, when she was talking to herself she often reverted to the descriptive phrases used by her own people.

But at least she had been sensible enough to sound a warning to herself in time. While not taking heed of half the things Sasha was talking about she must accept his advice on one count and keep out of the artist's way for the duration of the trip.

Since she could hardly be expected to take refuge in her cabin for the next nine days, she would have to latch on to Sasha whenever she was on deck. His hostility would drive the artist off.

Nine days of being preached at by Sasha was not an enticing prospect. Still, he was not always boring – he was intelligent and had a wide knowledge of many things that interested her; he was useful for teaching her French. The more time she spent in his company the more proficient she would become.

You would learn much from the artist, too, said the Devil inside her head.

God between us and all harm, Eva said back to the wicked fellow. But you won't win. God will prosper me. Away with your temptation!

In spite of her admonitions the Devil did not move that far from her over the days that followed. She stuck to her guns and stayed close to Sasha all the while. But He had her hoping that she would still get the chance to talk to the artist again.

God and Heaven won out. She saw the artist on a number of occasions, leaning over the taff-rail, and once or twice he, spotting her, acknowledged her stare with a smile. But Sasha was with her on each occasion, concentrating her mind on French grammar, and between his and Heaven's input, she managed to look away.

Soon enough, the artist and the Devil faded out of her mind. The *Vyatka* had reached Russian shores. Along with the other passengers, Eva rushed up on deck to take a look at Kahonerka island, at the west of the city of St Petersburg, where the ship was about to dock.

She had expected a rush of excitement to go through her but instead she was disappointed.

It was summer, she had not expected anything else; and yet her first thought on contemplating Russian shores was – why is there no snow?

9

The city remained tantalizingly out of her reach: since Uspenskoye was between Petrodvorets and Oranenbaum, off the road which flanks the Gulf of Finland, they went by ferry to the mainland and transferred at once to a private boat to complete their journey by sea.

It was ten in the evening by then and the sun was still lemon-yellow in the steely-grey sky.

'This is the time of the White Nights,' explained Sasha. 'You will get used to them in time.'

At the harbour a carriage was waiting to take them to the estate. Sasha had said that it was set in woodland, but the trees were very small and delicate – fairy trees, with roots treading warily in the marshy ground.

Eva did not see much more of the countryside then, for after going a very short distance along the road the carriage turned in at a gateway and went up a high slope. At the top stood a big two-storey house with white Corinthian and Doric columns and Palladian windows with a low red wrought-iron balustrade running along the front. On one side of it was a conservatory for flowers and on the other a carriage house and outbuildings, which she thought must be dwellings for the staff.

As soon as the carriage stopped the front door opened and a woman with fair hair and big hips came down the steps to greet them.

'My sister, Anastasia Ivanovna,' said Sasha.

Brother and sister did not look in the least alike. Tassya had a full, although not unappealing face which might have been pretty had its owner bothered to smile. That she looked disagreeable rather than receptive struck Eva at once.

'You are welcome,' said Tassya, when introductions had been effected, her intonation giving lie to her words.

And indeed Tassya was *not* pleased to have Eva in the house. For the last couple of years Tassya had been unhappy about her marriage to Lev. Without explanation her husband had gradually lost interest in his wife. He was polite rather than loving in his attitude to her, deliberately – or so Tassya thought – distancing himself from her, making love to her only occasionally and then with his body but not with his mind.

Tassya was convinced that Lev was having an affair. But with whom? She could find no evidence that her suspicions were justified. She was hurt and apprehensive and in the wrong frame of mind altogether to receive a beautiful woman into her house.

Eva's arrival seemed to her an imposition. When Alexandra had written from Dublin announcing imperiously (so her daughter had felt) that she had hired an Irish governess, Tassya had been outraged by what, to her, was another example of her mother's interference.

'Who knows what kind of a girl this is!' she had said to Lev, although Alexandra had described Eva precisely enough, explaining about her background.

Lev had shrugged. Weren't there hundreds of foreign governesses working for Russian families, he had said; Swiss, French and English, as well as Irish? If Alexandra wanted to hire one for her daughter and to pay her salary out of her own money, why ever not?

Don't bother me about it, he seemed to be saying, but Tassya, naturally, did, pointing out that in Russia governesses were made to feel at home, sitting with their employers at all meals, even festive ones, and attending important social functions where they were regarded as equal to the other guests.

It was not so in England, Tassya knew. There a

governess was relegated, along with the children, to a back wing of the house. But Russian children, once they were capable of sitting at the table, always ate with the family, so there was no way of avoiding their governesses.

Which was all very well, Tassya had thought, in the case of those pale, genteel Englishwomen who had made their way to Russia in search of a better life when her mother had been young. But times had changed lately. In recent years the girls who had come to Russia were younger and prettier and more adventurous. Some of them had caused trouble between husbands and wives.

Tassya had been certain that Eva would prove a threat to her own marriage. Had not Alexandra raved in the most nauseating way about the girl's beauty, saying that she was sure all the men in St Petersburg would fall in love with her? All the men. Including, thought Tassya, Lev.

How could Mama inflict such a person upon her? Tassya had lamented. And it wasn't as if she could have intervened to prevent Eva from coming. By the time Alexandra's letter had arrived at Uspenskoye, the girl was already on her way.

Fearfully, Tassya had envisaged being confronted with a beauty and had spent far too long trying to conjure up an image of the girl. Eva, she now realized, was even lovelier than she had envisaged.

'You are welcome,' she said – and didn't mean it a bit.

With a strained smile fixed on her face Tassya watched Lev as he came out to greet Eva. How could he not desire her? She led the girl away from him into the house.

From the hall they made their way towards a wide staircase on each side of which pot plants had been placed. In due course Eva would learn that the ground floor of the house was like a miniature factory with various activities allotted to each room. Apart from the kitchen there was a bakery in which fresh bread and cakes were baked daily, a wash-house, from which clouds of steam poured out whenever its doors were opened, a staff kitchen and servants' bedrooms.

The best rooms – the ballroom, music-room, drawing- and dining-rooms – were all on the first floor. They, too, had parquet floors and high ceilings and very tall windows. In contrast to Mrs Reardon's home this one was not over-furnished. Even though it had apparently been in the Melikov family for several generations, no memorabilia were on display.

Each room had a definite colour scheme supplemented by much use of gold. Tassya, who had excellent taste and was clever with colour, had a fondness for yellow and white.

'You will see a lot of yellow in Russia,' said Sasha. 'Dandelions in May, poplars in September, and in houses all the year round!'

He was aware that Tassya, for some reason, was ill at ease and was attempting to defuse the tension which seemed to have increased since Lev had joined them. Were husband and wife arguing? If so, Sasha hoped that they would not make Eva feel uncomfortable.

She, meanwhile, was assessing Lev, deciding that he was neither tall nor handsome, that his legs were too short for his strong body and his hands curiously small for a man. As well as that his hair was receding from a wide forehead. Fine lines splayed out from the corners of his eyes and trailed off in search of his hairline.

'Welcome to Russia,' he had said, looking with approval at Eva, and sounding as if he meant it. 'The children are looking forward to meeting you. They wanted to do so this evening but I'm afraid they fell asleep.'

Lev's mother, Babushka, who lived with the family, did join them at dinner along with her younger sister,

Aunt Masha. Out of courtesy towards Eva, English was spoken most of the time, although every so often someone forgot and lapsed into French.

'I hope you're not too tired,' murmured Sasha, as ever concerned about Eva.

'Not at all.'

The polite and inaccurate response. In truth she was exhausted. The conversation round the dinner table could have been in any language for all Eva cared. The insistent phrases reverberated in her ears like the buzzing of angry bees. Most of the time, hardly registering the sense of them, she contributed monosyllables.

Only Sasha seemed to notice how weary she was. Oh, it was not easy being a lady, unable to get up from the table and simply go to bed.

Eva was given a room of her own. Sasha, who was staying overnight, slept on a sofa downstairs. Russians, she discovered – even rich ones – were not always allocated guest rooms when they came to stay but quite happily camped out in the reception rooms instead.

'We are convivial people. Often quite large parties of relations arrive unexpectedly. As long as we are warm and comfortable we do not worry too much about having private bedrooms.'

So Lev explained. It was the last bit of information Eva assimilated that evening. As soon as she got into bed she fell into a heavy sleep.

In the morning Eva met the children, six-year-old Volodya and his five-year-old sister, Irina; after which a fat lady with her hair combed severely back into a bun came in, carrying two toddlers in her hefty arms.

'My babies, Pyotr and Alyona,' Tassya said, ungraciously. Forced to initiate Eva into the household she did so with scant courtesy.

The fat lady was Nyanya, the nanny who, Eva was

149

relieved to hear, would take much of the responsibility for the children. Her own duties would be light: simple morning instructions for Volodya and Irina, a few household tasks and a request to speak to all four children in English whenever she was with them. In the afternoons she was to take Volodya and Irina for walks around the estate.

'But not to the forest,' commanded Tassya. 'Bears live there. I do not want anything to happen to my *children* . . .'

How rude she was! How hostile! I wish I could get shut of *you* for once and for all, thought Eva. Soon, I will. Before too long I'll be out of your way for ever and then there will be no stopping me from going further up in the world.

Within a week she knew her way quite well around the house and garden and had explored much of the estate. There were two, quite separate, sets of stables, one for the work-horses, the other for the twelve best horses bred and trained to draw carriages in the summer months and sleighs in the snow; a dairy where cheese was made, and two greenhouses stocked with pot plants. Although the flower beds were enormous, because of the rapid weather changes in that part of Russia many flowers could not be grown out of doors.

The land was not very fertile, being marshy, and the season for crop-growing extremely short and plagued by severe frosts: only potatoes, carrots and cabbage managed to survive.

Eva quickly learned that, so far from all Russians being rich, many were impoverished – far too many, said Lev. He was a humane man with a political attitude quite different to that of Sasha: he was critical of his brother-in-law's illiberal view.

Yet when he spoke about the estate he invariably frowned, saying there were many problems.

'But everything is so gay – so colourful. What is wrong?' Eva wanted to know.

Lev was non-committal.

'Oh, yes, it is colourful, but –'

The village where the estate workers lived was gay certainly: the wooden dwellings – called *izbas* – painted brilliant shades of blue or green or yellow. Apple trees grew in the tiny gardens. Sometimes signboards, paintings of useful objects, were placed in front of houses. A drawing of a bucket indicated to those who could not read that it could be produced if necessary in case there was a fire.

The villagers were sturdy people, dressed in loose cotton clothes with padded jackets and, in the case of women, scarves pulled tightly over their hair and knotted at the nape of the neck.

Further exploration revealed that the estate had its own shop, the *lavka*, and a church with its own priest and deacons. Beside the church lived a seamstress who was an expert embroideress.

What a pity I can't paint what I see, lamented Eva. But between teaching the children and learning French herself she was kept busy. Sasha came once a week to continue her grammar lessons. He was useful in other ways, too, as Eva's etiquette instructor. From him she learned that she must never attempt to sit down at table until the under-butler, with white gloves on his hands, had stepped forward to ease in her chair. Nor must she ever handle her own luggage, something no lady would do.

A lady, said Sasha – not smiling – might well claim that she had never dressed herself, never had to bother. And she would most certainly understand the protocol involved in eating two lightly boiled eggs, served in a napkin on her side-plate, cracking them with a spoon, scooping the white into a glass, adding salt, and drinking it quickly down.

Meat had to be cut with a knife which was then positioned on one's knife-rest. You ate only with a fork. And it was essential to leave some food on the plate lest servants conclude that you were after a second helping.

But all this was as nothing compared to the art of officiating at the samovar. Eva watched Tassya carefully as the nickel samovar was brought into the room and placed in front of her. Under the samovar was red-hot charcoal, to ensure that the water was kept on the boil, and on top, keeping warm, was a small teapot which contained very strong China tea. The real expertise lay in determining just when to fill up the teapot and understanding how long it must stand while conversing with your guests.

Eva observed Tassya; Tassya, in turn, kept an eye on her. All the while she compared herself unfavourably with Eva, and fretted over Lev. And she desperately sought for an opportunity which would rid her of the girl.

All this time Eva had not yet been into St Petersburg. September came and with it cooler weather before those two weeks which are known as the Women's Summer sent the temperatures up again. But the poplars were already turning yellow and estate owners were deserting their summer residences for the delights of the city.

Eva had taken it for granted that the Melikovs would do likewise. She was looking forward to the move. The countryside, although beautiful, had not so far provided the glittering social life of which she had dreamed.

She was soon disillusioned. The Melikovs – so Babushka and Aunt Masha informed her – were no longer in society.

Babushka and Aunt Masha spoke freely about the reason for the family's social isolation. Their brother, the late General Melikov – Lev's uncle – had fought for reform in Russia together with the Grand Duke Constantine, the Emperor's radical uncle.

'He put forward a plan for limited elected representation on official bodies to be charged with advising the Tsar on legislation,' explained Aunt Masha. 'It was a very modest plan but people afterwards felt that it could be construed as a first step towards a constitution of absolute rule and they were frightened by it. Alexander II approved it the very day of his death. My brother was very excited. And then of course the Tsar was killed by a terrorist's bomb. His son, when he succeeded, did call a series of meetings to discuss the proposal but he is far less liberal than his father –'

'And under the thumb of Constantine Pobedonostsev, that is the most important point!' Babushka intervened.

'Constantine Pobedonostsev?'

'Sasha's and Tassya's cousin, who Sasha supports. He, too, is a reactionary although not a statesman, of course.'

'Constantine Pobedonostsev has far too much power over the Tsar,' agreed Aunt Masha, taking up the story again. 'He went to those meetings and afterwards he drafted an accession proclamation for the new Tsar which purported to pay respects to what he called the great reforms of the previous reign. In reality it simply upheld the autocratic principle, maintaining that it is God's will. My brother had no alternative but to resign, along with some of his associates. Count Dmitry Tolstoy, another reactionary, was appointed Minister of the Interior, and the ministry of education went to another of that ilk. And Constantine Pobedonostsev's ascendancy has been unchallenged ever since.'

The sisters left the story there, but in due course Eva was able to pick up the pieces as they related to life upon the estate.

None of what had gone on at the Tsar's meetings might have affected her own life had the Melikovs not felt that reforms were overdue.

None of it might have reflected upon Lev and his family, had Lev's father, in the years before his death, not spoken out forcibly in support of his brother. A little too forcibly, many felt. The storm which had gathered over the general's head clouded the lives of the younger generation. People began to feel that the Melikovs, as a family, were dangerous. They were dropped from a number of social events.

All this was depressing news for Eva. And to think that Sasha, who was welcomed in social circles, seldom bothered to go to town, although he frequently came to Uspenskoye.

On one of these visits he invited Eva to accompany him to Pedrodvorets.

'The Tsar's summer palace!'

'The Tsar does not live there any more. He prefers Gatchina which is quite near my own estate.'

'Then Pedrodvorets is unoccupied? No one will be there?'

'Yes, they will,' said Sasha patiently. 'Cousins of the royal family reside there during the summer months. A friend of mine, Olga Brodsky, will be giving a piano recital of Chopin's études and nocturnes. *Would* you like to come?'

Even if her presence would upset Olga . . .

'A piano recital . . .' repeated Eva.

Instead of a party or ball . . . But at Pedrodvorets, where cousins of the royal family lived?

'I'd love to go,' she said.

Here it all was, the world she wanted. She was standing on a marble terrace, facing the sea, gazing at the fountains of the Grand Cascade as her father must have done long before she was born. From twin masks dual streams of water spurted out to be joined by other jets of the fountains as they rippled down steps flanked by gilded bas-reliefs to oval terraces where sculpted figures waited. Still further the water tumbled, out of the mouths of dolphins into a pool paying homage to a statue of Samson. Behind her was the Grand Palace, the golden edifice set amongst maple, linden and chestnut trees, far more splendid than she could ever have imagined.

'If you think this is magnificent,' said Sasha, 'I wonder what you will make of the treasures you'll find inside!'

He was moved by Eva's delight. In that moment they were close for Sasha, like Eva, felt that she belonged in such a setting.

When he took her into the palace itself, drawing her attention to the silk ornamented with partridges, the Chinese satin that adorned the walls; the lacquered screens, the dazzling moulding and the gilded crystal chandeliers, she sighed, biting her bottom lip.

He had arranged that they be free to wander for a while before the recital began and, since she had said she was interested in paintings, he led her into the Study of Fashion and Grace where the walls were completely covered by female portraits.

'These were all painted by Pietro Rotari and his pupils,' he said, pleased with his own knowledge. 'You will see that in many, many cases, they have used the same model over and over again, dressing her in different costumes: Turkish or, here, Hungarian.'

Eva sighed, enthralled. And the recital itself went well, Olga Brodsky finding expression for her own wistfulness in the lyrical work.

'An evening to remember,' Sasha said as they travelled home.

From his point of view the greatest treasure was Eva; from hers it was difficult to be selective.

'It was all so wonderful,' she wrote to Dan the next day. 'I am in love with the glories of Russia. If only it would snow!'

She longed for snow to fall. In a childish way she believed that, when this miracle occurred, when the landscape took on the silver-white, gold-white tones she expected, when the trees in the forest were covered with myriads of delicate snow petals and flowers, then the magic of Russia would truly steep into her life, and she would be transformed.

It grew colder and colder. The landscape was frozen. Reports filtered through that the river Neva was already icing up.

And then it did snow! Bells were ringing to announce the astonishing fact – so Eva thought before she laughed at her own nonsense. Post was delivered twice a week to the estate post-house. What she could hear was the sound of the post-horse's bell.

Standing by her bedroom window she shivered. The night before she had opened the *fortochka*, the small hinged pane in the top corner of the window, in order to let in fresh air. She reached up and closed it and as she did so she saw Lev striding towards the house holding a letter in his hand. Perhaps it was another letter from Dan? She had heard from him several times since he was in London.

'From Mama!' she heard Tassya exclaim as she reached the dining-room. 'Lev, Lev, listen to this – she's going to remain in London.'

'Truly?'

Lev sounded just as surprised as his wife.

'Yes! She says that she is having a wonderful time and doesn't want to come back for the moment. But she suggests that we visit her in the Spring – without the children. They would be happy enough here.'

Eva, standing in the doorway, saw Lev frown. He paused, looking down at the floor.

'It is not until next April. There will be plenty of time to make preparations . . .'

Tassya sounded desperate. When Lev said, in an

unemotional voice: 'I don't think it will be possible. I'm sorry,' she put a hand to her brow.

'*Baryshnya*, excuse me.'

Had Eva not moved to allow the chef, in his starched white cap, to receive his morning instructions, she would have noticed Tassya glower at her, and the hatred on her face.

It was the beginning of a new year, 1890, and Christmas, celebrated on 6 January, was only a few days off. Much activity was centred on the ballroom into which a huge fir tree, felled in the forest, had been carried to undergo decoration.

Babushka, Aunt Masha and Eva, together with Nyanya and the four children, were centring their efforts upon this tree with varying degrees of enthusiasm and expertise. Already six crackers, each one almost a yard long, had been placed on its top together with paper lanterns with candles inside them.

'Once they have been lit someone will have to keep watch over them at all times,' said Babushka. 'In case we have a fire.'

'I will do it,' volunteered Volodya. 'I know what to do. You put wet cotton at the end of a long pole and –'

'You are not yet tall enough,' his grandmother told him. 'Next year maybe. We will see. Now hand me some of that tinsel.'

Better than the gaudy drapery, thought Eva, were the decorative edible goodies – all bought at Yeliseyev's, the best food store in St Petersburg which specialized in imported goods. Eva had not been taken to town when Tassya had gone there to shop.

Babushka and Aunt Masha laid the delicacies out on the floor – dates and chocolates; *pryaniki*, tiny cakes made out of honey; *vareniti*, small pies; sweet rolls cooked in the shape of a ring; *marmelad*, jelly sweets with a soft squashy centre; and walnuts on to which little stems had to be attached before they were dipped in glue and wrapped tight in fine gold- and silver-leaf paper.

All these small objects had to be tied with cotton and then looped so they could be suspended from the tree. It was tedious work but at last it was done and they stood back to contemplate the tree's final glory.

'Tomorrow can we put more things on top?' Irina wanted to know.

'But it is finished!' and – 'Tomorrow we have other things to do!' cried Babushka and Aunt Masha in chorus.

Eva kept quiet. Tomorrow, she, too, was going to have fun.

What she had in mind for the following day was neither objectionable from anyone's point of view, nor controversial. Quite simply she wanted to go tobogganing alone. In the last few months she had been continually in the company of others. The Slavs, she thought, did not appreciate the value of solitude. The mere suggestion of it made them feel uneasy, impelled them, in the most friendly way, to ensure that you were not lonely. Had she explained to the other members of the household that she enjoyed the solitary state, they would have been upset.

But that morning the children insisted that they did not want to leave the ballroom and their precious tree. Nyanya was quite happy looking after all four of them. Eva, wrapped up warmly against the cold, pulling her toboggan behind her, set off through the garden and orchard in the direction of the forest. Between it and the house ran a small river, now frozen.

It was snowing again and now, released from her duties, liberated from familial restraint, her face tingling and her whole self revelling in being alone she suddenly started to laugh.

She clumped up the bank on which Lev, at the end of the year, had taught Volodya, Irina and herself to toboggan, positioned herself, and selected her direction with care.

The river was straight ahead but she was confident of her steering. The idea that she might fall off did not worry her. Lev had taught her to roll clear if she fell, to avoid hitting trees.

She pushed off. As the toboggan gathered momentum, so did her exhilaration in the ride. The landscape was rushing past and the cold air was assaulting her cheeks and her nose, reddening them, but Eva didn't care. She was in charge of her little craft, of everything: in charge of all the world, a superior being, maybe even as mighty as God . . .

As God, as God! the wind seemed to echo as she shot past two trees and between two others.

As God!

And the huge dark outline of a bear loomed up before her path, and she lost control of the world, and the white snow turned black.

Lev and Tassya had begun that day with an argument. Like many rows, when the participants are already worried, it centred upon a relatively minor issue, that of whether or not Sergei Mikhaelovich – Seryozha for short – the family's long-time butler, should be permitted to play his flute at the gala celebration on Christmas night.

As always at this time the household servants, dressed in their best – the women in their *sarafans*, embroidered high-waisted dresses with very full sleeves, and *kokoshniks*, halo-like embroidered head-dresses – joined in the family party.

But Seryozha, although much older, was not nearly as good a musician as Kostya, the under-butler, and Tassya, whose ear as well as whose emotions were sensitive, said that Seryozha's playing grated upon her nerves and that Kostya rather than he should be encouraged to perform.

'Don't you agree with me?' she demanded.

There was no answer from Lev. He had not even been listening, Tassya realized, and on his face was that vague detached expression which she was beginning to dread.

Nevertheless she repeated her question, and explained her point of view.

'I don't see why we should ask Kostya,' said Lev, although he had just been given a reason. 'And if we exclude Seryozha he will be offended.'

'Why should that matter?' asked Tassya irrationally.

Tears were welling up inside her as she spoke and her head, from all her worrying, felt as if it were ready to burst. But Lev did not notice.

'Of course it matters,' he said, irritated. 'Why upset the poor fellow? Apart from the fact that it would be wrong to do so, Babushka and Aunt Masha would be unhappy as well. Seryozha played last year –'

'So badly,' cried Tassya, 'that my whole head split!'

But that had not been the reason for her discomfort then and she knew it perfectly well.

'I have enough on my mind without all this trivial nonsense!' Lev yelled, losing patience with his wife, and Tassya said that it was only too obvious and that she could bear living with him no longer, and began to pack a trunk.

'I'm going to stay with Sasha,' Tassya said, and now, hideously, tears were streaming down her face and her emotions were heightening her colour in what she was sure was a horribly unflattering way.

She had turned her back to Lev by then and her tone came over to him not as wistful, of one who longs to be loved, but as hard and aggressive and threatening.

He *had* a lot on his mind. He said to Tassya: 'Go!'

When, without saying goodbye to the children or to Babushka and Aunt Masha, she did indeed depart, Lev took his troubles for a walk. He had no idea that Eva too had gone out on her own that morning and it was pure coincidence that he took the same route.

Lev was worried, not about women but about Uspenskoye.

He had inherited it thirty months previously after his father's death and it had taken him six months to work out that it was in difficulties, the older man having neglected it and left it in the hands of a series of corrupt stewards.

Lev had sacked the previous steward and installed in his place a more trustworthy fellow. He had worked to his own utmost capacity in an attempt to redress the balance these last couple of years. But increasingly he was being forced to face the fact that it was all too late – that he could never save the estate.

Always hoping that by some unprecedented miracle they might, after all, pull through, he had refrained from confiding in Tassya and had thus exhausted himself by carrying the whole burden. Inside he was taut and terrified and longing for release. But if he relaxed he feared he might crumble, and where would they all be then?

So he had distanced himself from emotion and suffered for it, longing for comfort and love, wishing, at heart, that Tassya could sense the problem and offer him compassion.

Why should she – how could she know? Why wasn't she clairvoyant!

Round and round in his head went his worries and he very nearly failed to see the overturned toboggan.

And what lay beyond it . . .

The accident had only just happened but Lev did not know that. All he saw was the inert body of Eva lying in the snow.

At first he thought she was dead. Then, having ascertained that she was still alive, he wasted no further time. He lifted her up in his strong arms, acknowledged her moan with a grunt and strode back towards the house.

Under normal circumstances he would have encountered at least one if not several members of the household once he was indoors. But on that day everyone was in the ballroom, marvelling at the tree. Lev, uncertain as to the length of time Eva had lain in the snow, carried her upstairs, laid her on her bed, and went in search of vodka and a glass.

At that point he should of course have summoned female help – it was available in plenty. He did not look for it because he did not want to find it. He was in a particularly vulnerable state, worried, over-tense and deserted by his wife. Tassya had been quite right when she thought her husband was acutely aware of Eva's beauty. Men invariably were. But Lev was not naturally unfaithful: he had never before betrayed Tassya and, had she not walked out that day, he would have resisted temptation.

Still, Tassya was gone and Lev's vulnerability was heightened by Eva's plight. He went upstairs in the way of a man walking headlong into danger.

When he returned to the bedroom Eva had opened her eyes. She said, hoarsely: 'Did you kill the bear?'

'Drink this,' Lev commanded, having poured a generous measure of vodka into the glass. 'And then take off your clothes.'

'*What!*'

He said, in a reasoning voice: 'You could catch rheumatic fever. I'm going to rub you all over with vodka . . . Do any of your limbs feel numb?'

'No. I'm not sure. My arm is painful.'

'Let me see. It's not broken. In any case you must be rubbed, to restore your circulation.'

'I can't take off my clothes and let *you* rub me,' Eva protested. 'You must go downstairs and fetch Nyanya.'

'Please? *Milaya* – please?'

As he uttered the term of endearment Lev saw Eva's eyes widen. Then a woman screamed.

Tassya, in the three-horse *troika*, did not get very far before she met Sasha coming from the other direction.

Relieved to have a confidant, she poured out her tale of woe.

'I'm sure it's not another woman,' Sasha said when she had finished. 'Lev may simply be concerned about the estate. Has that not occurred to you?'

'Why should it?'

'Because he has reason to be concerned,' Sasha said flatly. 'I know for a fact that his father was highly irresponsible. It is common knowledge.'

'But *I* didn't know,' said Tassya. 'Why wouldn't he tell me?'

'Perhaps because he doesn't want to burden you with his troubles.'

This explanation for Lev's coolness was very much more attractive to Tassya than the possibility of another woman in her husband's life. She thought that she could cope with any emergency – even financial ruin – rather than that. She did not take much persuading to turn on her tracks and go back home with Sasha.

By then her mood was completely different. Poor Lev, she was thinking as she pushed open the door and went into the empty hall. I have not been at all sympathetic towards him lately. He has been carrying this burden of worry alone too long. I must make it up to him.

There being no sign of Lev in any of the downstairs rooms she left Sasha with the admiring crowd in the ballroom and went upstairs to look for her husband. In his excitement Lev had absently left Eva's bedroom door ajar. Tassya heard murmuring voices. She was just in time to hear Lev's last words and drew her own conclusions.

'Whore!' screamed Tassya when, out of her anguish,

163

she could articulate again. 'I knew you were sleeping with my husband! I knew it all along!'

'No, you are wrong – she did nothing . . .'

'Whore – whore – whore!'

Christmas or no Christmas, Eva would have to go. That was the general consensus. Even cool-headed Sasha agreed that the alternative was untenable.

If only, Sasha thought, he had put off his own visit for a day or so; not intercepted his sister. But he had been longing to see Eva.

Still, it was too late now for recrimination. A solution had to be found, and fast. So Babushka said, confronting him in the drawing-room. Upstairs, Eva lay in her own room. In the master bedroom, Lev and Tassya talked.

'So what are you going to do about the girl?' Babushka wanted to know. '*You* brought her here . . .'

Sasha rubbed his brow, digging his fingers hard against the bone. What indeed?

There was no doubt at all that, given time, Eva could be found another position as governess. He could journey into St Petersburg on her behalf, check at the Governesses' Club Room at the English Church of St Mary and All Saints to see if there were news of suitable vacancies.

Or perhaps at the British and American Chapel. That was more middle-class, less élite, of course, but it was a focal point of the British community; a social club as well as a place of worship.

Or, Eva being Irish, the Roman Catholic Church of the Assumption. Perhaps the priests there would help?

And there was yet another alternative . . .

Babushka was a down-to-earth, straight-talking woman.

He said to her: 'Do *you* think she encouraged him?'

Babushka did not hesitate. 'Only in so far that she is beautiful. That would encourage any man. Otherwise, no. She had fallen off her toboggan. The child was shocked. Lev was taking advantage. It was outrageous. I am ashamed of him . . . Tassya, naturally, rather than blame Lev, will condemn Eva. But in any case she will have to go. You can assist her to find another position? I will see that she gets a good reference.'

Sasha said: 'I have another idea.'

10

Sasha found Eva still reeling under the impact of Tassya's wrath. The lights in her glorious world had been extinguished all of a sudden and she was attempting to find her way out of the obscuration.

How was it possible to reconcile the turn of events at Uspenskoye with her vision of what fate had mapped out for her?

Her inability to answer this question rendered her temporarily uncertain. This lack of confidence communicated itself to the shy, insecure Sasha, and had the effect of making him braver.

'What am I going to do?' she asked him.

The question paved the way for an enquiry of his own.

'You could marry me,' he said tentatively. 'I would be honoured to make you my wife. Will you think about it? You don't have to give me an answer immediately.'

What to do with her in the interim remained his insoluble problem. Take her with him to Klyonovo? But I don't think I can bear having her with me while she is debating what to do, he thought, wondering what was going through her mind at this precise moment.

Eva had closed her eyes and although she had not physically budged an inch she seemed to be shrinking from him. She would turn him down. She must be working out how to do it without inflicting hurt.

Eva was not nearly so kind; Sasha, having an idealized view of her, could not be expected to know that her mind was actually blank.

His proposal had added to the series of shocks she had experienced this day and for the next couple of minutes her mind insulated itself from any more. She was ousted from this state by the notion that fate, as much as Sasha's evident affection for her, must have prompted his proposal.

After all, she was in destiny's hands. All that had led up to this offer – the accident in the snow, Lev's chivalry and prurience, Tassya's inopportune return – must therefore be part of a preordained plan relating to her life.

She was the daughter of Ulick de Burgh. She was intended to lead a glamorous life, to wear beautiful imported clothes as rich women in St Petersburg, like the women who had attended the recital at Pedrodvorets, did as a matter of course. As the wife of Sasha Pobedonostsev would naturally do.

But you do not find Sasha attractive, the voice of sanity butted in. On the contrary –

What queen has yet married for love? replied the madness in Eva. And there was, too, the fact that deep down inside her attraction was linked to danger and that she did not want.

With her eyes shut she managed to convince herself that this argument was beside the point. The matter was out of her hands; her fate pre-planned.

When she opened them she did not smile and Sasha was sure that she was going to reject him.

Instead Eva said precisely: 'I *can* give you an answer to your question immediately. I will become your wife.'

Unwilling to provoke further comment from Tassya, Sasha made no announcement about his engagement: he just took Eva away.

Until they were married she could live at Klyonovo, chaperoned by the two much older ladies who were already ensconced at the estate.

As the *troika* passed the Gothic gates of Count Orlov's estate he explained about these ladies.

'Aunt Lilya and Cousin Marisha. Aunt Lilya is bedridden. She has been with us for years. Cousin Marisha

167

only joined the household lately. I must warn you that she is a formidable lady . . .'

On another day Eva would probably have groaned at the prospect of spending time with more elderly women and hoped that they would not get in her way. But she hardly listened to Sasha, being still partly in shock.

'Cousin Marisha, in particular, will be delighted with our news. She has been telling me for years that I should marry and settle down. She is extremely fond of children.'

Any other time Eva would have been stopped dead in her tracks at the idea of bearing Sasha's children. Pregnancy and motherhood had no place in her life.

But when Sasha raised the subject in this somewhat oblique fashion Eva, in her imagination, was stepping into a white lace gown, reaching out for her furs.

'We will be happy together, I know we will,' said Sasha, happy himself already.

Eva did not reply. She was still in a *troika*, but heading for St Petersburg, on her way to a ball.

The vehicle in which her real self was travelling with Sasha did not go in to the capital but took the Kiev road towards Tsarskoye Celo.

The dark brown earth on each side of the road, the cherry trees struggling up out of it to take up position in the flat landscape were heavily coated with snow. She snuggled under the fur blankets which Sasha had provided.

They reached the base of the slope of Pulkovo Heights and took the left fork.

'Had we gone the other way we would have reached Gatchina Palace where the Tsar is living now.'

'In *winter*?'

'These are bad times. He's nervous. He lives under heavy guard and goes into town less frequently than before. In any case he is a man who prefers to lead a secluded life. He's very fond of musical soirées. He even takes part in them himself, on the French horn and the cello.'

'Will I be presented to him?' asked Eva.

'In due course,' Sasha said. 'My cousin, the statesman Constantine Pobedonostsev, is very close to the Tsar. It can doubtless be arranged.'

The reactionary Constantine Pobedonostsev, Babushka had said; but Eva, then, considered the man only in social terms, as an entrée into the Tsar's society.

And she was further dazzled, drawn further into dreamland, when Sasha said: 'Look! The Catherine Palace!'

'Stop – please stop!'

She was out of the *troika* before he could assist her up to the huge wrought-iron gates, inspecting the Baroque turquoise and white monument to Russian art, so striking in its dimensions, its golden domes glinting above the snow.

'Who lives here?' she asked Sasha when he came to join her.

'No one – now.'

'No one!' she exclaimed. 'But why not, for Heaven's sake?'

'That is – no one of consequence. It is fully staffed, of course. It was *Catherine*'s palace, Eva – Catherine the Great. Her descendants prefer other palaces. Pavlosk, also, is not in use at the moment.'

'Pavlosk?'

'The former estate of Paul I, Catherine's son. It is further along our road. It was never a gala residence like the Catherine Palace or Pedrodvorets but it is quite splendid and is filled with precious things. Sometimes concerts are held there, too. I will take you to one of them.'

'But the rest of the time no one sees these precious things? They are simply left there, unappreciated?'

'They are the Tsar's, to do what he likes with,' Sasha said.

169

He took her arm. 'Come. It is going to snow again. We must hasten on.'

Past the royal stables went the *troika*, across a river, along by the Rose estate, to where the climate was dry and said to be good for the lungs.

Klyonovo was set among the maple trees after which the estate had been named – klyon, the tree with leaves like hands. The estate was another sea of snow. It was indoors, not outdoors, that impressed Eva then.

The house in which Sasha lived was far more lavish than Uspenskoye, and therefore more to Eva's own liking. Alexandra liked grandeur and Sasha agreed with her. The Victorian influences which had permeated Russia from England had meant nothing to either of them. They had no time for the kind of simplicity which demanded that only four baskets of flowers be placed in a room instead of – delightfully – ten.

The house had always been known for its beautiful floors, a complex mosaic of rare and indigenous woods, palm ebony and Brazilian rosewood; and for its elegant, partly gilded doors.

Shortly before leaving for England Alexandra had acquired armchairs in poppy-red silk which Sasha thought complemented the dainty tables made from porcelain, mahogany and gilt bronze, one with a white opaline top; the classical blue smalt console; the two jewelled glass plaques engraved with the motif of a lyre, and the porphyry *torchère* which was the work of Strykov and Ivachev, the master stone-cutters.

When Eva commented on the beauty of the furnishings, Sasha was gratified.

'Stone-cutting is a Russian national art form,' he said, looking at the candelabra. 'The masters receive their training at the factory in Peterhof. I will take you there one day. The stones are extraordinary: agate, malachite – which is dark green – red granite, jasper. But you must be tired. Elizaveta, will you please see that a room is made up for our guest at once? Where is my cousin?'

'She is dining out this evening, sir,' the girl said, staring with interest at Eva.

'So she is. I remember her mentioning it. Well, it seems that you will have to wait until tomorrow to meet the rest of the family. Aunt Lilya is long since asleep.'

When the servant had left the room Sasha added: 'In a day or so, when you are rested, we can make our plans to wed.'

'Master Alexander?'

The voice itself was deep, a man's voice – the speaker a dwarf. At his side, most incongruously, was a huge dog, a St Bernard, Sasha said.

'Nábat has been missing you,' the dwarf said.

One of his small hands rested on his canine companion's head. Forgetting her manners entirely, Eva gazed at both of them in astonishment. The dog was so enormous; the little man so small.

She put out her hand and patted the dog's rump. The dwarf's expression softened.

Sasha said: 'Vanya adores Nábat. Don't you, Vanya?'

'Do you have any instructions for me, sir?'

'That will be all for now,' said Sasha. 'But leave the dog here.'

Sasha had already explained about Eva to Cousin Marisha by the time the two of them met. He had not worried about her reactions and in that he was right. She was delighted by his news.

She was a tall, heavy-bosomed woman in her mid-fifties with greying hair and piercing blue eyes. Hers was a power which had thrived in motherhood. She had been at her happiest when her five children had been under twelve. Later, she had longed to be a grandmother.

But two of her sons had proved delicate and were already dead. Only one of those remaining had so far married and his wife feared, resented and quite mis-understood her mother-in-law.

Seeing Eva, she scooped her up into the enclosure of her love, enthusing at the top of her voice over Sasha's wise choice.

'But she is so *beautiful!*' she exclaimed, as if to an invisible third party, although only she and Eva were present in the room. 'And I hear that the wedding is to take place quite soon.'

At the back of Cousin Marisha's mind was a suspicion that was virtually a hope – that the wedding had been brought forward because (shocking as it would be!) Eva had got pregnant.

'Yes. It is,' said Eva, referring to the wedding date.

She was disconcerted by Cousin Marisha's overt display of enthusiasm for her. Babushka and Aunt Masha had been kind to her; her own mother had doted upon her but, in the main, Eva was used to engendering in women not cordiality but jealousy, animosity and fear.

'Then Klyonovo will become a *family* home once more,' Cousin Marisha exclaimed meaningfully.

The innuendo was lost on Eva. She smiled uneasily at Cousin Marisha, uncertain how to respond.

Dushechka – poor little soul! thought Cousin Marisha. How shy she is – how much in need of my affection.

She would have been surprised to learn that Eva was not normally viewed by women in such a compassionate light.

Predictably, Eva's relationship with Nábat, the big St Bernard, was problem-free. The animal took to her at once, following her around like a baby anxious not to lose sight of its mother.

So Vanya said. He, too, had taken to Eva and she to him, in the way of queens who like their subjects loyal.

'You must make sure Nábat does not bring mud into

172

the house on his paws,' fussed Sasha, looking anxiously around at the furnishings, but Eva only laughed.

They were going to be married in the Russian Orthodox Church. Sasha took it for granted that Eva would agree to this and she did not argue, although she was not entirely sure that Father Coen would have seen hers as a real marriage.

Cousin Marisha, on the other hand, believed in it implicitly, insisting that Eva wear the wedding-gown that she had worn as a girl.

'In those days, of course, I was more slender – although perhaps not quite as – Still, the dress can be taken in.'

The gown – sent from St Petersburg – turned out to be a fortunate success, made of flimsy tulle with a low neckline, a raised back collar and long, frill-etched sleeves. With this went a long tulle veil which was to be worn with a chaplet of fresh flowers. What pleased Eva less was Sasha's insistence that theirs be a quiet wedding with very few guests.

'Afterwards we will let the rest of the family know about it. It is better that way. Otherwise we may have interference through Tassya from my other sisters.'

For that reason they were to be married not in a big cathedral but in the little estate church.

The night before the wedding Eva got out of bed and tried the dress on again, looking at her reflection in the glass. Once, so Aunt Masha had said, the Russian Church had forbidden the use of mirrors until Peter the Great – sensible man! – had ruled otherwise.

Still wearing her wedding gown she crossed to the window and pulled open the heavy brocade curtains so that she could gaze out into the gardens.

It was the kind of night to which Muscovites, as she now knew, would be well accustomed: the climate in St

Petersburg was less equable than that of Moscow, the marshy land often reducing the snow to slush.

But tonight was a treat, the snow matt, the moon full and bright in the blue-black sky. She stared at the moon. Wasn't it weird that, wherever you were in the world, at some stage you would be able to see that yellow disc?

Maybe at this very minute Dan, too, was standing at a window looking at the same sight. Or was he merely in bed asleep? She must write to Dan and tell him about her marriage to Sasha, and the beautiful dress she had worn.

But then she remembered their last meeting, his declaration of love. It might be cruel to go on too much about the wedding and the dress.

I'll just tell him I got married, she decided. It probably won't come as a great surprise to him – he would be expecting me to make my way up in the world.

Being who I am . . .

'Eva de Burgh? What's wrong with Eva Dillon?'

It must be moonlight madness but she was sure she could hear Dan's voice. There was a scathing quality to it and worse was still to come.

'What do you think you're doing, marrying a fellow you don't love?'

His presence was so strong. If she turned back from the window surely Dan would be there.

And then she'd tell him off.

'You don't understand,' she said to him, still looking out at the moon. 'I'm not like other people. *My* life was planned out, even before I was born!'

At this pronouncement – this statement of fact – Dan actually laughed.

'We're all the same!' he said. 'What are you but a good Irish country girl out in a foreign land? And what's *wrong* with being what you, Eva – Eva Dillon – are?'

'I am Eva de Burgh,' she riposted. 'And tomorrow, as is destined, I will be Eva Pobedonostsev, wife of a wealthy man.'

174

'And what good will that do you?' the wretched man went on. 'And what will you feel, when his hands are all over your body?'

That was too much. In her wedding gown she swung around to face him.

Who would listen to a man who wasn't there?

Soon you will be fulfilling your destiny, she said to herself instead.

The church was yellow with four white columns in front and a wrought-iron balustrade and a woman who could not be herself was stepping out of a sleigh.

Cousin Marisha was fussing over the woman's dress.

'It is much, much too summery. I am cruel allowing you to go out so lightly clad in the middle of winter!'

'I am quite warm,' said the woman who was not Eva.

In truth, this woman was cold all over, numbed and detached from what was going on.

She certainly knew nothing of the amount of trouble to which Sasha had gone to ensure that the traditions of the wedding ceremony would be observed without it including relations or friends who did not live at the house. Someone had to be enrolled to play the part of the bride's father. He asked the estate steward. Then there was the question of the best man. A minimum of four were required, forcing him to engage Vanya and three other servants.

In the church the rest of the staff were waiting. The priest and Sasha were at the altar when Eva was brought in. On a small table draped with silk was a copy of the Bible and a painted icon depicting the enthroned Christ flanked by the Virgin Mary and St John the Baptist. Vanya and one of the other servants held candles in each of their hands. In the hands of the other two best men were two crowns – one for Sasha, one for herself – fashioned out of metal. These crowns which, many centuries earlier, would have been made from

flowers, were copies of those worn by the Tsar and
Tsarina.

A crown for a queen . . . She thought of that and only
of that as she stood on Sasha's left side, and the priest
produced the rings, placing them on the third finger of
Eva's and Sasha's right hands before swapping them
over three times between the bride and bridegroom.

In response to a signal from the priest they began to
encircle the table, Eva and Sasha and the four best men
holding the crowns and candles. Once, twice, three
times round the table before proceeding to the altar to
kiss the sacred icon.

Then – she and Sasha must have exchanged their
vows; must be married although she was barely conscious of having participated in the exchange – the priest
read the final prayer.

'Kiss your wife; and you, Eva, kiss your husband.'

Sasha bent and kissed her on the lips. She shivered and
he took her hand again and held it tight in order to
reassure her. Then he was leading her back down the
aisle, out into the cold, helping her into the sleigh.

Sitting beside her, he squeezed her hand. Eva did not
respond.

The reception supper was over. Cousin Marisha, after
hugging Sasha and Eva and kissing them three times on
alternate cheeks, had finally gone to bed.

Eva walked slowly up the wide staircase towards the
bedrooms, noticing the fresh plants which Vanya had
placed there in honour of this day. Sasha, following,
looked even more serious than usual.

When he opened the door to the conjugal bedroom
and stood aside to allow her to enter, Eva saw that his
hands were shaking.

The big four-poster bed dominated the room – seemed
for a moment to be growing, stretching out the folds of its

canopies to encompass both of them like a gargantuan bird of prey.

A screen had been placed in the room, behind which a bride could modestly undress. The wick of the oil lamp had been turned tactfully low.

'You see, my dressing-room is through here,' said Sasha.

He gestured towards a door. When he had disappeared inside the dressing-room, having shut the door behind him, she slowly began to undress, taking off the tulle veil and dress and draping them over a chair, untying the laces on her corset, sliding off her silk stockings.

A Parisian night-gown, white for the virginal bride, had been donated by Cousin Marisha, and she slipped it over her head before pulling down her hair and brushing it fiercely.

All this took a long time, far longer than Sasha, in his dressing-room, needed to get undressed himself. He put on his dressing-gown and sat stoically on a chair, trying to estimate how many minutes Eva would need for her *toilette*.

Finally, even his quantum of patience ran out and he re-entered the bedroom. He had hoped that his bride would be under the bed-clothes by then, waiting for him to join her. Instead, she was sitting in front of the dressing-table and did not turn her head when he came in.

She would be shy, he thought – all brides were on their wedding night. He came up to her, put his arms around her and kissed the back of her neck. She stiffened – as any new bride might.

He wanted to pick her up and carry her to the bed in the romantic fashion and if her response to him had been loving he would have found the courage to do that.

As it was he only whispered: 'Come, you are tired. You must sleep now,' and when she got to her feet, he took

177

her hand and, more like a nurse than a lover, led her across the room towards their gargantuan bed.

In his most optimistic moments Sasha had looked forward to reciprocating passion on his wedding night; in more down-to-earth considerations he had anticipated bridal shyness and nerves. Since Eva had accepted his proposal he could not but see himself in a fortunate light: he had not expected to feel unhappy after making love to his bride.

Unhappy and inadequate and ashamed. He should not have forced himself on her, he told himself over and over, long after Eva herself had fallen fast asleep. Not tonight when she was tired and strained – not ever. And the justification – the overwhelming strength of his desire for her – was also inexcusable.

Not that Eva had resisted him. On the contrary, he thought, it might have been easier for him now if she had pushed him away, said that she was exhausted, instead of submitting in that frigid, detached way.

She had hated his love-making – he knew that, although she had not said so. Her body told him so, even if words did not. The whole business had been an ordeal for her rather than a pleasure and now he was paying himself for having subjected her to it.

Another man might have shrugged his shoulders, taking the attitude that many women disliked love-making, or so it was supposed. They got used to it with practice and became resigned. Relieving a man's frust-rations was part of the duties of marriage. Why should either of them make a big fuss about it, over-dramatizing and depressing themselves? Another man might have gone to sleep.

But Sasha did not think along those lines – could not bring himself to do so. Loving Eva, he wanted her to be happy above all else. And this night he had made her suffer instead.

But it was the *first* night, the first time. In the morning, tomorrow night, in a week's time it will be better, he tried to persuade himself. Eva will be relaxed.

He was not convinced by his own argument. And when the morning and the night and the week passed with Eva enduring but not melting, he was miserable, but not really surprised. He had never had a high opinion of his own worth, and her attitude only confirmed it.

To the world at large he imagined that he was giving the impression of being a happily married man, but Cousin Marisha for one, saw right through his façade.

She was not an inhibited woman and neither her femininity nor the fact that she was Sasha's cousin rather than his mother deterred her from making enquiries about his marriage.

Finding him alone one morning she came straight to the point. 'You are not happy in this marriage, I would say. The love-making is not right?'

Sasha went red. It was not necessary for him to answer for Cousin Marisha to know she had been right in her assumptions.

Poor, poor boy, she thought.

'Would you like me to talk to Eva?' she asked Sasha. 'Sometimes young girls need the advice of older women. Remember her own mother is dead.'

'No!' he said. 'Please!'

Another wave of colour flooded Sasha's troubled face.

'Don't worry,' Cousin Marisha said reassuringly. 'I won't tell her you and I have talked. I shall be very discreet. Tonight, you will see, all will be very much better.'

Sasha, usually so courteous, did not express his gratitude which rather surprised her, as did the low moan he emitted before, still blushing, he made his way to the door.

* * *

'Eva,' said Cousin Marisha, *'Dushechka!'*

Eva, with Nábat at her side, had just come in from a walk. It was much too cold to be out of doors in Cousin Marisha's opinion, but she did not want to lecture the child about that as well as about the other, more important matter. She had given a great deal of sincere thought to what she perceived as Eva's dilemma –the predicament of many a beautiful woman forced into bed with a dull, unimaginative husband. A kind man – that went without saying – but better a brute than a dullard when it came to making love. The child would ultimately find her reward in babies. Meanwhile, she must learn how to make her husband happy in bed.

'Dushechka! Come here, child.'

By Eva's side, as usual, was the dog, its air of incipient tragedy accentuated by the way its upper eyelids fell well over its eyes. Behind both of them lurked Vanya, the dwarf. Eva had thought that man and dog made an incongruous combination: Cousin Marisha felt that they went well together, their heads enormous, their faces wrinkled (Vanya was not young), their upper lips pendant, their legs heavily muscled; both of them with an inherent tendency to rush to the rescue.

'You wanted to talk to me?' enquired Eva.

In response to a nod she sank down into a chair. Cousin Marisha gestured to Vanya to leave, which he promptly did. Nábat, by contrast, positioned himself between the two women, blocking Cousin Marisha's view of Eva's face, tilting up his snub nose and letting his mouth hang open to reveal his shiny red tongue. The animal's presence and Eva's concentration upon him did not assist in creating an appropriate ambience for a serious discussion about love-making, but Cousin Marisha forged ahead.

'It can be difficult for a young bride, the first nights,' she said; although for her it had been the reverse. 'Perhaps you did not know the facts, and now you feel besmirched? But it is good, natural, to make love with your husband.'

Eva's hand was caressing the strong neck of the dog. Since her face was hidden, it was not possible to gauge her reaction. But then she said: 'Yes, I knew what would happen,' and if Cousin Marisha had been asked what her tone conveyed she would have replied, disinterest.

But that could not be so . . .

'At the beginning it is often difficult for many girls. But it becomes pleasurable with practice.'

'I understand all that,' Eva said in the same indifferent manner.

The time had come for a good lecture, with a warning at the end of it. Without any further ado Cousin Marisha explained to Eva about the nature of men: how beauty alone was not enough to retain their interest, how a woman had to work at marriage, learn the art of making love.

'Because if she does not, if she is cold and unresponsive, her husband might be forced to take a mistress,' she ended.

At that point Eva stood up and Cousin Marisha was able to see her face. It looked quite cheerful. Her little talk had not fallen on deaf ears, she concluded. Eva had listened and taken note. All would now be well with the children.

In fact, Eva had registered a few – just a few – of those carefully selected words.

Her husband might be forced to take a mistress. If Sasha chose to do that, she would be perfectly happy.

Then her thoughts went back to where they had been for most of Cousin Marisha's lecture: to the British embassy ball.

11

Her first social engagement as Sasha's wife was to be a ball at the British embassy – now that was fate at work!

Ever since Sasha had raised the subject of the ball, Eva had been thinking of how the ambassador and his wife and all their guests would receive her as Lord Clanricarde's daughter – the offspring of a man who had held with distinction this top diplomatic post.

And she would finally see St Petersburg itself. For a whole week she and Sasha were to stay at the Pobedonostsevs' apartment in the fashionable Sergeyevskaya Street, in the Liteinaya quarter.

The apartment in Moscow, Sasha explained, was far less frequently used.

'Moscow is an arts and industry centre. It is for academics and musicians. It is less élite than St Petersburg which is a city of the court and the civil service. You will find that people in St Petersburg do not think very highly of Moscow. Muscovites feel much the same about us us –'

He paused, raising his eyebrows, intimating that Muscovites could not be right.

It had occurred to Sasha that Eva would need new clothes. Jewellery, too. If only his mother had not stayed in England. She could have given advice – far better than Cousin Marisha who knew more about loving than style. And it was pointless asking Olga. Apart from the fact that, however politely, he had spurned her love, she had no taste in clothes.

Eva and he would have to do their best together. He said to her: 'In St Petersburg you and I will do a little shopping.'

* * *

Such an elegant city, so perfectly planned. The boulevards so straight and so wide, almost as wide as the frozen river Neva.

The houses so cheerful, painted in bright colours, the bridges red or blue. And soaring above them all the domes of so many churches.

How regimented it all was – so well-behaved! Even the streets! Although their pavings might be defective they were neatly divided into first, second and third ranks. Adding to the impression of general regimentation were the large numbers of military officers in uniform. Not to mention the women in bright, rich national costumes, with white mantles ornamented with silver tassels, their headgear shaped like diadems, adorned with pearl and silver, who – in their way – were also graded since their apparel was either pink or blue.

'Who are those women?' Eva asked Sasha curiously.

'Wet nurses. You see them everywhere in this city. They wear blue if their charges are boys, and pink if they are girls.'

Some people were less well-organized: the pedlars offering a variety of goods; Tatars selling linen and old clothes. They shouted: *'Khalati!' 'Tsreti, tsvetochki!'* and the beautiful, circumspect, classical city seemed to sigh with resignation at the amount of noise they made about dressing gowns and potatoes.

Sasha was enjoying himself showing Eva around, but he had not forgotten that they also had a practical purpose in town.

Eva must have gowns, the best gowns, imported from Paris, made by those couturiers of whom his mother spoke. He planned to take Eva to Merten's to buy furs for her, and to Morozov's the jewellers in Gostiny Dvor.

They went to Merten's first to buy Eva two full-length fur coats, one for day-time wear and the other to wear over her ball-gowns when she finally acquired them.

'And fur blankets for wraps,' said Sasha, even though

there were several fur blankets in the apartment already, left behind by his mother. But he wanted the most fashionable, the very best of everything for Eva.

He explained this to the staff at Merten's and the correct coats were brought out – sables, blue and silver; white Arctic fox; snow leopard and lynx and wild mink, some with trims of ermine. Alongside these were wraps made from bear and beaver, and yellow-throated marten.

'Which do you prefer?'

'I'm not sure,' said Eva, hesitant for once. 'They're all beautiful.'

'Sable is the lightest and softest – look,' Sasha urged, picking up a blue sable coat and refraining from mentioning that it was also the most expensive fur. 'I think you should take this for evening, and perhaps wild mink for day.'

Eva nodded agreement, acquiescing, Sasha felt, to his superior knowledge in this, for her, new world. He gave an order for beaver blankets and, feeling pleased with himself, decided to postpone the visit to Morozov's until the afternoon, and to take Eva straight to the House of Fabergé in Bolshaya Morskaya which had been granted a Royal Warrant and had recently doubled in size.

'What do they sell there?' asked Eva, gloriously ignorant.

'Oh, this and that,' he said mysteriously, wanting to surprise her. 'I think you'll enjoy going there.'

On his own previous visit to the House, Peter Carl Fabergé had been present in person, and Sasha had hoped that the master-jeweller might be there today.

Intent on enquiring for him he nearly missed Eva's ecstatic reaction to the treasures on display – gold cigarette cases and powder boxes, clocks, animal carvings and the enamelled Easter eggs for which Fabergé was famous.

'Look closely and you will see that there are many

shades of gold,' he said to her. 'If he varies the alloy a goldsmith can produce not only yellow, or green or red or white gold but also the more *recherché* effects such as blue, orange or grey.'

'But at Fabergé we tend to stay with the more usual colours,' an assistant, to Sasha's discomfort, butted in. 'Just as we rarely use precious stones, unless for special commissions and Imperial pieces. The Master is particularly fond of Siberian emeralds and the grey jasper of Kalgan.'

'We have come in order to speak to M. Fabergé about a special commission,' Sasha said. He did not have any particular article of jewellery in mind for Eva, but was irritated by the way the assistant had cut into his little speech. 'It's a great pity that he is not here.'

'Did you have a specific item in mind, sir?' enquired the assistant, annoying him even more.

It was only then that he noticed Eva's enthralled expression. She was standing in front of a collection of carvings of animals, fishes and birds looking, Sasha thought, like a small, enchanted child. He followed her gaze, assimilating the collection, the giant agate anteater, the varicoloured ostrich with green garnet eyes, the dogs and owls and kingfishers and the large frog with gloriously distended stomach and happy, satisfied smile.

'They all look as if they have been very well fed!' Eva remarked, unable to look away.

'Would you like one of those pieces?' he asked her, puzzled by her taste.

His own choice for her would have been one of the exquisitely enamelled Easter eggs, the rose trellis and pale green enamel one which, opened up, revealed a model of the Gatchina palace executed in gold: a device to hide the jewel, an oval locket, which the Master had placed beneath it.

Or, possibly, the silver pen holder, enamelled a translucent orange rust with a red-gold mount.

'I'd like that one!' Eva said, raising her big brown eyes to him and then dropping them again in contemplation of a carving less than three inches tall of a brown-grey agate dog. 'He's exactly like Nábat!'

There was no accounting for taste! Buying the carving Sasha also placed an order for a head ornament for Eva.

'Something like that one,' he said to the assistant, pointing to a spray with floral diamonds on red-gold stalks in a rubbed-over silver setting.

'The master never repeats a piece!' the assistant told him, shocked. 'Every piece is unique.'

'Well, whatever he wants to create,' Sasha said irascibly.

It hardly mattered. Nothing appeared likely to give Eva as much pleasure as the little agate dog.

Outside in the street she insisted on removing the carving from its box so that she could look at it again. Holding it in her hand she said to Sasha:

'Let's walk.'

'In the snow?'

'Why not?'

With the *troika* following them they strolled back along the avenue. The drinking fountains had frozen over. The dignity of the sculpted gods and goddesses looking down from the façades of houses was in shreds – they had icicles on their noses. In Senate Square the equestrian statue of Peter the Great was similarly afflicted, as well as his rearing horses, and the dome of St Isaac's cathedral.

The snow was falling quite heavily when, in the afternoon, they set out for Morozov's.

'Garnets for everyday wear. A single string and dropping earrings,' Sasha was saying when a man stumbled out of Ulitsa Plekhanova and skidded in front of the *troika*, narrowly missing the horses' hooves.

The driver pulled up.

'For God's sake be careful!' shouted Sasha.

The man did not look around but floundered on to the other side of the road and disappeared from sight.

Seconds later three other men appeared from the direction that the fugitive had come, waving sticks and shouting drunkenly.

'Where did he go? Where did he go?' one of them yelled at Sasha.

'That way –'

Sasha was about to point in the direction which the man had taken but Eva held his arm.

'There – there!' she insisted, pointing in the opposite direction, back along the Prospekt.

'He went that way?'

'Yes. Indeed. Hurry!'

'Eva, there was no need to protect that fellow,' Sasha said when they were alone. 'He was a Jew. You didn't notice the black cap he was wearing?'

'Why should we not protect a Jew, as well as anyone else? And who were those other men?'

'Just students, a bit merry,' said Sasha, answering her second question first. 'As to the fellow they were chasing, as the Tsar himself said, we should never forget that it was the Jews who crucified our Lord and spilled his precious blood. Apart from that it is rumoured that the murder of Alexander II was the work of Jews. Certainly one of the accused was a Jewess. They have doubtless been inspired by the German Jew, Karl Marx, who propounded the theory that only labour counts. You must know that Jewish lawyers are banned from the Russian bar and that as many of them as possible are prevented from attending educational institutions. Many have been deported *en masse* from Moscow and Kiev, which, of course, is all to the good.'

Eva frowned, taking in – Sasha presumed – the wisdom of what he had said.

'Drive on,' he commanded.

The jewellery was duly purchased. It was their final outing that day.

There was white lace around the shoulders of the gown which Eva was to wear at the ball – a gown which plunged down to a low *décolletage* and was caught there by a bow. Its bodice and hipline were made from rose satin, the skirt of white ruffles and there were flowers on the tiny sleeves and a band of flowers underneath the hips.

With this she was to wear white gloves and to insert the same colour flowers, pink and blue, into the back of her hair.

Before the dress could be slipped over her head there was the serious business of putting on what went underneath, her frilly drawers, specially designed for wearing under very smooth, very tight-fitting dresses, as, in a subtle way – in spite of its flounces and flowers – was hers; and over this her corset, red and tan, with cream lace and trimming and a blue satin bow. Her corset was reinforced with leather and stiffened with whalebone with an oval spoon busk designed to compress the stomach. On her bottom was perched a small wire bustle, consisting of six little hoops intended to support the heavy drapery at the back of her skirt. The bustle was light but strong. When she sat down the six little hoops folded in together.

An hour before they were due to leave for the ball Eva was almost ready. At Morozov's Sasha had purchased a costly diamond bracelet, pressing it upon her almost in the manner of a supplicant wishing to win her favour.

Slipping it over her gloved hand she thought: Tonight I will forget that my father was a womanizer and remember only that he honoured the name of de Burgh by the distinguished post he held. Tonight they will acclaim me as his child.

'You are beautiful, *baryshnya* – so beautiful!' the maid

who had dressed her whispered. She wondered what it would be like to be a great lady, born to wealth like this one, who thought nothing of going to a ball.

The *troika* crossed the Winter Canal at its junction with the Neva by the Hermitage Bridge and continued on along the Dvortovaya Naberezhnava towards their destination.

'You will create a sensation tonight,' Sasha said. 'You are bound to be the most beautiful woman present.'

If my father could see me he, too, would be impressed, Eva thought. Walking up these steps, as he must have done so many times, and I in my sable coat and diamond bracelet, and Mr Worth's white and rose satin work of art.

Acting like a *scubaide bheag leitheadach*, her country-women might have added – swollen with the swank.

She *was* a bit full of herself, but not for long for, right at the top of the steps, she was struck by a terrible thought. Why had she never considered the matter before?

'What is it?' asked Sasha, since Eva, having paused on the top of the steps, seemed to be rooted there. 'What's the matter? Are you·not well?'

Eva turned a stricken face towards him.

'What *is* it?'

There was no alternative but to tell him, although she did not want to confess, neither to him nor to anyone else.

She said, thinking – after all that preparation; the certainty that my presentation was perfection: *'I can't go to the ball. I've never learnt how to dance!'*

'But that is of no importance,' Sasha said, after a couple of seconds. 'Now listen to me Eva, it is very, very simple: we will intimate that you are *enceinte* – in a delicate condition, you understand? That way, people will think that it is quite natural that you would want to sit rather than dance. And, even though we have not been married very long, people in St Petersburg do not know when the ceremony took place – only that I have been abroad and have taken an Irish bride.'

Eva smiled at him gratefully, if not with great love, and he slipped his arm under hers.

The crisis averted, they were admitted. With Sasha by her side Eva lined up to be received by the British ambassador and his wife: '. . . Pobedonostsev,' she heard a man's voice call, and she found herself in front of two affable faces.

Acknowledgements were made. Eva heard herself responding. A surge of triumph went through her.

'See! See!' she said in her mind to her father's ghost. 'I am here!' and, with no credit given to Sasha, she added: 'I got here by myself!'

Under the brilliant chandeliers the revellers danced sedately. By her side a couple were animatedly discussing the Tsar's favourite opera: 'So melancholic – so full of passion. Poor Lensky – so jealous of his friend . . . "*Kuda, kuda, kuda vy udalilis*" – that moment when he confronts his possible death!'

'You are not too tired?' enquired Sasha, playing his role well.

Eva shook her head. The evening was going well enough, she thought, in spite of the drawback of not being able to dance. Still, she had taken careful note of what was going on on the floor and she decided with a little practice that this matter would soon be rectified.

Meanwhile, people were very obviously impressed by her appearance – she saw admiration on their faces, heard them whisper as she passed.

And all this, notwithstanding the fact that – as yet – no one knew who she was. She was looking forward to telling them that she was Lord Clanricarde's daughter which Sasha, she thought, should have done already.

'My dear child, are you feeling all right?'

The British ambassador's wife, her supportive duties completed for the time being, appeared on her left side.

'We were very pleased you could come. You're Irish, I hear?'

It was the moment for which Eva had been waiting – the opportunity to talk about herself and to make her impressive announcement.

She allowed the English woman to sit beside her in a whoosh of ruched satin.

'Yes, I am Irish,' she said. 'I am – I was Eva de Burgh. The daughter of Ulick de Burgh, Lord Clanricarde, the former ambassador to Russia.'

In the long silence which followed this announcement her neighbour on the other side said sadly: 'Her voice is too *full* for Tatyana at the beginning, although I agree that in the last act her soprano copes with Tchaikovsky's vocal demands . . .'

'I see,' said the British ambassador's wife. 'Really – I had – no idea.'

'I wondered – are there any mementoes of my father in the residence? Perhaps a portrait? He died when I was very young but I know that he was handsome.'

There was a curious expression on the English woman's face, something which Eva was experiencing difficulty in reading. Pity? Surely not? And yet – it was not one of respect.

'He must indeed have been handsome – very handsome to have such a beautiful daughter,' said the British ambassador's wife. 'Now, dear, tell me, how are you enjoying living in Russia?'

The subject had been changed. It was almost as if the British ambassador's wife did not want to discuss Ulick de Burgh.

She stayed talking amicably to Eva without once referring to Lord Clanricarde again, and then, with a motherly smile, left again on her conversational rounds.

Beside Eva the talkative couple had moved on from *Eugene Onegin* to Mussorgsky.

'In the reign of our Tsar Russian music and literature have reached great heights . . .'

'But, of course. Although the foundations for that were laid in his *father's* reign.'

It was much later in the night when Eva overheard a conversation relevant to herself.

Both the British ambassador and his wife were, as befitted their diplomatic status, the most tactful of people. They would not have discussed Ulick de Burgh between themselves that night, had they thought Eva could hear.

But when the subject came up Eva was out of sight of both of them, although not out of earshot, behind a Corinthian column, adjusting one of the flowers on her hip band which seemed to have worked itself loose.

'Extraordinary thing – Clanricarde's daughter married to young Sasha!' an English voice exclaimed.

Eva's ears pricked up.

'A lovely creature,' said a woman. 'His *daughter*? But Clanricarde was too old . . .'

'My dear, that man had bastards all over the place, up to the very end! After all, his womanizing contributed to the political defeat of the Whigs and to Lord Palmerston's temporary retirement from office. Clanricarde fathered an illegitimate son, a man called Delacour, by the wife of one of his friends. Delacour inherited his mother's property after her husband's death. Her family – the Handcocks – objected, attempted to regain a proportion of the property by persuading the heir to settle. Wouldn't do it, of course. Action brought against him in the Court of Chancery. Clanricarde a witness, damningly said to have schemed to secure the inheritance for the bastard son. All in the papers at the time. *Very* bad for the Whigs.'

'I knew there was something,' the woman sighed. 'I

knew Clanricarde was disgraced – I couldn't remember the details. Poor child – so proud of being his daughter.'

'Not much merit in that!' said the man. 'Well, my dear, shall we dance?'

Bastards all over the place!

How she wished she could curse her father as their ancestor, Nuala the Dagger Woman, had done, she who had stabbed her own sons to death and solemnly fulminated against those who dared to lay hands on as much as a stone of her many castles!

With tears of hurt and anger trickling down her cheeks, Eva stood rigid behind the pillar.

Her father, having done so little for her in material terms, had not even left behind a shred of his reputation! That he be tormented in Hell!

And as for the ambassador and his wife, she hated them, too, for pitying her, forgetting that there had been compliments as well.

A few hours before she had been quite sure that she would be welcomed with open arms into Russian society, simply on the basis of being her father's daughter. Now she was equally convinced that, deep down, she would never be accepted; that she might be admired but not respected.

Acceptance, then, still mattered enormously to her. But the conversation she had overheard had also planted a tiny seed of rebellion within her. It was so minute that Eva did not know that it was there.

Having regained control of herself she saw the evening through, and if she looked a little weary at the end of it, that only contributed to her being thought of as *enceinte*.

'What a charming wife you have,' the British ambassador's kindly wife said to Sasha as they left.

Eva managed a wan smile.

'Good-night,' she said, thinking – May the Devil roast

193

the whole lot of them! as she made her way down the steps.

It was quite the wrong night for Sasha to try to make love to Eva. When he reached out for her he surprised upon her face a look of such hatred and contempt that he winced and turned away.

He was not to know that this rancour and scorn were directed, not particularly at himself, but at all seducers, all those profligates and philanderers who attempt to take advantage of women.

Categorized thus now, never at any stage desired by his wife, Sasha told himself that Eva would never warm towards him in bed. He thought that she was by nature frigid; that she would never have been interested in any man in a sexual way. How wrong Tassya had been – how far removed from the truth in her accusations.

Next day he left Eva in the apartment and walked alone in the city until he found himself outside the Alexander Nevsky monastery.

Still thinking about Eva he wandered across the bridge over the canal and into the monastery courtyard. At the church door he hesitated, then stepped inside. Beneath the enormous gold sunburst and the painting of God the Father, a priest in a red cassock was chanting and crossing himself. At a white and gold side altar a woman lit a candle and kissed a depiction of a saint. His own favourite icon, an exquisite Madonna in beaded clothes, reminded him of Eva. He began to hate himself for making love to her, for making her as unhappy as himself.

He stared up at the Cross. From its zenith a slender silver rod fell down to grip a trio of chains and another, thicker candle. The priest bowed his head.

On his way out the urns and the lamenting figures in the graveyard were snowmen of a kind, poking fun at death. He knew by then that he could not go on for very much longer in the same humiliating manner. Something had to be done.

The snows melted and turned into brown slush. April became May and fat, flaunting scarlet poppies bloomed, and the pale mauve lilac. The air was crisp. The White Nights kept the sun up late.

On one of those elongated days they went by carriage to Pavlosk. The practice of holding recitals at the railway station hall, initiated by the Tsarina Maria, was still popular. Strauss himself had performed there, Sasha said to Eva on the way. But on this day he intended not to listen but to talk, and in an appropriate setting, which meant in the palace. Although he knew that what he had to say would be only too acceptable to Eva, it was still a delicate subject to broach.

Over the entrance gates the two-headed eagle proclaimed Pavlosk's royal status. Gilt lettering on a black plaque recorded the foundation of the estate. In front of the yellow mansion a statue of Paul I gazed serenely over their heads.

'Why did you bring me here?'

'To prove to you that there are things that we *can* share,' Sasha said earnestly. 'This vista. The temple with the sculpture of Maria inside it. The treasures inside the house.'

'Which, once again, is not in use?'

'At present, no. I can come here whenever I like.'

Above them the poplar trees bowed in deference to her beauty, or so Sasha thought. He wondered where to make his announcement. In the room of Peace, surrounded by sculpted flowers; by peacocks, symbols of family happiness – the irony in that! And had not Paul, father of ten, dedicated an ivory temple within this palace to that very theme?

The Room of War then! Or in that room where a

195

painted Cupid pointed an arrow at your heart and would not let you escape . . .

Other Cupids adorned the empress's gilded linden wood bed.

'You said you had something to tell me.'

'Yes,' he said, 'I did.'

The conclusion was neither war nor peace. He would try not to bother her again, would take a mistress. No one in society. In order to avert a scandal a peasant woman from the estate would be recruited. Vanya would see to that. Otherwise nothing would change. Their pleasant life would go on.

In the empress's room was a toilet set fashioned from silver and enamel, a gift from King Louis of France – a treasure so precious that it had not been used but placed in a special case. Instead, an alternative set made of Tula steel had been purchased for practical use.

'There is so much else to see,' Sasha said. 'The crimson Tapestry Room. A gilt clock in the shape of a lyre. The ceiling in the Throne Room.'

So many treasures to share . . .

Why remember the look of relief on Eva's beautiful face?

12

Stronger by nature and more certain of himself than Sasha, stimulated by the development of his career on *The Times* of London, Dan might have been expected to relegate Eva at least to the back of his mind as time went by. He did nothing of the kind, neither immediately after her marriage nor in the two years following it, by which time he had been working for the paper in Paris for almost three months.

This appointment, he knew, was partly due to the unexpected friendship shown him by Henri Stefan Opper de Blowitz, a Bohemian immigrant to France who, having joined *The Times* at the age of forty-five, had made himself its Paris correspondent.

Blowitz had scooped the world with his exclusive report on the Treaty of Berlin. The story of how he did it, depending more on guile and quick thinking than on gentlemanly behaviour, had long been a Fleet Street legend.

Blowitz, as Dan knew well, was very far from being a gentleman. He was an egoist and, outside his trade, a liar. He caused monumental headaches at Printing House Square by writing his dispatches in French.

But he was a brilliant foreign correspondent. When Dan, spending a holiday in France in order to improve the French which he was doggedly studying in London, called upon him and said so, Blowitz was flattered and amused.

In due course an arrangement was made with Printing House Square – Dan would act as Blowitz's assistant for two years, basing himself in Paris and leaving the great man free to roam further afield when necessary.

On a March morning in 1892 the two men, one short with greying hair and bushy side-whiskers, the other tall and clean-shaven, walked together along the Avenue de Suffren discussing not the affairs of France but, rather, those of Russia.

'An empire governed by fools – imbeciles!' Blowitz asserted loudly. 'The bad harvest of last year leading inevitably to famine now. All the time the peasant becomes poorer, the soil declines in fruitfulness, the population increases – and the State grows more and more exacting in the collection of taxes! In Vyatka, for instance, the governor is so determined to lay hands on the taxes that he sends out the vice-governor with police officials and soldiers and Cossacks with sledge-loads of birch-rods on a tour of inspection of the villages. And what is it they do? They select the wealthiest peasants and they flog them until the taxes are produced. But in many cases there is no money and so they sequestrate the private property of the villagers – not only their tea-urns and their fur coats and their cotton clothing but also their agricultural implements!'

'And at the same time the Council of the Empire is proposing to introduce a scheme whereby the authorities can lend the peasants seed-corn in the Spring which they will have to return in the Autumn when the harvest is gathered!'

'Exactly! And what will they use in the interim for implements? It is absurd! On the other hand the scheme, if it goes through, will only come into effect *next* year – after so many are dead! Not only of hunger but also of influenza of which there is currently an epidemic . . . *Mon Dieu*, Dan, but do you have to walk so fast? I do not have legs like you!'

'Sorry!' Dan said, grinning and modifying his pace to the other man's requirements.

'To run cannot be healthy! The Council has no idea . . .'

At the end of the Avenue Suffren, Blowitz and Dan turned right into Avenue Gustave Eiffel and the former, catching sight of the Eiffel Tower, switched abruptly from discussion of Russian affairs to a diatribe on this three-year-old construction: 'A two-and-a-half-million-rivets steel monstrosity!' he observed, grimacing. 'It has ruined the Champs de Mars, bestriding its formality like a gigantic pike-staff!'

'Eiffel did say France would be the only country in the world with a 300-metre flagpole,' Dan said as Blowitz paused for breath.

Artists and writers were appalled by the tower, but Dan rather liked it. 'At least it gave employment to 300 steeplejacks!'

'Let them starve rather than do such work!'

Averting his gaze from the tower the senior man began to give his instructions for the day: 'M. Burdeau's election as vice-president of the Chamber will be held in the room of M. Viette –that is for you to cover. There is also the trial today of Eugène and Archilles Dourches for forcibly taking Louise Dourches from the Ville Juif lunatic asylum. And I am told that the so-called Rajah of Benares may be evicted from that house at Suresnes . . .'

What a genius the fellow had for picking up news, Dan thought, thinking of the third story. Probably a tip-off from a woman. Blowitz got on well with women and they, in turn, confided in him. For all I know, mused Dan, grinning, the informant could be the so-called Rajah's wife.

But when he and Blowitz had parted company and he was on his way to his first assignment of the day his thoughts reverted to Russia. From there it was a short, inevitable step to thinking about Eva. There had been other women in his life but none equal to her.

Remarkable how the two of them had continued to keep in touch. It was more understandable from his side than from hers: she was married, after all. But marriage had not deterred Eva from putting pen to paper. Over the years since she had been in Russia her letters – originally guarded, like herself, boasting about her finery and her jewels, the grand people she had met – had become a bit more open, hinting of dissatisfaction with her affluent life.

At the beginning, too, she had still gone on about the de Burghs, reminding him (as if he could forget!) that her father had been an ambassador to Russia, and asking him if he ever heard any news in London about her brother Hubert. Maybe he had even met him?

Eva's obsession with the de Burghs had never ceased to irritate Dan. With satisfaction he had been able to tell her that Hubert de Burgh had a reputation in London of being a miser and a recluse – that his greatest extravagance was laughingly said to be a meal of two boiled eggs.

At the time he had made this report he had been piqued himself, hurt over her marriage: that must have been obvious because Eva's next letter had been more sensitive and concerned.

That was the one in which she had revealed her own distress, telling him of her father's involvement in the Handcock marriage. The old scoundrel's behaviour in this connection seemed to have been a turning point in her life.

The affair must have been reported in *The Times*. One of these days, when he was back in London, he would go to the archives and read about it there.

Eva had indeed been brought to a crossroads at the British embassy ball. Afterwards she turned off in a different direction, but no one saw her go.

Sasha – believing that she still wanted to go to parties and balls – accepted the invitations he would previously have turned down. Eva *was* taken up in society – she even met the Tsar.

She learned German as well as French. Ostensibly she appeared to be at ease with the glittering people. But she never rid herself of the conviction that she did not belong.

Nor did she feel a true member of the household at Klyonovo, in spite of Cousin Marisha's mothering or her own growing affection for the Russians as a whole. Warm, volatile and passionate, their emotions ran deep. Elevated on good days to the heights of glory, or plunged, on bad ones, into the depths of dejection, they reminded her of the Celts.

However dissatisfied Eva might be with her life, she remained cloistered in a world of gaiety and affluence, hardly aware of the devastation wrought by the bad harvest until Marisha's sister died.

Would Eva travel with her to Sandomir, in the Radom region, where the funeral was to take place? Marisha wanted to know.

So while Dan was striding along the Avenue Gustave Eiffel, in the company of Henri Stefan Opper de Blowitz, Eva was in Sandomir, in a house filled with incense and the non-stop chanting of priests.

She was gazing out of a window at a garden covered in snow, thinking of what she had observed since her departure from Klyonovo.

The weather for the excursion had been much worse than either she or Cousin Marisha had anticipated. Meadows and cornfields had been buried deep in snow and as they had journeyed on, worried all the time lest the roads on which they were travelling become impregnable, they had been forced to confront the fact that a number of farms had been destroyed beyond redemption.

It had been the plight of the animals which had brought home to Eva the reality of what was happening in Russia. The severe frost of January had decimated horses and cattle which were unable to live in the cold without being properly fed. Their corpses, half-covered in snow, lay rotting on the sides of the roads.

Or some of them did. A huntsman whom they had encountered along the way had revealed that he was paying a mere fifty copecks each for a dead horse off which his dogs could feed because so many were available.

'Russia has not ever sustained such a loss in horses as during this last year,' he maintained vehemently. 'Even in the famine of 1840 it was not like this.'

Then, when Cousin Marisha had drawn his attention to the ploughed but unsown fields, he had told them: 'In many parts of Sandomir there *is* no seed corn. These fields will probably not be sown for weeks. The transport of grain on the railways is very slow and by wagon it's even worse. The horses, of course, are half-starved and unfit for work.'

More evidence of the seriousness of the situation was brought to Eva's attention when she arrived at the house of mourning. Cousin Marisha's family was large and very widespread: relations had journeyed from many parts of the country in order to pay their respects to the dead woman. Each one spoke of what was going on in their area.

In Roslav, in the Government of Smolensk, there was much distress, with villagers living on bread made of rye and hempseed and many, unable to find work, reduced to begging. There was no prospect of relief: the provincial Government of Smolensk had spent 15,000 roubles on the whole district, reported Cousin Marisha's youngest brother, Grigory – a minimal amount.

A cousin, Pyotr, said that in Nizhni-Novgorod the streets of the bazaars were filled not with merchants but with snow drifts. In the Government of Tobolsk disturbances had broken out and the situation there was said to be so serious that Prince Galitzin was about to be posted in as Imperial Commissioner with unlimited powers to act.

Back at Klyonovo, Sasha spoke angrily of the numbers of peasants who had failed to pay their taxes.

'They must be forced to comply,' he maintained. 'Once again I blame Count Tolstoy for these instances of resistance. He is an irresponsible man, giving the people ideas beyond their comprehension. Many have felt – rightly, in my opinion – that the fellow should have been detained rather than merely confined to his estate for publishing these anti-government articles about the famine. He is mad – an anarchist. A revolutionary!'

'So your cousin Constantine says.'

'The Minister of the Interior should know what he is talking about.'

'Has *he* been to Sandomir lately?'

'I have no idea,' said Sasha. 'Excuse me. I must leave for the city at once.'

Bad harvest. Starvation. Taxes – the peasants forced to pay. For Eva it was an all too familiar theme. She had taken it for granted that conditions at Klyonovo were good.

But was that the case or had the bad harvest also had repercussions at the estate? How just an employer was Sasha? His harsh words troubled her.

She was not in the habit of touring the estate: its running fell to Sasha and his steward. But after all she had seen these last few weeks, she wondered at herself for remaining remote from the land and its people.

'Vanya,' she said. 'Come with me. I would like to be taken right round the estate.'

It was not a day for going outdoors. The sky was leaden grey and it was sleeting. Still, no one had taken *her* furs away: she would be muffled up.

'Do you wish to visit each family?' Vanya queried, his brow more furrowed than ever.

'Every one,' she said. 'We must ascertain who is in need of food or money or clothes.'

Thirteen roubles each, she knew, would see the people through to the new harvest. A tidy sum, if she considered the numbers of workers and their families, but not, she felt, unrealistic.

With Vanya on one side of her and Nábat on the other she set off by sleigh. Nábat, the most amiable of animals, had one curious habit: seated next to anyone else but Eva he invariably moved even closer to his neighbour and, with a peculiar jerk sideways, attempted to push them away with his rump. Having twice seen Vanya flung sprawling into the snow, Eva ensured his protection thereafter.

Thirteen roubles each, she repeated silently. That money Sasha must fetch from the Gunzburg bank.

In fact, Sasha's visit to St Petersburg was directly concerned with the Gunzburg bank where much of the family fortune was currently amassed. But the bank, along with several big financial houses, was in trouble. When Sasha got to town he discovered that up to six million roubles of assets were in difficulty of immediate realization.

Other men were worried, too. Meeting somebody he had previously thought of as only an acquaintance he was surprised when the fellow detained him, eager for someone to whom he could pour out his woes. He spoke of his wife's penchant for imported clothes, something which women of her ilk had formerly regarded not as a luxury but as a necessity: he had been forced, he confessed, to refuse to buy them for her. Her anger had appalled him. He, too, was worried sick about the Gunzburg bank's affairs.

'*Spokoinoi nochi!*' Sasha heard one peasant say to another after he and the man had parted – *A good night!*

At the end of that week the bank announced that its problems were alleviated. The men of the city relaxed.

For the time being, Sasha thought, going to bed alone.

Spokoinoi nochi! For how long would life be good – trouble remain averted?

Towards the end of that first day Eva had a good idea of what conditions on the estate were like. No one was actually starving. Nevertheless when she suggested that the workers be provided with bread and meat soup and dishes of peas and beetroot, many faces lit up.

'Orders must be given to the kitchen as soon as we get back,' she said to Vanya. 'No, don't turn back yet. I still want to go on. I did say I wanted to visit *every* worker's house.'

'I think there is no one in this one,' Vanya said categorically, as they passed another *izba*.

He flipped the reins and the sleigh bells tinkled.

'But there *is!*' protested Eva. 'There was a girl – a woman standing at the door. Surely you must have seen her?'

'I'm sure Madam is mistaken,' Vanya said politely. 'No one was there, I am sure.'

And I am equally sure I am right, thought Eva obstinately. For some reason Vanya did not want to stop at that particular house.

Was it because of the girl?

It was a question which Sasha could have answered with consummate ease, for the woman concerned had been his mistress for the last two years.

From Sasha's viewpoint it was a good enough arrangement: Evdoxia, Dusya for short, was, by nature, maternal, and it was this kind of motherly sex that Sasha had always craved.

He was somewhat disconcerted, although flattered, to discover soon on in their relationship that Dusya adored him. Although she was only a peasant her adulation propped up his sagging confidence which Eva, on a daily basis, threatened to knock down. He felt no guilt about taking advantage of his *droit de seigneur*, for Dusya revelled in his doing so. But sometimes her intensity startled and disturbed him. She loved him far too much. It could not be healthy.

Still, he did not spend too much time considering Dusya's ways. There were too many other, more important things to think about.

The effects of the famine were soon shown on the Exchequer returns. Receipts showed a falling off of 29,000,000 roubles as compared with the estimates.

The country staggered on.

That year Dan was transferred back to London for three months. There he made a discovery that would ultimately alter all of their lives.

It was triggered off by a conversation between two senior journalists about the Prince of Wales's circle.

'They lick his boots,' one of them said scornfully. 'I wonder if he has any real friends – men of integrity?'

'Delacour was a worthwhile chap,' said the other man thoughtfully. 'Do you remember, years ago, when the Prince instituted a social boycott against Randolph Churchill? Delacour stood up to him – said he allowed no man, not even the future king, to choose his friends.'

Delacour? The name seemed familiar to Dan, but at that particular moment he could not remember why. Then that night he dreamed of a black-haired woman with whom he had been briefly involved in Paris. She was wearing a pretty gown and a jet brooch set in gold and studded with pearls on a ribbon around her neck.

Suddenly Dan knew that the dress belonged to Eva and that she would be extremely angry at his old girlfriend for daring to put it on.

He was anticipating no end of trouble – for Eva could be clearly seen walking along the street towards them –

but instead of taking action to head it off he burst out laughing.

'It is not funny!' his old girlfriend said. 'That woman will attack me!' But Dan was chortling his head off and quite unable to stop.

The cachinnation woke him up with a jump and he guffawed again at the idea of Eva being so cross.

Eva, he thought – Eva and Delacour and the Handcock affair. I meant to go to the archives to look the matter up. He went there at lunchtime, and was handed the file in question.

What he read did not at first surprise him very much. *The Times* had not been easy on Eva's father. The story itself – so typical of Clanricarde, he thought – only served to depress him.

He was about to close the file, return it to its source, when the date of the birth of Mrs Handcock's son leapt up at him from the page.

John Delacour – originally known as John de Burgh, an appropriately damaging name from Clanricarde's point of view – had been born in 1841.

Clanricarde had denied intimacy with Mrs Handcock in 1840, but had stated nothing else in his own defence. Not even the fact that he had been in Russia between 1838 and 1841, as Dan knew very well from Eva.

He could smell a story. There was the possibility that Clanricarde had returned to England in that time, but that was unlikely.

In any case, it could be checked out. He was not a reporter for nothing. Clanricarde's situation could be proven one way or the other by reading through the passenger sailings' lists for 1840.

As he left the archives, Dan was convinced that Ulick de Burgh would not be listed. There was something fishy about the case; above all about Clanricarde's hesitant self-defence.

A man known for his golden tongue to say so little? It did not make sense.

Not unless Eva's father had been protecting someone else.

When the lists in question revealed no record of Ulick de Burgh, Dan almost cheered aloud. Here was he, attempting to prove the innocence of a man who had wronged his own family, and being pleased with the results.

But that was not the point. It was Eva who mattered to Dan – her peace of mind. It would be wonderful for her to feel her father wasn't quite so bad.

On the other hand he was not ready to tell Eva what he had found out – not yet. Because there was surely more to unearth? If Clanricarde had not been John Delacour's father, who *had* been – and why had the boy been called at the outset after Eva's father?

Damn it! Dan thought. The whole thing happened such a long time ago – over fifty years. The main characters in this drama are dead. I don't know if Delacour is still alive – he probably wouldn't know the truth himself.

Or would he? And if so, would he be prepared to discuss such personal affairs?

Lost in thought, he slowly made his way back to the newsroom. He *had* to find out whether or not Delacour was dead.

Wondering if they would only tell him that they had never heard of the fellow, he mentioned Delacour's name to the same journalists who had been discussing him yesterday.

'John Delacour?' said one of them promptly. 'But he's well known in London society.'

'Dan's been in Paris for the last couple of years,' the other journalist explained. 'He wouldn't know that.'

'What's your interest in the man?' the first journalist, sensing a story himself, immediately asked.

Dan fobbed him off, but not before finding out where John Delacour lived.

He decided to write to Delacour, putting his cards on the table and telling him about Eva and how the truth about Delacour's parentage could affect her. It was a difficult letter to compose and he felt downhearted after he had posted it, sure that it would not get a response.

A week went by and then, as he was about to give up hope, Delacour wrote back. He, too, came straight to the point, as his very first sentence showed.

'You are an impudent fellow,' Dan read, 'but you appear likeable enough, and I am prepared to give you such information as I have concerning my father on condition that it goes no further than the girl. Otherwise I will sue.

'Although he did not officially recognize me as his son, I believe that my father was Sir John Burke, Clanricarde's cousin, who met my mother in the company of his own wife and their son, Thomas. I understand that a serious liaison developed between my mother and Sir John while Clanricarde was abroad, and that I – the result of it – was named for my father. To avert a scandal the surname was later changed.

'Clanricarde's friendship with my father, family loyalty, would have been enough to ensure that he would defend him against scandal, even at the cost to his own name and political career. From all accounts, he was that sort of man . . .'

As well as a landlord who didn't always care, thought Dan ruefully, putting the letter down. The good and the bad in the man . . .

But it was the good that Eva should know about. The letter he wrote to her contained details of his own discoveries and the lists of sailings. Delacour's missive he copied for her by hand.

At the end of his letter he added another thought: 'Has it ever occurred to you that maybe your father *did* make

provision for your mother and yourself – that maybe
Hubert countered it? For how would you have known,
two country people, what papers he had in his hands?
Your mother took everything your father said on trust –
she never had it in writing. She wouldn't have thought of
asking for a copy of his will . . .'

Aren't I the generous fellow? he said to himself. If
Clanricarde is watching down from Heaven (no certain
thing!), I hope he's impressed at what I've done to save
his illustrious name!

When Eva first read the letters she was unable either to
feel or comprehend the value of them.

When the information had gradually seeped into her
consciousness, the effect was remarkable: it was as if Dan
had thrown open the shutters of a room in which she had
been a prisoner for most of her life; allowing the sun to
stream in; saying to her: Look, here is a key to the door.
Why don't you go on out?

Her father *was* the man she had worshipped as a child,
a good man who had maybe loved her mother, not the
callous philanderer she had suspected him of being
throughout her grown-up years.

From this it was only a short step to the conclusion that
since her handsome, attractive father had turned out to
be far less of a devil than she had thought, maybe other
personable men might be seen in a different light. A short
step; though, since it is almost as hard to come to terms
with people being better than we expected than with
people being worse, it took her a bit of time actually to
reach the door.

Going out of it she took with her a new-found courage
with which to face the world of desirable men; with
which to confront love – or the possibility of it. She did
not have a candidate in mind. Sasha was not attractive to
her, she did not love him; he was her husband only in

210

name. As for Dan, he was hundreds of miles away, back again in Paris.

It was almost Easter, the most important church festival in Russia. In churches throughout the country the peasants would spread out their cakes and eggs, so that they would be blessed.

Eva had decided to get away from Klyonovo – to go to Moscow, to stay in the other apartment. Her excuse was that she wanted to visit the shops. To get there she had to travel into St Petersburg, and catch a train from St Nicholas station in Znamenskaya Square.

She felt perfectly safe travelling alone. Special carriages were set aside for the ladies on this train. Relieved to be free of her unsatisfactory marriage for a couple of weeks she settled into the sealed world of her sleeping car with its brown plush seats and wash-basins and divans. It was an additional bonus that she was alone, not forced to share her compartment with a lady anxious to make conversation.

She had brought two books to read, recently published, *In Tent and Bungalow*, a collection of Anglo-Indian stories, and *The Lady of Balmerino*, by Marie Connor-Leighton, which came in three volumes. Since she had no intention of hurrying home she would need a lot of reading.

She picked up the first volume of the trio and began to peruse it. It was a story of the last century in which the jewels of Queen Marie Antoinette, Royalist fugitives and Jacobite conspirators played an important part.

But after a while she found that she could not concentrate upon life on a Scotch farm a hundred years before. The heroine of the book, by name Rochilla, began to irritate her.

Why was it that, having achieved her ambitions – become a great lady, with power and beautiful jewels and clothes, she should remain so dissatisfied? The motion of the train, which should have soothed her, was having the adverse effect, working on her nerves, mocking her empty life.

The wild thought came to her that she should go away for good, leave Russia altogether and return to Ireland. But that would be absurd. Didn't she and Sasha have a perfectly good basis for living together? What need was there to go? Only –

Thoroughly annoyed by both the heroine in her book and by herself she got up and went into the corridor, looking to left and right. A few yards away from her a big man was standing alone, smoking. He glanced up, caught sight of her and did not look away. Was that out of impudence, or because they had actually met? He did look familiar. One way or the other he was not going to content himself with looking: he was making his way down the corridor in her direction.

Eva stood her ground, returning his stare with one of her own. He was a fellow in his thirties with a black beard and hair striated with grey. He wore a blue-black fine wool suit, a purple jacquard woven waistcoat, a silk tie with a pre-formed knot. All this she noticed, as well as the fact that there was something of the schoolroom about him, before he began to talk.

'We have met before,' he said, when he had reached her, and one of his hands went up to adjust his spectacles which were sliding down his nose.

Of, course, she thought – the *Vyatka*. And you, my friend, are the artist who made me laugh.

He managed to do that again.

'Do you know that this railroad is almost completely straight all the way to Moscow?' he began. 'But not altogether, and this is why. The engineers asked the Tsar where the line should go and he drew it for them with a ruler. There was only one hitch. The Tsar's finger protruded over the ruler's edge, so they constructed a loop!'

'Is that really true?' Eva asked, amused.

'Of course it's true or I wouldn't tell it to you! But it's not all that funny. In Russia even the experts believe the Tsar must always know better. What has happened to you since we met on the boat? You are just as beautiful but very much better dressed!'

'How would you remember what clothes I was wearing on the boat?'

'It's the artist's job to observe. I see also that you are wearing a wedding ring. You are happily married?'

'You're very inquisitive!'

'Then that means you're not. If you were your face would light up at the question and would answer it for you. Will you be in Moscow for long?'

'For two weeks,' Eva said, although she should just snub this nosy man. 'And you?'

'At least that long. I know who you are. I made inquiries on the boat. Eva – that's all that counts. Did you marry the man you were with then?'

Cheekier and cheekier. But she said: 'Yes, I did. And your name?'

'Karol Helfmann. I am a Jew. The day after tomorrow I will be at the School of Painting in Moscow, at an exhibition of student work. Why don't you come?'

Back in her compartment she asked herself what harm would it do if she went. Wasn't she interested in painting? Always had been since she was a child and her father had played that game. So why shouldn't she look at student work?

The Head Guard, in his black blouse and his wide trousers tucked into his boots and his round fur cap, came to examine her ticket, and the *provodnik* made up her bed.

She had brought her own pillows, towels and soap. The carriage was steam-heated. The *provodnik* had hoisted up the back-cushion of her seat in order to form an unwanted upper berth. She was warm and comfortable and well looked after. There was no apparent reason for not being able to sleep. No one would interrupt her. But instead of sleeping she tossed and turned, over-conscious of turning wheels.

In the middle of the night she was still considering whether or not to accept Karol Helfmann's invitation. Before she finally dozed off she concluded that she should not. In the morning she had changed her mind again and was disappointed not to see him when the train disgorged its passengers to Moscow.

It would be undignified to wait for him to appear. The encounter had lifted her out of the lethargy. And in contrast to St Petersburg, where the streets were sometimes quite empty, Moscow was gloriously alive.

This was a different Russia, a city with an Asiatic influence – so sacred that visiting peasants doffed their hats and blessed themselves reverentially as they entered its portals. It was the centre of all national and religious feelings, with 450 churches and 25 convents, but it was not of God Eva thought so much when she was there, but of food and drink. The air was rich with smells of fowl and game and other less definable odours. Men selling a delicious honey-flavoured beverage which she loved, stood near the *chainayas*, the tea-houses where vodka was also sold.

There were hawkers of all kinds in Moscow and all kinds of merchandise could be purchased in the streets: stockings, door-knobs, carpets, brooms and baskets. Saintly men, *startsy*, mingled with beggars in straw boots. German dress predominated but bearded peasants in bast slippers and patched caftans strolled by, and men in old-fashioned fur caps, and women with genuine pearls – Circassians and Tatars in national dress, and Greeks in red fezes, and Persians with high conical caps made from black sheepskin.

How could anyone be lonely in such an environment?

She told herself that she did not suffer from this complaint. All that was missing was her beloved Nábat: on Sundays in Trubnaya Square dogs and birds were bought and sold; perhaps she should purchase another dog.

Meanwhile, wasn't she happy? Of course she was. She *liked* being alone, enjoyed solitude, did not even need to talk to the driver as – responding to her instructions – they stopped on the Moskvaretsky Bridge for a view of the Kremlin. This ancient irregular triangle occupying a quarter of the city, boasted twenty amazing towers, every one of which had a name. The Belfry of Ivan, the tallest building in Moscow. The grey domes of Archangel Michael where the graves of princes lay. The huge rich gold-leaf domes of the Assumption Cathedral. The Grand Kremlin Palace.

When she had tired of counting them up she gave orders to the driver to take her straight to the apartment. It was on the Nikolskaya, the third street of the Inner City, which ran off the Krasnaya or Red – meaning beautiful – Square. The Pobedonostsevs' apartment was in number five, a four-storey grey house on the same side of the street as Upper Trading Rows, the smart shopping centre. Although only rich people lived on the Nikolskaya, the impoverished, beggars and prostitutes inhabited the same area, and bordellos had opened up.

The servants were expecting her. Her luggage was unpacked, her clothes hung up. Cakes had been purchased from the Filipov bakery on the Tverskaya; poultry from the shop on the Okhotny Ryad which offered the very best.

In the afternoon she would shop in Muir and Merrilees on the Petrovka, and potter around the most fashionable dress shops by the Kuznetsky Bridge. In the evening she would go on her own to the Maly Theatre where Ostrovsky's comedy, *Poverty Not a Vice*, was playing.

It never occurred to Eva to share these expeditions

with a friend. Most women were wary of her – it suited her to keep them at a distance. Cousin Marisha had succeeded where others had not in getting close to Eva, but she seldom visited Moscow, insisting that it smelt.

And there *were* times when summer rains flooded Theatrical Square and the Alexandrovsky Gardens, and the sewers discharged their unsalubrious contents; when the underground river, the Neglinaya, was filled with waste and excrement.

But not today! On this glorious day the sun beamed on the greenest city in Europe. On this day she was happy.

In the morning she put on a ruffled overcoat over a pale blue dress with a high lace collar. Her boater hat had a blue feather in it that stuck up like an arrow.

She walked down the Nikolskaya and paid homage to the Cathedral of St Basil the Blessed for no other reason than that its wonderful onion-shaped domes – green and yellow and red – would make anybody merry.

In the late morning she joined a small crowd making its way into the School of Painting. At the end of the corridor a door was held open by a leg from a broken easel. Beyond that she could see sections of canvasses, mostly unframed, displayed on a long wall.

Since she had met Karol Helfmann on board the *Vyatka* she had learned about Russian painting. She knew that for centuries the Church had insisted that only icons be painted, that many icons, of the Blessed Family or the saints, had been adorned with gold so that they could be given to the Church by members of the congregation; that icon artists had not been permitted to sign their work, it being thought of as God-inspired.

And this when the Renaissance was at its zenith in Europe! No wonder Russian artists were conscious of lagging behind; that their excitement had mounted when Peter the Great had invited foreign artists to Russia and permitted the painting of portraits.

Standing in the queue Eva remembered with amusement Sasha's tirade on board the *Vyatka* against the Itinerant Artists, The Wanderers. How indignant he had been, how convinced of the decadent ethos in the work of Perov and Zhuravlev. Since that time she had been privileged to see for herself both the *Monastery Refectory*, which depicted drunken and gluttonous monks, and *Before the Wedding*, Zhuravlev's visual protest against arranged marriages, and she knew where her sympathies lay.

The crowd moved on. She reached the exhibition room and looked around in search of Karol Helfmann. Loquacious, gesticulating students blocked her view.

Then she saw him. He was talking to an earnest young man who was pointing to one of the paintings on the nearest wall and waving his hands as if to express despair. Karol Helfmann was nodding occasionally but his eyes were darting about the room as if he were looking for someone else.

When they focused on Eva their owner smiled, terminated his conversation, and made his way over to her.

'I was waiting for you,' he said, as if he had been certain that she would come. 'Are you going to enjoy this? What do you know about painting?'

He asked this gently, not aggressively. Eva said: 'A little. Just now I am very interested in Ilya Repin's work.'

She said this not to impress him, but because it was the truth. But Repin did not appear to have won Karol Helfmann's respect.

He said: 'Repin? And how acquainted are you with his recent development?'

'I once saw *They Did Not Expect Him*,' said Eva. 'Isn't that enough?'

Her new friend shook his head. He looked distressed, as if he was suffering some intolerable inner pain. Perhaps he was naturally melancholic?

'It is a great painting,' he said finally. 'But Repin has

moulded his talent to meet the ideals of The Wanderers. It has become diluted in a dead atmosphere.'

'You don't approve of The Wanderers?'

'Like most revolutionary movements which endure and become accepted it has become an establishment – nothing more. Look around you today and you will soon see what I mean. The younger Moscow painters – Pasternak, for one, myself for another – see things differently. We wish to move on so that we can contribute to the mainstream of Western culture. The Wanderers would have us isolated.'

'But Pasternak himself exhibits with The Wanderers,' protested Eva, having seen Leonid Pasternak's large *genre* canvasses exhibited on a number of occasions. 'He seems content to work in the realistic manner of which they approve.'

'He is not a fool. He knows that rejection by The Wanderers would be a serious setback for a young painter,' said her companion. 'But his thoughts are moving elsewhere.'

This was all deliciously different from the conversations Eva had with Sasha, or his circle. With Sasha she could predict his argument the very minute a subject was raised. His would always be a conservative view. But this man was a nonconformist, a rebel like herself and to converse with him would be to begin on a journey that would have no known destination.

What would his paintings be like?

'I would like to see *your* work. Is that possible?'

'Of course – if you care to visit my studio.'

'You have a studio here – in Moscow?'

'Yes. And I work here much of the time. My home – my family, they are in St Petersburg. And you?'

'I live in the capital, too.'

He took off his glasses and dangled them from thumb and first finger.

'I often return to St Petersburg. Here I rent a house

218

from a merchant – a single-storey house, not at all grand, opposite the Church of St Nicholas in Tatars' Lane. It is very easy to find. It is the building on the corner, the one nearest the blue house with the red window frames. But I will take you there if you like.'

'When?'

He shrugged. 'Today – this afternoon? Whatever suits you –'

'*Karol!*'

The young woman who had joined them was in a shocking rage, and breathing very deeply. Her wide nostrils flared so that Eva was at once put in mind of an untrained but well-bred horse.

'You said that you would come for me,' said the young woman furiously. 'I have been waiting for you. I thought there was some mistake – that our rendezvous should have been here!'

She glowered at Eva. 'Who are you?'

Whatever his paintings will be like, thought Eva, at least they will not be dull!

'I look forward to seeing your work as arranged,' she said, ignoring the question that had been put to her. 'Now I must look at the exhibition. I wish you both good day!'

The sheer villainy of it – going all on her own to visit Karol Helfmann!

But, of course, she was not just going to pay him a visit – she was going to inspect his work. And if she liked it, she would buy one of his paintings and hang it in the apartment and Sasha would be shocked.

For doubtless Karol Helfmann, who had spoken on their very first meeting of havoc and bloodshed, of new societies emerging from wreckage, would produce unusual work.

She hardly knew the part of Moscow in which he had rented a house, but her driver assured her he did, and they crossed the Moskvaretsky bridge over the canal and took a left fork.

Soon they were in the Zamoskvorechye, an old merchants' centre, in search of the Church of St Nicholas. The problem was that there were so many churches in this vicinity, said the driver, less certain of his route than when they had started out. They stopped in front of one which on investigation proved to be dedicated not to St Nicholas but to St Clement. Much later they came across the Danilov monastery and the driver announced in a holy voice that the Patriarch of the Russian Orthodox Church dwelt behind its doors.

A priest in a brown cassock with a gold cross around his neck and a *klobuk* on his head sorted it all out. But even so it was late in the afternoon when Eva found Karol's house.

She told the driver to wait. Karol had told her that the house was not at all grand. It was even smaller than she had expected, made of wood and painted a dull cinnamon brown.

But when she knocked on the door Karol opened it almost at once, as if he had been standing all afternoon in the little hall awaiting her arrival.

'You had difficulty getting here?'

'A little.'

She could smell the paint. Karol opened another door and she stepped through into a big white-washed room that had obviously been made from two small ones. It was immaculately clean and neat, containing a huge table on which paint-brushes had been tucked into jars, and pots of paint laid out in symmetrical rows, and an easel, holding a fresh canvas, turned to face the wall. Other paintings, framed, had also been stacked so that only their backs could be seen. Karol Helfmann was not in the business of exhibiting his work to every visitor who came into his wooden home.

'When you were talking earlier today about your

220

family, did you mean that you were married, that you had children?' asked Eva. At that moment it seemed to be more important to have his answers to those questions than to attempt to estimate the quality of his work.

But I know already that his paintings will be aggressive and turbulent – filled with disquiet and change, she thought, just as I am certain, too, that they will appeal to what is in me.

'Yes, I am married. I have two children, a boy and a girl, twelve and ten years old,' said Karol carelessly.

'Your wife was the lady whom I saw at the exhibition?'

He laughed, losing his schoolroom air. 'No, that was not my wife,' he said emphatically. 'My wife is very kind and very boring. I see as little of her as I can. As for the lady at the exhibition, she is not at all kind and there was a period in my life when I found her exciting. However, that was some time ago. Let us discuss neither of them . . . Do you also have children?'

'No.'

'I am sorry.'

'There's no need to be. May I see your work?'

'Sit down,' he ordered, pulling out a plain wooden chair. 'First, I will make us some tea. I presume that you are not in a hurry?'

After an infinitesimal pause she said: 'No, I am not in a hurry,' and he smiled, satisfied, and, pushing open another door, disappeared into a kitchen.

She had expected his paintings to excite her, but not as much as they did. Beyond that certainty she had not attempted to guess whether they would consist of landscapes or figurative work. Or portraits . . .

In the event, he explained that he did not paint from life.

'Only landscapes.'

She recalled once seeing the work of one of the three Russian artists who had created *genre*, landscape and historical pictures which had a distinctly national flavour – Shishkin who, later on, had been Pasternak's teacher of etching. Shishkin's vast landscapes had impressed her as being serene: Karol Helfmann's paintings could not have been more turbulent.

These large canvasses, depicting land, rivers and sea in storm and devastation, screamed the painter's anger out in the meticulously tidy room; their colours – in contrast to the sober suiting of their creator – were crude and violent and sad.

She had risen from her chair to look at them. Now, shocked, disorientated and stimulated, she backed into it again.

'You must be a supremely angry and unhappy man,' she said, and realized she was whispering.

Karol Helfmann shrugged and, again, she marvelled at the disparity between the way he looked and worked.

'Jews, generally, do not have an easy life in Russia. There is plenty to be angry and unhappy about.'

'I thought things were easier for your people since Ignatiev was dismissed,' said Eva, referring to the man who, as Minister of the Interior, had been responsible for introducing legislation limiting Jewish movement within the country, and forbidding them from acquiring land, trading in alcohol or opening their shops on Sundays.

'I see that I have much to teach you,' said Karol, the schoolteacher again.

He did not look angry now, but deceptively gentle and engaging.

Eva, imagining Sasha's expression should she purchase one of Karol Helfmann's violent paintings to hang in the apartment, suddenly wanted to laugh.

It was Karol who, in an abrupt mood swing, re-introduced anger.

He said: 'You were not here, of course, in 1881. Even if you had been, you would probably have been too young to understand what went on.'

'When Tsar Alexander was killed?'

'When five young agents of the People's Will were hanged in Semyononsky Square in St Petersburg,' he said, and he looked at her in such a way that she felt he had known at least one of them. 'It was a public hanging in the presence of troops, crowds, officials, priests and foreign diplomats. Were you aware of that?'

'I think I heard something about it – yes.'

'Were you aware that the execution was horribly bungled? Of the time they took to die?'

'That is the basis of your anger?'

He said: 'My sister Jessie was one of the five who died.

'Until then I had no real sympathy with the aims of the People's Will,' he said quietly. 'When Jessie spoke about what they intended to do – how they had met in a forest to formally pronounce sentence of death upon Alexander Nicolaevich Romanov, I thought that they were romancing. After all – even if the assassination succeeded – what hope did they have of assuming power in Russia? The death of Alexander II would simply make way for the reign of Alexander III.'

'You knew about the assassination plan?'

'Jessie confided in me. She knew that, although I might not approve of what she was doing, I would never betray her. In any case, as it happened, there was not one plan but several – they tried several times to kill the Tsar by planting explosives on the railway line at a time when he would be travelling from Livadia to St Petersburg. On the first occasion he eluded them by following a different route, on the second because the detonation did not occur at the crucial moment. The third time they struck at the wrong train. Then they put a bomb in the dining-room of the Winter Palace. It was intended to go off during dinner.'

'And?'

'Lack of punctuality saved Alexander's life. A number of others were killed or injured, most of them soldiers of the palace guard. The Nihilists were literally forced underground, renting a basement in Maly Sadovy Street, driving a tunnel under the road so that they could blow up the Tsar's carriage as it passed above them. They were that determined. When the Tsar switched routes again they had an alternative plan – a mobile strike-force armed with bombs. One of them exploded under the back axle of the Tsar's carriage as he was driving to the cavalry parade. You know the rest, I am sure – how Alexander escaped unhurt but was stupid enough to insist on walking back to the scene of the explosion, to talk to his assailant who had been put under arrest.'

'Not knowing that there were others in the crowd . . .'

'My sister amongst them. The second grenade was effective. It was then that I began to understand the necessity for chaos – the fertility of devastation, and to study the sources for my own work. At the same time I began to read, not only about Russia, but about other countries where people have been similarly oppressed. About Ireland.'

'And to travel there?'

'Later on. Before that I read enough to make me realize that the life of the Irish peasants, society as a whole, will only be bettered when the landlord–tenant relationship is destroyed.'

She began to talk to him then of her own experience of eviction. He listened without interrupting, but when she had reached the end of her story he said: 'How can you, who have suffered so much, be content with your present life?'

'People would laugh at you for asking that question! Am I not rich? Don't I live in luxury – instead of a makeshift shelter?'

'And aren't you married to a man you don't love – no, don't even bother to answer! You'd only tell me a lie!'

'I wouldn't lie –' Eva started to say.

It was as far as she got. A woman outside in the street

shouted over her words – 'Karol!' and banged upon the door.

And Karol Helfmann, who had been so confident, who had been in charge of the conversation, looked sheepish, like a small boy caught out.

'Who's that?'

He groaned, raising his eyes heavenwards.

'Ssh!'

'Aren't you going to let her in?' Eva mouthed.

Karol shook his head. I must go – shortly, Eva thought.

The knocking was repeated. Eva remained quiet. Her mouth was dry. She looked at the samovar. When this absurd situation has resolved itself, she thought, she would ask for a drink, then demand to be taken home.

Another knock, louder, very loud.

'Karol?' aggressively. 'Open the door if you're there!'

He shook his head, unsmiling.

'Ssh!'

How undignified, thought Eva. Why should we hide like this? Recognizing the voice of the unseen caller, she knew that it was the girl from the exhibition. From whom Karol Helfmann, supremely talented artist, victim of life, was hiding. She was not sure why she should feel so intensely about what was happening – only that she was filled with rage by the circumstances. Why couldn't Karol Helfmann open his own front door?

Finally the knocking ceased. The caller had apparently given up and gone away. Eva heard what she had failed to hear earlier – the movement of another vehicle. Now it was heading back towards the centre of the city, she imagined, or wherever the other girl lived.

At once Karol Helfmann got up and went into the kitchen, to return with a bottle of vodka and two glasses.

'Will you join me? I think we need a drink, don't you?'

'Why didn't you open the door?'

And why am I shaking all over? thought Eva, willing her hand to keep still in order to hold the glass. She gulped at its contents and coughed, hot and sticky all over.

'It was better not to let her in,' said Karol in answer to her question. 'She is a very emotional girl. Very – unafraid. She might have harmed you.'

'Harmed *me*?'

More than anything, she thought, this is a most caring man: she valued his compassion above the other qualities which he had displayed, forgetting altogether that when Sasha showed her consideration it only bored her stiff.

'Let me tell you about Sophia,' Karol said. 'In many ways she is a wonderful woman, full of passion and life and strong feeling, but, you understand, my love for her has gone.'

'Have you told her so?'

'She refuses to accept the situation. I will talk to her again. You must not worry about it. I will not hurt her . . . And it has nothing to do with us. You said that you intended to be in Moscow for two weeks. Can we spend that time together?'

13

There were drawbacks to freedom. Now Eva, the very one who had lauded solitude, began to admit – only to herself – that she hated being alone. Most of all she loathed the loneliness of night.

There were, of course, the servants. Although the Pobedonostsevs only rarely visited Moscow, a full staff was retained at the apartment in the Nikolskaya all year round.

But Eva – needless to say – was not hankering to discuss menus at 3 A.M. She was missing love.

On an impulse she went to Trubnaya Square and returned not with a dog but with a marmalade cat. The creature could be looked after by the servants in the apartment when she returned to St Petersburg, and be cosseted by her when she was in Moscow.

She was now visualizing being much more often in the City of White Walls. And why not? She could do as she pleased. Sasha might miss her but – since he desired her happiness – he would not object if she said she wanted to go.

Having worked that out she dismissed Sasha from her mind and thought about Karol instead. In connection with their meetings he had explained to her that these must fit in with his painting. He could not work according to a schedule. When he began a picture he might continue painting throughout the whole night or, conversely, go for two days without drawing a line. He sounded very serious about all this – a far cry from the man whose art had once made her laugh.

Eva teased him: 'Is that because you're being inspired, like the icon painters?'

He gave her a sharp look.

'It *is* creation,' he said, the severe teacher, not sounding amused.

Karol was not only interested in painting but in literature and music as well. On his first free evening he took her to one of the symphony concerts founded by Nicholas Rubinstein which were held in the large concert hall of the Conservatorium, and to the Bolshaya Moskovskaya Gostinitza for dinner.

'For a slender woman you eat voraciously! Women with healthy appetites are immensely attractive! Have you ever thought about that?'

'You eat well yourself!'

The next day they were going together to buy books at Tastevin's.

'You must read Pushkin's poems,' Karol insisted. 'He used to be like you, mixing in society. He was a man of fashion more than a poet at first. If his *Ode to Liberty* had not attracted the attention of the Tsar, if he had not been exiled to the south and involved himself in the secret societies there, he would never have written so superbly later on.'

'Are you a member of such a society – of the People's Will?'

'No. But because of my sister I sympathized with its ideals. I know people who are aiming now to revive the practices of the Narodovoltsy, the Populists, and others who are formulating their own doctrines: a young man named Vladimir Ulyanov, for instance, a law graduate who's living at present at Simbirsk, but whom I occasionally encounter in St Petersburg. He is an authority on Karl Marx's work. His brother, Aleksandr, was also executed for his part in the Tsar's death.'

He paused, frowning – then said abruptly: 'Shall we talk of something else?'

* * *

Still, he was funny as well, pointing out the idio-syncrasies of people in the streets.

'Have you ever noticed how animalistic they are? See, that woman with the long face is not a woman at all but a horse in female clothes! I will draw her for you as she truly is underneath her gown! And as for that man who is not a man but is, in fact, a bear . . . !'

These humorous drawings were the only ones he ever did of people. Man was too monstrous to depict, Karol said – too warped. How could he ever compare with a tree or a river or a hill?

Eva was not sure how serious he was when he came out with such statements. They were almost invariably followed by a sketch designed to make her laugh.

She loved being with him – was having what she regarded as the best time of her life, except, of course, at night. All too quickly, the time passed. Then she had only three days left in Moscow.

With the marmalade cat on her lap she considered the evening ahead. Karol had said that he would take her to the ballet at the Bolshoi Theatre, although she had yet to find out the details of the programme, and who would be dancing. Ballet dancers were *demi-mondaines*, elevated to the status of goddesses, living in splendid houses. Their lovers were said to spend millions on their jewellery – to strew violets in front of their sleighs.

Kept women then, many of them. And yet in all sorts of ways, in spite of her own newfound freedom, they were less constrained than herself.

And less lonely at night . . .

Lucky dancers, thought Eva. *They* can invite anyone they like to visit them at home.

Lucky dancers . . .

But perhaps even they did not like incurring scandal. Perhaps, when their lovers called, they told their staff to go off.

There was no reason why *she* should not dismiss the

servants this evening. It would be pleasant to talk to Karol out of the public eye.

With such an evening in mind she went to meet him beside the sculpted fountain in Theatrical Square.

'My apartment is very near here,' she said to him. 'And I have to show you my cat! Later we can dine in a restaurant.'

He looked pleased.

When she had shown off her new pet he said: 'You like animals, *all* animals, don't you?'

'Naturally.'

'Not everyone feels as you do. I remember an incident that happened when I was at school. We had a very pretty young teacher and we all vied for her attention, bringing her gifts, a flower, sweets. There was a boy called Tolya who loved her more than any of us. He brought her presents, too. One day he appeared with a baby snake tucked inside his shirt. In class, he let it loose near her desk. She didn't scream. She *was* like you – she loved all animals – even snakes. Tolya was amazed that she could have such feeling for the creature. In fact, he was not altogether pleased . . .'

He laughed. The marmalade cat leapt off Eva's lap on to one of the tables.

'That's the end of the story?'

'Not quite. Next week, Tolya brought along a baby mole to class. Once the teacher got over her initial surprise she was as pleased as can be. She thought the mole was sweet.'

'Draw it for me?' pleaded Eva, but Karol did not oblige.

'Let me tell you my story first. Tolya told us that, the following week, he was going to bring along a practical present for his love. "A mole is not useful," he said. "So I'm going to take it home."

'A week later he came to class with a gift wrapped up in paper. He took it up to the teacher's desk. She was intrigued. "What *is* it, Tolya?" she kept asking. She had the prettiest face.

'Tolya told her to open the packet. As she was doing so he said: "I made it for you myself."

'Then she saw what was inside. She burst into tears. The contents of the packet fell on to the floor. It was a moleskin purse. You understand what I am telling you, don't you? *She* didn't. Tolya knew even then, at the age of eleven, that creativity, at its best, grows out of destruction and death. If you are to create you must not be afraid of destroying all that you have in order to build upon the ruins. You must risk yourself completely – consider embarking upon complete self-annihilation. Tension, devastation, is essential to real art. Many times I have been tempted to kill myself.'

From the table the marmalade cat was making her way to Karol.

Eva said: 'What stopped you?' and he answered angrily: 'Giving others the satisfaction of saying that I had failed.'

The cat had reached him. Her green eyes glinting, she jumped on to his knee, nuzzled purring against his chest.

'They're perverse creatures, cats,' said Karol. 'They often offer love to those who do not like them.'

At the same time his hand was sliding slowly down the heavy back of the cat, pausing at the base of the spine, moving clockwise – round and round and round.

The animal arched in ecstasy. Karol said: 'We're friends.'

And Eva threw off the suspicion she had that Tolya and Karol were one.

The cat, having established proprietorial rights over Karol, abandoned him, strolled to the door and waited for Eva to open it.

'You contrary thing!' she said, obliging. 'You'll want to come in again.'

Karol, too, had got to his feet and was crossing the room to the door.

He said softly: 'There's no one here but the two of us?' and took her hands in his.

Imprisoned as she had then been in her cell, she had been frightened of kissing Dan. She had disliked being kissed by Sasha even more than their actual act of coition. That mating she had attempted to disregard, to categorize as brutish coupling, not requiring spiritual intimacy, whereas Sasha's kisses had begged her to respond to his need for emotional love, a concept that repelled her.

She was over her fear. She wanted Karol on many levels, for many reasons: one of them the recognition that she and he were similar people, kindred spirits banding together to combat the hostile world.

They kissed at first as friends, with Karol's hands resting lightly on her shoulders and Eva in no rush to move beyond cordiality. She was delighted just to have found that bond of compatibility. But she was still not afraid when he began to coax her beyond friendship, drawing her in to him, mouthing: 'Too many clothes!' kissing into her smile.

After many kisses he held her away from him and looked at her quizzically.

'Yes?'

Holding his hand tight she led him into the bedroom where she and Sasha had never made love and allowed him to undress her.

Naked, he was less handsome himself, his arms too thin for his body, his stomach inclined to paunch. Next day, she would recall, with amused tenderness, that his feet were ugly, splaying out, with odd, prehensile toes.

She had set off on the precarious pathway side by side with a friend, believing herself sure-footed. In bed with Karol she was soon lost, and he the dragoman.

There had been no dream – no colour and luminosity in

the love she had made with Sasha: not excitement; not the anger that can accompany love – merely endurance.

Karol led her through desire to deprivation and fret and silent pleading right out into the lake of passion. Her body was a water dwelling, the lake a whirlpool. For only a moment – fear.

Then he thrust into her, forcing her down into the maelstrom and, drowning, she entered the silver land that was waiting beneath the depths.

'How often do you propose to dismiss your servants?' Karol asked mischievously.

'We can't meet at *your* house?'

He grimaced: 'There are canvasses everywhere. It is more pleasant to make love away from the smell of paint! Also there is the problem of Sophia.'

'Sophia? Do you still see her?'

This was an unforeseen development from Eva's point of view. Another woman setting herself up as a rival? Unthinkable!

Karol, as she might have expected, said: 'No, not in that sense. But I don't want any embarrassments. I met her through Bakhrushin. He's a young but important patron who lives in the blue house, the one with the red window frames. You remember seeing it when you came? Bakhrushin is particularly interested in theatrical art – paintings of actresses, of the ballet and so on – as is Sophia herself. The proximity of our establishments makes it even more difficult for me to avoid her altogether. She watches me from Bakhrushin's window. The obvious escape is for me to return to St Petersburg, but I have work to do here.'

'In that case my *servants* will have little to do this week!' said Eva lightly.

Underneath she was cross – annoyed that another woman should have the temerity to dictate the terms of her life, even a woman as patently stupid and as unmemorable as Sophia. Eva could not even recall a feature of her face!

Still that was not important. Sophia did not count.

'I am going to stay in Moscow for another ten days,' said Eva's letter to Sasha the next morning, not giving any reason for her sudden change in plans.

'Remain here for that time and I'll travel back to St Petersburg with you,' Karol had said last night.

In any case, it would have been ridiculous to have left Moscow so quickly, now and she and Karol were lovers. In St Petersburg it would be less easy for them to meet frequently; in public hardly at all.

The logistics of that she would put out of her mind for the time being. There was the present to enjoy. This evening she and Karol were going to the Truzzi Circus to enable Eva to marvel at horses and bears.

'Please see that this is posted,' she said to her maid, Vera, handing her the letter.

She was used to having servants. Remembering her own working days she was much kinder to them than to almost everyone else; certainly kinder than she was to those women she encountered at parties and balls.

'Yes, madam,' said the maid. 'Are you quite sure that I can take the whole day off?'

'The rest of the week, I said!'

Love painted Moscow in even brighter colours. Every church spire, every monastery or bell-tower – even the people in the streets – seemed to glow with a supernatural light.

Small wonder that the artist Konstantin Korovin, whom she met with Sasha, said that what was needed in painting was more of the bright and joyful; that colours should be a feast for the eye.

They had come across the young artist one evening in a restaurant and he had shown them some of his work, including a portrait he had painted of the actress Tatyana Lyubatovich. When Eva had enthused about it, Korovin had said that he would like to paint her.

'In the blue dress that you are wearing now,' he said meditatively. 'On a balcony with a garden for a backdrop.'

'You have already made such a painting,' Karol told him coolly. 'Of a chorus girl, I think –'

The young artist looked crushed. When they were alone again Karol said: 'He was hoping for a commission from you. On graduation from the Moscow School of Painting, he was not awarded the rank of commission artist – he was not that highly thought of,' and Eva detected jealousy in his voice.

On their last evening they went to the Inner Town to walk hand in hand through the Voskresenskaya Gate which stood opposite the end of the Tverskaya.

'Which way through?' Eva asked, for there were two openings, over each of which was a pointed tower.

'*This* way,' he said, as if it was a matter of extreme importance, guiding her to the left.

From here they could see the Chapel of the Iberian Virgin, one of the most revered churches in Russia.

A contradiction in Karol was that, while on the one hand disdaining both the royal family and the Church, he was proud of the palaces and chapels.

Now he said:

'Did you know that each time he comes to Moscow the Tsar visits this chapel before entering the Kremlin? There are, however, less salubrious visitors. We must ensure that neither of us is robbed.'

The danger came from elsewhere. Nor were they destined to visit the chapel that particular evening. When they stepped through the left-hand opening a woman came forward to meet them.

Her eyes flashed acrimony, her nostrils were dilated, but her mouth was quivering in misery.

Still she shouted at Karol: 'What are you doing with this woman? You told me you were meeting an art patron! Is *she* the reason why you have left me alone in the house!'

At that point Eva walked away, heedless of Karol's earlier warnings that robbers were about.

Her thoughts were in a whirl. Karol had said there were canvasses strewn around his house – he had not mentioned women!

She isn't even pretty, thought Eva unjustly, considering Sophia's face. Her brown hair is nondescript, and her fashionable clothes do not conceal the fact that her breasts are small. What use could Karol have for such a creature? How could he lie to me about the need to get away from paint?

I shall have nothing more to do with him, vowed Eva. He can remain in Moscow with this ugly woman and I shall return to St Petersburg. I shall never see him again.

She determined not to think of him – not hope that he would abandon Sophia to rush after her. All the same she did. But Karol did not pursue her. She reached the apartment without hearing his footsteps behind her, and without being molested.

'Vera, I would like some tea please.'

There was no reply. Of course, she had let the maid go off!

She made tea herself. There was no knock on the front door. In bed her only company was the marmalade cat curled up on the opposite side.

He was waiting for her on the station platform, a suitcase by his feet. 'I owe you an explanation.'

'There is no need for that.'

'But there is. I know I inferred that Sophia did not come to my house any more,' persisted Karol, picking up his suitcase and following Eva along the platform to the compartment she had reserved. 'But I was telling the truth in the sense that we are not lovers any more.'

'Then why permit her to come?'

'A reasonable question – only Sophia is not reasonable. I suppose I should have told you but each time I try to end the friendship that remains between us she becomes irrational – even violent. Once she tried to slash her wrists. Out of compassion for her I have found it difficult to reject her completely. Before now there was no reason why I should. But now, after all, there is you.'

They had reached Eva's compartment. She boarded the train with Karol behind her.

'So?' she said, when the porter carrying her own luggage had gone. 'What do you intend to do about Sophia?'

'I think if I remain in St Petersburg for several months without going to Moscow that it will be easier for her. I have written to her telling her that I do not intend to return to Moscow this year. It will give her time to recover. Will you try to understand? I do care about her, but only – now – as a friend.'

'You risked losing me!' cried Eva, and she remembered her father all of a sudden – another compassionate man who had stood in danger of losing much for the sake of a valued friend.

'*Have* I lost you?'

Through the carriage window she could see passengers aboard other trains, eager with anticipation about the journey ahead.

Whereas her journey would only culminate in a meeting with a man she did not love.

'I love you,' Karol said.

The train was starting up. The last door had been slammed. In the corridor outside, a late comer stumbled against the door.

'*Can* we travel together?'

On all roads, always . . .
She said: 'Indeed we can.'

14

This left them with the serious problem which besets all illicit lovers – where to meet to make love. It was not feasible to avail themselves of the Pobedonostsevs' St Petersburg apartment – Sasha had taken to coming to town more often than before for meetings with the bank. Karol's studio was in the garden of his family home.

'We must rent another apartment,' Eva said. 'The only question is where.'

'And how much it will cost,' said Karol.

The days when she too had worried about money seemed long past. Financial considerations never affected anything she wanted to do.

She reminded herself that Karol was an artist – that creative people worked on an aesthetic rather than a commercial level. Her lover was concerned with depicting the truth as he saw it, not with high fees.

Of Karol's need to support a family she did not want to think. They could both contribute to the rent. All that mattered was that a suitable apartment be found as quickly as possible.

Meanwhile their being together at all was proving frustratingly dangerous. Having rendezvoused by the bridge with the golden gorgons that flanked the Moika they were each wearing invisible masks to disguise their true feelings. Eva thought that the encounter – like an alchemist's art – had turned all things to pure gold: the graceful Dutch church, the sun-touched classical buildings, even the unhealthy yellow waters of the river. So charismatic is love.

As if they had coincidentally met, they walked sedately together to the palace of Count Stroganov, and anyone seeing them might have thought that they were more interested in Rastrelli's *bas-reliefs* and lion masks than in each other.

'I will look for an apartment at once,' promised Karol.

He found a third-floor dwelling consisting of two small rooms and a minute hall, in a building which overlooked the Mikhailovsky Palace with its earthen ramparts and moats.

'Paul I lived there,' said Karol, looking out, 'but only for forty days. He thought he would be safer there than at Pavlosk but his so-called close associates hit him on the temple with a snuff box and then killed him – all with the complicity of his son. Alexander was that eager to be Tsar! Next time that husband of yours takes you to Pavlosk ask him to show you the drawing-room downstairs. Alexander had to face his mother in there. When he came into the room Maria was sitting in front of a table. On it was a basket containing Paul's blood-stained shirt. But perhaps your husband is more concerned with Pavlosk's treasures than he is with people's lives!'

There is no need for you to be jealous of Sasha, Eva might well have said. I share nothing of significance with my husband.

The apartment was sparsely furnished with two chairs, a small table, and a bed.

'We lead very different lives,' Karol said, at the window. 'You, I suppose, are a frequent visitor at the Summer Palace as well as everywhere else,' and he went on staring out.

'I am not interested in the social life of St Petersburg,' Eva said truthfully. 'I would rather be married to you.'

But how could that be possible? Karol certainly did not offer a suggestion to bring it about. Soon they were both too engrossed in love-making to consider anything else.

In summer the leaflets on the birch trees changed from light green to emerald before they unfolded. Roses briefly bloomed.

Eva, having turned down a proposal of Sasha's that they should holiday in one of the German spas or in the south of France, was greeted with the unwelcome news that Karol intended to take his wife and children to Yalta, in the Crimea, for their vacation. A duty, that was all . . .

But that was the time when Eva began to find out about love: to understand that, having been freed in one sense in order to experience passion, it could trap her, too.

How could she exist for a month – a whole month! – in a world from which, summer or not, the colour had been erased?

A dull, dark, drab prison of a world; an ugly, revolting cell!

Close your mind to the thought of that, she urged – think of one pleasant thing!

One outing that I might enjoy sharing with Sasha. And there *was* one such event.

'I shall be going to hear Chaliapin, the new bass singer from Kazan.'

'He used to sweep the streets,' Karol said. 'Are you going with your husband? Yes, I suppose you are.'

And after all it was pleasurable to see the jealous expression on Karol's face; hear his promise to return to St Petersburg after only two weeks in Yalta; his reversal of his decision not to work from life but instead to paint her portrait.

He talked of depicting her: 'Perhaps as a Russian! As an earth mother, maybe, with attendant animals! The way she is shown in embroideries from the north, and from the Baltic States and Byelorussia. Or possibly wearing a muslin bridal veil, your face half-covered. You are, after all, *my* bride! Tomorrow we will buy you the very thing to wear – a semi-transparent veil, with floral designs woven in scarlet and light-blue and green and white silk . . .'

An easel was set up in the second room of the flat. Almost at once the glamorous prospect of being immortalized on canvas was eclipsed by the tedium of sitting still. And it was equally frustrating not being permitted to look at Karol's painting.

'When it is completed,' he said severely, the teacher yet again.

On the small table was a bottle of vodka from which Karol drank as he worked. He drank a lot – more than he had done when they had dined out in Moscow.

'Do you always drink when you work?'

He frowned: 'An artist needs to relax. For me, without alcohol, it is almost impossible. Eva, please keep still!'

Between one thing and another Eva was hardly aware of Sasha any more. Ignorant of much of his life she certainly did not know that his mistress, Dusya, had given birth to a baby boy that same summer.

Cousin Marisha knew all about the child – including the fact that he was called after his father, and that Sasha took little interest in him, which naturally she deplored.

Cousin Marisha had been to see the baby on several occasions and while Karol and Eva were making love in their newly acquired apartment, this kindly lady was trying to persuade Sasha to acknowledge his little son.

'You should bring him into the house, allow him to be part of your life.'

'That is a mad proposition!' exclaimed Sasha crossly. 'There is no possibility of my ever permitting that!'

'But he is your child, Sasha,' protested Cousin Marisha. 'The only child you have.'

'That has nothing to do with it,' said Sasha, unmoved by this argument. 'How do you think Eva would react if I were to confront her with the boy?'

'I don't think she would mind at all,' Cousin Marisha said. 'Eva is not a real wife to you. No, don't deny it! I know that. She does not share your bed and I do not think she would object to Dusya in principle.'

'She is aware that I have a mistress,' Sasha said coldly. 'Other than that, we do not discuss the matter.'

'Then she will not be shocked to hear about the boy.'

'Perhaps not,' said Sasha. 'But I object to the concept of introducing her to him. After all, his mother is only a peasant!'

'As was hers!'

But Sasha was walking away.

Dan knew that he could be transferred from Paris at any time, but did not know to where he might be sent.

'Where would you like to go?' Henri Blowitz asked. 'Russia, I suppose! You are obsessed with that country!'

'There is trouble afoot there – isn't that reason enough for a journalist?' demanded Dan, grinning.

Blowitz, he knew, would promptly challenge this view.

'It's not the *only* country in the world that is true of!' he said, sure enough. 'What about South Africa? Gold may have made the place rich but it's inevitably going to lead to a collision between the Boers and the new immigrants. If you must leave Paris, go there, get yourself acquainted with the situation. You'll be on the spot when the whole situation blows up!'

'I want to work in Russia,' said Dan obstinately.

'Good God, it's a woman!' Blowitz shouted in glee. 'Aren't there enough of them in Paris for you? Am I not a fine example to follow in that connection? Still, I agree that if you start from the premise that the new Tsar is likely to be even more ineffectual than his father, you may well be right in anticipating trouble.'

It was October 1894 and Tsar Alexander, having contracted nephritis, had been dead for over a week.

'Nicholas is an unimaginative man,' Blowitz continued, referring to the new Tsar, 'and irresponsible.

243

Look at the disrespect he showed towards the Japanese temples during his world tour. No wonder a Samurai tried to kill him. All he's ever shown interest in is skating, dancing, stag-hunting and the ballerina Mathilde Kschiessinskaya!'

'*You're* criticizing him for womanizing?'

'His own father said his infantile thought processes made him an unsuitable chairman of the Siberian railway committee. You're right – there's trouble a-plenty in store for Russia. Perhaps you'll get there yet!'

The portrait of Eva hung proudly in the apartment on the wall that faced the bed. To celebrate its completion Eva suggested that they visit a gypsy house.

The gypsies lived on the outskirts of the islands of St Petersburg. It was a fashionable and amusing *divertissement* to go to that area. Sometimes wild parties were held in gypsy houses that lasted till after dawn.

Sasha would not be there, she was sure of that: he was in Klyonovo. Karol's wife never went to so-called smart places. And as for the risk of being seen by Sasha's friends, it was time to gamble, she said.

The room into which the gypsies ushered them was extremely simply furnished except for one beautiful chandelier which Karol maintained was stolen. The walls were whitewashed.

'In Moscow I will take you to the best gypsy restaurant,' vowed Karol.

'The Yar? Yes, indeed you must.'

'Or have you already been there with your husband?'

Eva sat down at the table, ignoring this remark. The gypsy musicians were getting ready to play and sing and dance. Their songs were of death and suicide and of girls who went away from the world, having refused to marry.

This environment made a welcome contrast to the ballrooms and drawing-rooms in which Eva spent much of her time, and was all the more fun because of it. She enjoyed watching the gypsies as well as listening to them, steeping herself in their world. They were poets and bear trainers with a knowledge of horses and herbs and although Sasha insisted that they were originally from the low-caste people of India, she was sure that they were wise.

'A basket of champagne!' called Karol, leaning back in his comfortable chair.

When their order came he drank quickly and refilled his glass at once.

'Thank God there's no one here we know,' Eva said, and she caught the eye of a gypsy man and gave him a cheerful smile.

'You know that fellow?'

'No.'

'You behave as if you do. But I forgot – you must have a fellow feeling for these people. In countries where it doesn't snow so much they also live on the side of the road.'

She looked across at him, hurt.

'In Poland,' Karol said, 'there is a gypsy king called Gregory Kwiek. He spends his life making kettles and touring the gypsy camps of Europe.'

He raised his glass to her. And the other gypsies sang, of love and life and death.

New Year followed and Christmas and with them the inevitable family involvements on both sides which separate such lovers.

When they were over Karol said that he wished to live in the apartment on a permanent basis.

'You are leaving your wife? And the children?'

'It is better this way. Provision has been made for them,' was all that he would say.

That winter Cousin Marisha had been more often in

the city. She was still in the Sergeyevskaya Street apartment in April when she fell ill.

Then Karol said that he would have to spend several weeks in Moscow.

'So long?'

'Moscow is the centre of the arts. I have been out of it too long. That is bad for my work. It is a pity you cannot be with me.'

'It's not possible with Marisha unwell.'

She hated that April – resented the Easter feast. But Marisha recovered from her illness and returned cheerfully to Klyonovo and now Karol was due home.

Going to the apartment to meet him, Eva arrived with time to kill. It was the first time she had gone there since Karol had been away. She wandered into the second room where Karol had set up his studio and which he saw very much as his own private place. He was secretive about his work and did not like anyone, even Eva, to inspect it in its formative stage. It was several months since she had been permitted to look at his paintings. Still, she remembered with clarity the two on which he had been working. She imagined that these would long since have been completed, that there would be other paintings in the studio.

Two canvasses had been turned with their fronts to the wall. She turned them round to face her and was shocked. They were the same paintings she had seen at the beginning of February, still at the same stage.

She was still gazing at them when she heard Karol's footsteps outside the door, and his key turn in the lock.

He was drunk. That was as patently obvious as the scratch mark on his face.

They embraced and she could smell the drink on his breath.

'What happened to you?'

'I slipped,' he said, 'against the edge of a door.'

246

He was lying. Now that they were close she could see the scratch more clearly. Fingernails, not the edge of a door, had inflicted that damage.

A woman's fingernails? Each time I try to end my friendship with Sophia she becomes irrational, even violent, Karol had once said. Sophia was in Moscow. Had the two been meeting again?

It was asking for trouble to subject a man who was drunk to an inquisition, to accuse him of infidelity; but Eva could not help herself.

'Sophia did that to you, didn't she? You've been with her again.'

He stared at her, puzzled.

'Sophia?' he repeated. 'No, I was not with her.'

'Then who scratched your face?'

Without being aware of it, Eva had taken up a stance in front of her own portrait. She said again: '*Who?*'

'My wife scratched me,' he said.

'But you have been in Moscow!'

'She lives in Moscow now.'

'You stayed with her in Moscow?'

'Where else would I stay? She is living in my house.'

'You told me you had parted.'

'I was short of money,' he said. 'I sold the St Petersburg house, moved the family to Moscow. That is the artist's life.'

'You lied –'

'– said I made provision.'

This was the appropriate moment to either forgive or leave the apartment, not to stare at that scratched cheek, surmising about the circumstances under which it had been inflicted.

She said again: 'You stayed with her. But you say you love *me*!'

'You talk of love as if it is a refuge – a comfort . . .'

'Is that so wrong?'

He sneered: 'Love should never be a refuge. Comfort is

a dirty word. Why won't you accept the fact that all of us live *in extremis*? Life is nearly always ugly. Once, in this city, I took a peasant woman, a prostitute, home. When I got her into my bed she cried out with pain. She had taken so many men that day. What would *she* know about refuge and comfort – or love? She worked for her family – that was her life. There was no alternative for her but to accept pain as part of living. You have never known that.'

'I have never resorted to prostitution!'

'You live off a wealthy man!'

'And if you concentrated on your work – finished it, sold your paintings, you might not be poor!' cried Eva, stung.

Karol's reaction was to push her aside and take her portrait off the wall.

'Eva,' he said, 'my so-called bride who lives with another man!'

'And you live part of the time with the woman you call your wife!'

He smashed the portrait then, ramming the canvas against the table's edge and throwing it derisively on to the floor.

She looked down at it, saw that it had been ripped across the painted breast. Her own face still stared back at her from behind the muslin veil, but Eva herself felt dead.

'I am sorry. I'll paint another portrait of you, exactly the same.'

So promised the letter which was delivered by hand to the Sergeyevskaya Street apartment.

'I miss you desperately. I'll try to curtail my drinking. This has been a bad period for my work. It is so with artistic people.'

This was tempting stuff. Was not Karol the one person to whom Eva could truly relate – except, of course, for Dan.

But when she thought about Dan she wondered if he had progressed as far as herself. His letters were splendid, it was true, but they were letters – Dan wasn't there, and Karol – intelligent, stimulating, funny, talented Karol, so full of wisdom when he wasn't drunk – was a matter of streets away.

Without Karol she felt in physical pain. What they said about love was correct – it did affect the heart.

'This has been a bad period for my work.' Should she not sympathize rather than attack? Poor man, thought Eva. But she didn't care two hoots either about Karol's wife or Sasha: she was not that human yet.

She saw him again. Their affair was resumed. Next time he visited Moscow, swore Karol, the two of them would go.

The year slipped by, became 1896. The coronation of Tsar Nicholas was scheduled for that May. All over Russia plans were being made by people of all classes determined to be in Moscow on that day.

'Even Jews!' said Karol caustically.

The Tsar's government were said to have reconsidered their decision to exclude Jews from the coronation: three rabbis were to represent Jewish subjects in Moscow.

'And yourself!' joked Eva, for Karol was going to be in the City of White Walls in connection with his work, as were – to attend the celebrations – Sasha and Eva.

'I'll be there ahead of him so you and I can meet,' she suggested.

And when Karol growled: 'Your damned husband!' she didn't mention his wife.

In Paris Dan and Blowitz were also talking about the coronation.

'Nice little story here!' said Blowitz. 'The State carriages which the French envoys will use in Moscow were designed by Ehrler. Apparently at one stage Empress Eugénie, having tried to sell them and failed, said that they should be destroyed. She had a dislike for their being used by wedding parties in the Bois de Boulogne. You're looking very pleased with yourself.'

'I'm being transferred,' Dan said. 'Sent on another assignment and then back to London. But first I'm going to Moscow to cover the coronation. My French did the trick!'

15

Alexandra Pobedonostsev was not a good correspondent. She wrote to her children when she had something to communicate which she considered to be of major importance, and then briefly.

'I am due to arrive in St Petersburg on 26 April,' said her letter. 'I am looking forward to the coronation celebrations. I intend to return to London after they are over.'

Noting the handwriting Cousin Marisha said: 'Perhaps your mother will help you to see sense about the boy. He is, after all, her grandchild.'

'My mother has never been particularly maternal,' Sasha said bleakly. 'I see no reason why she should change her attitudes where the boy is concerned.'

'Where little Sasha is concerned,' Cousin Marisha corrected. 'But he has her blood in his veins, too.'

'As well as peasant blood! Do you think she will be pleased about that? I don't want this matter discussed with my mother – please!'

Cousin Marisha retreated. But she would resume the battle in due course, thought Sasha, sighing deeply and wishing the position of the women in his life could be arranged with the same ease as figures on a chessboard. If he had been in charge of the game, Alexandra would not even be thinking of coming home – not as matters were between himself and Eva; Cousin Marisha would be moved to the furthest possible space; and Eva would be in Klyonovo with him, instead of going on ahead to Moscow.

Along with the letter from Alexandra had come another addressed to Eva. Sasha glowered at it. That damn' reporter, he thought. How dare he write to my wife! He was always slightly put out by the arrival of Dan's letters, which Eva invariably greeted with enthusiasm and read in privacy, but he had never snooped upon their contents.

But this was a bad day all-round. The letter from his mother worked on his sensitivities like a pinched nerve, making him overly conscious of how he would soon appear in her eyes – a man whose marriage was a failure, whose wife was cold, whose son had a peasant mother.

When Cousin Marisha, wearing her most disapproving expression, had left the table, he tore open the offending envelope.

> My dear Eva,
> Exciting news, *I* think! I am being sent to Russia to cover the Tsar's coronation! I shall arrive in mid-May and I envisage being fully occupied until after the event. Then I am hoping that you and I can meet. I shall call at your Moscow apartment and if you are not there I will travel to St Petersburg in search of you . . .'

Dan's imminent arrival was too much for Sasha. He felt guilty afterwards for his bad behaviour but by that time, in a fit of pique, he had already hurled Dan's letter into the fireplace and the flames had eaten it up.

For Eva, too, this was a bad period. Karol's wife had fortuitously gone away, taking the children with her. There was every reason to believe that Eva and Karol could have a splendid repeat of the May of two years previously when they had met in Moscow.

Things went wrong before then. Karol was working late, or so he purported, putting the finishing touches to a painting Bakhrushin had commissioned.

252

Because of that Eva went alone to the opera and there met Konstantin Korovin.

'Karol Helfmann's friend!' he exclaimed. 'What a coincidence. I do not see either of you for two years and then – both of you, on the self-same day!'

'Where was Karol?'

Korovin said: 'At a café – with Bakhrushin and Sophia Milyukova!'

Seen in the light of her own beauty, Karol's behaviour was incomprehensible. But Eva was beginning to think beyond looks: to realize that while Karol was possibly quite sincere in declaring his love for her, when it came to women he had other needs as well. He required them, probably not even for sex, but for applause – adulation. He might maintain that his wife was boring, that he no longer desired Sophia, but he held on to them. He was a collector – not, like Bakhrushin, an assimilator of specialized treasures, but a ruthless collector of love. Who knew how many other women were in his clutches on this basis. But no longer myself, she swore. I will not join a queue.

All this she threw in his face the following day when he came to the Nikolskaya.

His eyes darkened. He scowled. He pushed past her into the drawing-room.

'In that case,' Eva said, 'I am going out.'

For refuge, she went to the cathedral of St Basil, remaining there until she could be fairly confident that Karol would have gone.

When she opened the drawing-room door her first thought was that, in her distraction, she must have blundered into someone else's apartment.

Ever so slightly, the furniture in the room had been repositioned. The richly carved, gilded sofa which had originally stood with its back to the wall now rested at an angle to it. The ornamented armchairs, too, had been displaced; the console moved around. The paintings on the walls were crooked, tilted in different directions as if the men and women depicted in them were drunk.

One of the paintings was gone. In its place, pinned to the wall, was a drawing of a hideous gargoyle with a long, lolling tongue.

She might have done better to laugh at Karol's venom, but few are so tough in love. This was a badly damaged man that she didn't really know, might never know – a gaoler. Sinking on to the repositioned sofa, she burst into floods of tears.

Apologies arrived in the form of letters which Eva ignored. Karol called four times at the apartment and was told that she was out.

But this show of resistance on Eva's part was deceptive. She had reached the stage of being able logically to reject her lover, whilst remaining emotionally tied.

Thus it was with her by the middle of May. Although the coronation was scheduled for the twenty-sixth, Moscow was already crowded with foreigners from all ends of the earth. The Khan of Khiva. The Crown Prince of Rumania. Twenty-eight more princes due to arrive over the next week.

In the streets massive preparations were under way. The entire length of the Tver highway, from the Kremlin to the palace of Petrovsk – where, in customary fashion, the Tsar would reside just before he was crowned – was to be deeply sanded. Every inch of the triumphal way was to be decorated with flags, banners and escutcheons emblazoned with the Imperial initials. Streamers were to be stretched over the roadway, poles adorned with garlands of heather, and drapery in white, red and blue to be hung on balconies, scaffolding and the frontage of houses.

Electrical illuminations were being tested – and while the rain fell and the temperature remained obdurately low, the leaves on the trees refused to turn to green.

In spite of the rain the city could hardly contain its excitement. Those who loved music looked forward to a grand vocal concert in which forty-nine famous singers from all over the world were going to perform; and to Mme Sigrid Arnoldson's appearance in the Imperial opera.

The German ambassador was to supplement his musical entertainment by bringing to Moscow a Berlin Philharmonic Society. A regimental band from Vienna would play at the Austrian embassy ball. Women thought of nothing else but what they were going to wear.

Even the poor were going to be catered for at the Tsar's expense. Opposite the Petrovsky Palace, on the Khodynka meadow, a fête was going to be held at which it was planned to distribute mugs, sausages, gingerbread cake and bags of sweets and nuts. A pavilion had been erected to enable the Tsar and Tsarina to appear there in person on 30 May.

'You'd like to go, wouldn't you?' Eva asked Vera.

'Oh *yes*, Madam!' said the maid.

'Then do – but stay here in the meantime and if that gentleman calls again, tell him I'm not here!'

It was one thing to fend Karol off by using a third party, another to meet him in person. On the day before Sasha and Alexandra were due to arrive in Moscow, Eva went shopping in Upper Trading Rows.

When she made her way back on to the Nikolskaya he was waiting in the street.

Mother of Mercy! she muttered under her breath. Her heart was an eejit – why did it have to thump?

And why, under the circumstances, was he so insouciant, grinning away at her and, when she attempted to snub him, singing aloud the popular song, 'Strolling along St Peter's Street', in which the singer addresses a girl?

255

It was wrong, inappropriate, for a man who had done such disgusting things to try to make her laugh!

And succeed!

'I have with me,' he said solemnly, 'an invitation to join me at the Yar restaurant on a date of your choice. You did promise you would come.'

He held out a piece of paper. On it was a drawing of two asses, dressed in swanky human clothes, sitting at a table.

'I've had other things on my mind – or soon will have!'

At least this was true, what with the banquet that was to be given by Sir Nicholas O'Conor in honour of the Queen's birthday, the balls that were to be held at the French and Austrian embassies, and the coronation itself.

To all these functions she was to be escorted by dull, worthy Sasha!

'I know you are busy,' Karol said in his most considerate voice, the reasonable, sober one.

When you listened to that voice you thought that was the way the man always talked!

'– but maybe when the coronation is over, when you have time between your parties . . .'

They weren't finished yet!

'I might be able to see you on the twenty-ninth for a while,' Eva said slowly. 'That's the night before the French ambassador's ball. I can't be certain but I might – possibly – get away.'

'I'll go out there beforehand and book a room,' he said eagerly. 'I'll wait in the hope you can come.'

'And don't you come to this street in the meantime!' said Eva. 'My husband is bringing his mother with him. What would I do if you met the two of them!'

Dull and worthy Sasha might be, but Alexandra was neither. Eva had forgotten her vivacity and charm – her determination to extract the best out of every day. She was a greedy woman but she was great fun and always surrounded by people. Meeting her again, the two women were on an equal footing, at least in the social sense.

'There are thirty-four foreign princes and grand dukes and thirteen foreign princesses and grand duchesses in this city, not to mention eleven heads of foreign embassies; and I swear my mother knows them all!' observed Sasha, when he thought she was out of earshot. 'Have you noticed how she flirts! I hope she doesn't do so with the ecclesiastical deputations!'

'What are you saying about me?' Alexandra demanded, entering the room. 'What a pity! I hear that the splendid entertainments which the Austrians were going to provide have been cancelled because of Archduke Ludwig's death. I'm sure he wouldn't have minded if we had enjoyed ourselves without him!'

No, Alexandra had not changed one whit. And she was looking much the same as before: just as smart, wearing a figured red and black brocade and silk day dress by the designer Worth.

The dress was cut on the new, smoother line with a minimum bustle and emphasis on the sleeves, giving its wearer an up-to-date western European look. Russian women, while not exactly out of fashion, no longer seemed to be buying the latest clothes. Every so often there was a frown and a mutter of 'Expense!'

'What do you think of the Tsarina?' Alexandra went on. 'People tell me that she is not popular in court circles, being shy and rather dull. Deeply religious in quite the wrong way! I suppose it's the result of being reared by her grandmother, Queen Victoria!'

'Please don't make these observations in public, Maman!' said Sasha, looking pained.

In time for the Tsar's official entry into Moscow the weather had taken a turn for the better. The morning of 21 May dawned bright and warm. As the Tsar and

Tsarina left the Petrovsky Palace the sun actually shone and men took off their coats.

The Pobedonostsevs watched the royal procession from the covered balcony of a window in the Tverskaya, directly opposite the house of the British embassy on which a banner called on God to bless the Emperor and Empress.

From one P.M. the cavalcade was seen to approach, headed by the Grand Duke Vladimir. At half-past two cannons were fired, church bells clanged, hats were removed and the sign of the cross was made. Soldiers stood to attention.

Gendarmes rode by. And then – in the distance – Eva saw the scarlet tunics of the Cossacks of the Kuban and Terek, His Majesty's personal escort, and the first sotnia passed on dappled greys.

Hundreds of troops – the Asiatic vassals and tributaries of the Great White Tsar; Turkomans from the deserts; Kalmycks from the south-eastern steppes; nomadic Kirghiz; territorial troops from the Don to the Amur.

Farriers and lackeys and footmen in scarlet plush breeches. Court runners with white and black and yellow feathers in their hats. Negroes in Oriental costumes. Huntsmen in Lincoln green.

And – when it seemed that thousands had passed by – the Tsar clad in the dark green colonel's uniform of the Preobrazhensky Guards rode by on a milk-white horse.

I wonder if Karol is watching, Eva thought. And the ladies, the Dowager Empress Maria Feodorovna and the Empress Consort, Alexandra Feodorovna, in their Russian costumes of white and silver brocade, went by in their gilded coaches.

'With white mantles around their shoulders,' wrote Dan, 'and coronets studded with pearls adorning both their heads.'

He had a place in one of the tribunes in front of the Monastery of Our Lord, but Eva never knew.

Dan was just as well placed to observe the coronation itself. When Eva was putting on her cream satin gown that morning, and long before the cannon was fired at seven A.M., Dan was already installed inside the Kremlin walls.

The sun, too, had risen early that day and was pouring fire on the gilded cupolas of Moscow. And even when Dan took his seat the square was packed by early risers, amongst them guards in gorgeous red, white and gold uniforms. A crimson carpet had been laid on the Red Staircase.

Red, red, red – a mass of scarlet alternating with crimson. The colour predominated, eclipsed all other shades in the endless variety of uniforms. The uncontrolled thought entered his head that red was the colour of blood.

For God's sake, stop being so morbid, he said to himself. Just because you see colour – because there are policemen positioned on the rooftops, you have to think about death.

Especially in a city which is, literally, gleaming with cheer. Everyone was marvelling at the electric illuminations, which would be even more spectacular this coming night. And if you looked over at the uncovered stand between the Red Staircase and the Cathedral of the Annunciation you saw not crimson or scarlet but the white gowns and light-coloured parasols of the ladies.

From the Church of the Assumption, where the coronation ceremony was to be held, the voices of the clergy celebrating a *Te Deum* were lost amongst those of the diplomats, princes, potentates and troops outside. The gold brocade canopy embroidered with the Imperial eagles was carried to the foot of the steps. Somewhere in the distance a gun was fired and the clamour of the crowd intensified.

It was nine when the procession began. 'Pages with white horsehair plumes,' wrote Dan. 'The ladies of honour in Russian national dress, their white veils flowing, their trains made of red velvet.'

The women who read *The Times* would be much more interested in what the ladies wore than in the actual ceremony, but how was he, a mere male, going to describe the complexity of their attire! He, who had difficulty distinguishing satin from silk! If only Eva was with him, he thought – she would be able to help.

The empress dowager who, by right of precedence, was to enter and leave the cathedral before anyone else, appeared at the top of the staircase and, as the national hymn was played, the spectators burst into spontaneous applause.

'. . . small diamond crown on her head. Train held up by high dignitaries . . . accompanied by the grand dukes and duchesses. After them the Queen of Greece and all the foreign princesses . . .'

Wearing? 'Elaborate gowns,' Dan scribbled, wondering if that would do.

There was a tremendous burst of cheering. Military bands in the outer courtyard, cannon thunder and the bells of hundreds of churches proclaimed that the Tsar had come.

'I must admit that the empress looked magnificent,' Alexandra said when all this was over. 'That silver brocade gown is very flattering cut in the ancient fashion and the marvellous brown hair falling down in ringlets and dressed so simply without ornamentation – it suited her very well. Now, what are our plans for tonight?'

While Sasha wondered how his mother could maintain such enthusiasm for party-going, Eva was working out how she could manage to get away from both of them on the twenty-ninth.

On that evening they had been invited to a private musical *soirée*. Since this was not part of the official entertainments, there was a slim possibility that she need not go.

She would plead a headache, exhaustion after all the social round and then, when Sasha and Alexandra were safely out of the way, she would slip off herself.

This unoriginal but plausible excuse was accepted by the others without question, although Sasha seemed concerned.

'Eva just needs to rest,' explained Alexandra, eager to be going and mystified that any woman would miss the opportunity to socialize, but an ally nevertheless.

Eva waited for half an hour and then explained to Vera that she was feeling better after all.

'And I haven't forgotten that tomorrow you are going to the fête,' she added. 'May both of us have fun!'

The Yar restaurant was a few miles out of town near the Petrovsky Palace, a fashionable place where it was possible to hire private dining-rooms with balconies over the floor – perfect for lovers' trysts.

But Karol said that the private rooms had long since been booked.

'They had none left. The city is very busy. We can have a table in the public restaurant instead.'

This room was extremely large with a high domed ceiling from which three white and gilt lamps had been suspended. The wall furthest from the entrance was supported by black and green marble pillars. There was a stage at both ends of the room.

They walked diagonally across the restaurant to a table set for two. From this point you saw that above the long red glass windows which lined the other long wall were five gilded balconies with arched glass doorways. Behind these were the private dining-rooms. Of the doors that led into them, three were intriguingly shut.

'And behind them,' said Karol, 'other lovers like us!'

On the stage nearest the entrance door a gypsy band played.

'Don't you find it contradictory that, in a restaurant like this, we can eat caviar and bliny instead of gypsy stew!' said Karol. 'So the Tsar has been crowned without threat of assassination!'

'You sound as if you are sorry rather than glad! Have *you* ever been a member of the People's Will?'

'Art is distinct from politics,' Karol replied. 'Artists should remain uninvolved on a personal level whatever they show in their work. Think of Goya in terms of the French revolution. Beethoven's dedication of the *Eroica* to Napoleon.'

'Beethoven struck Napoleon's name from the score in the end!'

'After he became angry at the emperor's betrayal of the cause of liberty. Well, artists should transcend politics. In any case, I did not share my sister's involvement with the People's Will.'

The restaurant *was* full. Their food had not yet been served when Karol looked up.

'What are you staring at?'

'Other lovers – as I said. Or possibly not lovers – they look too alike. Up on that balcony, gazing at us. They must be mother and son.'

'They are mother and son,' Eva said faintly. 'My husband and his mother.'

'Your husband?' enquired Karol. 'Yes, it must be! Look at his jealous face! The fool is suffering. I'll enjoy my dinner all the more. I've waited years to reduce him to what he is! Was this a surprise you prepared for me – or didn't you know he'd be dining here tonight?'

'How could you, of all people, have confused the dates –

you who are so precise?' Alexandra said when the discovery was made that the *soirée* was for the following week. 'We can't go home – not when Moscow is so alive! You'll have to take me to dinner.'

'But what about Eva – shouldn't we make sure that she's all right first?'

'Eva was quite happy to stay at home when she thought we were going to the *soirée*,' said his mother innocently. 'Why should this make a difference? We'll go to the Yar. It's one of my favourite restaurants.'

'We'll never get a table . . .'

Alexandra sighed in exasperation.

'Of course we'll get a table – we'll get a private dining-room. I love coming out on the balcony and looking down at the crowd, listening to the music. I know the manager well. He'll do anything for me. If the private rooms are already booked he'll cancel one of the bookings!'

When this did in fact transpire, Sasha's prime thought was how soon that night he could get to bed. The next night, he recalled wryly, was the French ambassador's ball.

While their meal was being prepared he followed his mother on to the balcony. It was Alexandra who first saw Karol and Eva and although she said nothing Sasha saw by the start she gave that she had had a shock. Then he, too, saw them.

The anguish he felt at seeing them together, the realization that Eva had lied to him, was terrible to bear. Even worse was the humiliation of being shown up in front of his mother.

He stood beside her for what seemed to him an age, not because he wanted to inspect Karol and Eva, but because he could not conceive of his legs being strong enough to carry him away. Much as he wanted to, he could not even bring himself to cover his eyes with his hands.

It was Alexandra who made the first move.

'Sasha –'

I must go, he said to himself, and found the strength to back into the room.

Must . . .

But even then he remained polite.

'Excuse me,' he said to his mother, and he bowed before he went.

'You are very cruel,' Eva said slowly. 'I realize that now. And you are not brave. It was your sister, not you, who had courage. Even if I loathe what she did I know that she was brave.'

'She was brave. Must we talk of Jessie?'

'You do so frequently. You use her death as an excuse – a disguise for the fact that you enjoy destruction. Until you painted – and destroyed – my portrait – you never worked from life. Only from chaos – and you need to create that in order to feed your work.'

'All this because you have seen your dull husband?'

'Don't denigrate him!' she said.

Sasha had intended to confront the lovers and in that way to attempt to retrieve a vestige of his dignity; but Eva emerged from the restaurant alone, leaving Karol behind.

The sight of her impelled him into bitter speech.

'I believed you cold – not wanton. I suppose it was also true about Lev!'

When Eva flinched but did not reply he forged ahead with insults: 'I should, of course, have been warned, remembering from whence you came. Was your mother as devious and unchaste? Your father appears to have known no more about women than me! I sympathize with him! Another cuckold – another fool like myself!'

'What do you mean by that – a cuckold? My father a cuckold?'

Sasha might have said: 'Even now, you think of your father first!'

But Alexandra was coming out of the Yar and Sasha strode away.

16

Sasha was in a daze of misery. Instead of going home he headed by foot in the opposite direction, walking past the Petrovsky Palace and then crossing the *chaussée* of Tver to the Khodynka meadow where races, military reviews and popular fairs were held.

On this night – even at so late an hour – others, many others, were heading in the same direction: men, women and children of the muzhik class who were looking forward to next day's fête.

On the big, flat, treeless field, music platforms, round-abouts, refreshment stands, tightropes for acrobats and greasy poles had been set up and, on the border nearest the Tver highway, a line of small, wooden stalls from which it was intended to distribute the Tsar's dole.

Small passages had been made between these stalls, which were set close together, and barriers erected to prevent more than three people getting through at a time, an arrangement which meant nothing to the unhappy and humiliated man who slipped between one of them now. All he could see was a vision of his beautiful wife in bed with another man. He did not think of the woman who waited for him at Klyonovo or of his baby son, only of Eva and her lover.

The people who were gathering for the fête stared at him, wondering why a man of gentle breeding, well-dressed, should be wandering amongst them tonight.

Hundreds of people had already gathered – thousands; some said as many as 800,000 would ultimately squeeze in and many were settling down for a few hours of sleep, curling up on the grass.

Sasha did not lie down but this was not because pride

prevented him from sleeping amongst the common people. He was beyond searching for self-respect, for he knew in his heart that to embark upon such a quest would be fruitless – that it was now out of his reach for ever.

In any case he noticed no one else: he was cut off from awareness of others and their sufferings, imprisoned in the cage of self-pity those who love enter voluntarily when they have been rejected.

For a long time he stood on the other side of the barriers gazing vacantly over the heads of those who were coming through. The moon was shining as brightly as the electric lights in town, lighting up the open-air theatre platforms, promising a day of gaiety ahead.

Isolated in his pain Sasha remained motionless. Eventually, without making any attempt to find a more comfortable position on the uneven ground away from the ditches and holes, he sat on a clump of grass.

Vera the maid had reasoned that, with all the crowds that were expected at the fête, she and her friend Milochka would be best advised to get to the plain early.

'Otherwise we might not get in.'

'We should sleep there,' suggested Milochka. 'It is a fine night – why not?'

So, while the drama at the Yar restaurant was unfolding, the two friends had set off.

They, too, positioned themselves just inside the barriers but, unlike Sasha, they lay down and managed to fall asleep.

When they woke the sun was rising out of a hazy sky. The field was dotted with dandelions which had reached the puffball stage and were being tramped into the ground by thousands of peasant feet.

But it was not a member of the peasant class whom Vera noticed on waking but – to her astonishment – Sasha, sitting on the grass.

Convinced that she must be dreaming, Vera rubbed her eyes and shook her head as if to clear it, but her employer was still there. She could not imagine what had brought him to this place. She thought that he must be drunk although, to her knowledge, this was not Sasha's habit.

Still, only drink, she thought, would account for the vacant look on his face.

'Look!' she said, nudging Milochka. 'That is the man for whom I work!' and the two girls giggled.

They were both feeling hungry. Knowing that the Tsar's dole was to be given out at ten o'clock they had camped near the stalls.

'Sausages!' Milochka said wistfully. 'How long do we have to wait?'

The question was unanswerable since Vera, like herself, did not have a watch.

'Ask *him*!' said Milochka, pointing cheekily at Sasha and at the suggestion of such temerity they both giggled again.

Meanwhile the people were crowding in. Vera could not remember when she began to feel afraid. Was it the sensation of overcrowding that triggered it off, or the first shouted demand for food?

That shout was followed by many others.

'Feed us *now*!' the crowd yelled. 'We're hungry! How can we wait until ten o'clock!'

People began to talk amongst themselves of the money that was being spent on food and on entertainment for the wealthy while they went unfed. Arguments broke out between those who resented the Tsar and those who believed him sacred. This led to cursing and, inevitably, to fights.

The workmen began to join the revellers in a clamour for sustenance. A suggestion – which became a general cry – was made that they should storm the booths.

'What's going to happen?' whispered Milochka apprehensively.

On the stalls the distributors were talking amongst themselves.

'They're frightened of being attacked,' Vera said. 'I suppose all the police and troops are being used to take care of the Tsar.'

A little while later the panic-stricken distributors took a decision. Small bundles of food were thrown among the crowd.

This gesture, designed to save the workers on the stalls, led to pandemonium. The hungry, desperate crowd pushed forward, shouting and scrambling.

'We're going to be trampled!' Milochka wailed as she and Vera were shoved this way and that.

Vera did not know what fate pushed her against Sasha. She had lost Milochka by then and her one thought was how to get out of the Khodynka plain before she was crushed to death.

'Save me!' she pleaded, not prefacing her words with ones of respect for Sasha, for deference fell away under the threat of death. 'Save me!'

His mouth fell open. He looked only half-awake but he had recognized her and he pulled her to him and into his arms and with an amazing dexterity, under the circumstances, lifted her up above the crowd.

'Save her!' he commanded.

To the terrified maid, what happened next was a miracle designed especially for her. A band of stalwart muzhiks, obeying Sasha, had taken her from him and, while one of them was still supporting her on his shoulders, the others had formed a circle around the pair of them and were fighting their way out of the mêlée.

Behind her people were screaming and pushing and being flattened underfoot or squashed against the barriers. She could not see a trace of their bodies but she knew with as much certainty as if they were lying on the highway in front of her that her friend and her saviour were dead.

Twelve hundred people trampled to death in one day in the Khodynka meadow. It was a gruesome story for Dan to file to London – a sickening memory to stay with him all his life.

Along with the other journalists he had been forced to witness what in effect was the aftermath of a battle. Red Cross wagons, fire brigade carts and furniture vans had been ordered to transport the corpses into town, but many still lay in heaps five or six deep, exactly where they had fallen, their faces black and purple. In the now tremendous heat the stench became unbearable.

After the event the would-be wise were observing that so many people should never have been permitted to assemble in one spot. Others, crossing themselves, murmured uneasily that the tragedy was an omen that boded ill for the Tsar.

The Tsar and Tsarina had gone ahead with their plans to visit the pavilion at Khodynka. From there it was impossible to see the heaps of bodies that lay over to the left, only the pavilions and tribunes from where the gaily dressed spectators shouted a great welcome, most of them unaware of the extent of the disaster.

The imperial hymn was played, and extracts from Glinka's opera, *A Life for the Tsar*. Bells rang, military salvoes were fired, and red gas-filled balls let up.

All this Dan put into his reports, as he did the fact that Tsar Nicholas had elected to go to the French ambassador's ball that same evening.

By that time most people knew what had happened at the Khodynka meadow. Foreign journalists, as well as many Russian people, were asking themselves from what source the Tsar could find the spirit to dance.

'Nicholas is a fatalist,' said one journalist sagely. 'He's

simply bowing his head in resignation to the will of God – that's all.'

'The peasants will forgive him,' someone else maintained. 'They call him their Little Father.'

But they themselves are known as 'dark people', Dan thought grimly. They have had enough in recent years. He knew, too, that many educated citizens of moderate political views, who might appear to be loyal to the Tsar, were beginning to regard Nicholas and his court as an anachronism.

'I suppose now there will be another assassination attempt by the People's Will,' a cynic said, jokingly, but none of the others laughed.

Because of the tragedy, Dan's visit to Eva was postponed as a matter of course. Naturally, it never occurred to him to think that she – as well as so many others – had been personally involved in the whole disastrous affair.

When Dan eventually found the time to go in search of Eva, he was seized by a terror lest Eva had changed beyond recognition – grown fat on Russian food.

He felt nervous about seeing her – concerned, too, that her husband might object to his presence; regard him as an interloper in Eva's life.

His old affection for her sustained him. Arriving on the Nikolskaya he knocked on Eva's door.

The maid who opened it had red-rimmed eyes. Dan's first thought was that this was because something had happened to Eva.

'The mistress is not here, sir,' she said sadly. 'You will not have heard but the master is dead. Madam Pobedonostsev and the master's mother have returned to the estate.'

He wrote to her offering sympathy, asking, in the usual way, if he could be of assistance.

Eva wrote back thanking him, saying there was

271

nothing he could do. Nothing except see her if he could. He was busy – it was a lot to ask, but if he could spare the time to visit her in St Petersburg before he returned to London they would all be glad.

A lot to ask? That doesn't sound like Eva, Dan thought. But she was in mourning for her husband. Her grief must be softening her.

He let her know that it was not a lot to ask. He would certainly come but it wouldn't be for a month. Would she write and let him know if that date would suit?

But the weeks went by and there was no second letter from Eva. This was not because she did not want Dan to come to Klyonovo but because – in the light of what happened next – she thought she did not deserve a visit from him, or indeed from anyone else.

Now that Sasha was dead, Cousin Marisha felt more than ever that his son should be accepted into the house. Surely they could not continue to behave as if the child did not exist? she asked herself. He was a person, a member of their own family, not an animal who could be left to graze on the estate for the duration of his life.

More than that, he was a most beautiful child, with curly hair and big brown eyes. She had seen him on a number of occasions with his mother as she herself wandered around Klyonovo checking on this and that. As her interest in him grew she began to make a point of visiting that part of the estate where he and his mother lived. She watched him grow from a baby into a toddler. In recent months, as her interest in him deepened, she found herself waiting for Dusya and the child to appear, so that she could talk to them, and stroke young Sasha's hair.

On these occasions she noticed that Dusya was uneasy, even frightened. Perhaps she believed that she should not be making contact with the master's relations?

Cousin Marisha wanted to reassure her – to ease her fears, but all she could do was show by her attitude that this relation, at least, did not want to snub her.

When Marisha heard of Sasha's death she thought almost immediately of Dusya and the boy. Provision must be made for both of them. The child's future had to be discussed.

Did Dusya know that Sasha was dead? His remains had been interred in Moscow and it could well be that the news of the tragedy was still known only to the staff at the house. She must visit Dusya and speak to her about the matter.

Without saying anything to either Eva or Alexandra she went to Dusya's house.

'My dear,' began Marisha, to whom all young women, peasants included, were in need of mother-love, 'have you been told?'

Dusya looked at her blankly. Very gently, Marisha began to explain. At first there was no reaction from Dusya. She stood, seemingly frozen, in the doorway of her *izba*, holding the boy by the hand.

Had she even heard what had been said to her? Cousin Marisha wondered. She was steeling herself to repeat the phrase when, to her horror, Dusya screamed. She did not simply utter a single cry, although that would have been startling enough, but emitted a prolonged wail of horror, seemingly endless, that tore through her listener's head.

Not surprisingly, young Sasha, too, was affected by the sound, and burst into tears himself, rubbing his eyes furiously as if to extract further moisture from them.

'My dear,' began Cousin Marisha again, shocked by this reaction. 'My dear, please don't worry too much. You will be looked after, I can assure you of that. Sasha's family will not abandon you.'

At the mention of Sasha's name, the girl screamed again. *Dushenka*, thought Cousin Marisha, distressed by the visible pain. She stepped forward, intending to take Dusya into her motherly arms.

But the girl eluded her. Instead, she bent and scooped up the toddler, holding him to her, stroking his damp cheek.

Then to Marisha's astonishment she said: 'Take him – please?' and pushing the child towards her Dusya went into her house.

Alexandra had been quite splendid to Eva, saying over and over again that she understood it all.

'As a woman, I know how you felt,' she said. 'Sasha was my son but he was also my husband's child, and my husband was very dull.'

If anything, this approach was worse than castigation. It sent Eva up to her room to come to terms with her guilt. So Alexandra was alone in the drawing-room when Marisha and the boy arrived.

'But, really, it is all too much! Sasha of all people!' protested Alexandra, holding her hand to her head. 'Where is the boy's mother?'

'Presumably still in her house,' Marisha said.

'Then you must send him back to her. It cannot be possible –'

'I assure you, Alexandra, that it *is* possible!' said Marisha firmly. 'In fact I would say proven! Look at the boy. He is the very image of Sasha. Of yourself –'

'Is that any reason why his mother should abandon him? Hand the responsibility to *us*? It is outrageous of her. You will have to sort it out, Marisha. I shall be returning to London this week.'

'I thought you might be.'

Alexandra glanced at her sharply but her cousin's expression was bland.

'All the same, we will have to summon his mother. Vanya must be sent for her first thing in the morning. Has Eva seen the boy?'

'Not yet.'

'It may not be necessary for her to do so.'

Cousin Marisha said obstinately: 'I imagine that it will.'

Afterwards, Eva was to marvel that she should have slept in the same house as the boy, without knowing that he was there.

In the morning she left the house early for a walk, taking Nábat with her, unaware of the new drama unfolding on the estate.

It was, she thought, the best time of the year. In early spring, the thaw had turned the fields into a sea of mud.

'Sow in mud and you will be a prince,' the peasants often said. When the fields were muddy they prepared the land. This month, they were sowing summer grain.

It was a strange day to be thinking of Ireland, but she found her mind straying back to the fields of her youth, imagining the turf-bog near her old house, and wild flowers and ferns that would be growing there now. Then this vision was put out of her head by Nábat's peculiar behaviour.

'Nábat!' she exclaimed, for the big dog was rushing ahead, struggling against his lead. 'Where are you taking me? Slow down, for Heaven's sake!'

Nábat did not obey. His massive, muscular body pounded ahead on its straight legs, dragging Eva behind. When she was beginning to pant with the effort of keeping up with him, he stopped in front of a wooden *izba*, nuzzling at its door.

'What is it? No, you can't go in – !'

But his huge head had pushed open the door. He was already inside the house.

'Nábat!'

At least the *izba* seemed empty. No partially clothed, embarrassed peasant was making his presence felt.

'What are you looking for?'

Nábat began to bark. Only then Eva saw what had led

him to this place: he, the rescuer of men from the days of the Greek empire, was now too late. The body hung from a beam in the centre of the ceiling.

That a woman was dead, had killed herself, was all Eva knew when she ran to summon help.

Dusya – Sasha's mistress – to have been driven so far. It was a spiral of destruction, Eva thought miserably when the pieces of the jigsaw were assembled. And she the cause of it all.

Where, now, were her dreams? The blood of the de Burghs that ran in her veins was of no consequence. To be rich mattered nothing in the face of the havoc she had wrought.

She sat in her room torturing herself with the horror, refusing to come out, even at meal-times.

In vain Alexandra and Marisha pleaded with her, sure that the shock of finding Dusya's body so soon after Sasha's death had disturbed the balance of her mind.

The child, the child, Marisha pleaded, offering little Sasha as a bait. That only served to make matters worse. How could the child want *me?* reasoned Eva. If it were not for me, his parents would still be alive.

On the purely practical level Cousin Marisha wanted to talk to Eva. Since Sasha had no legitimate heir, Eva had inherited the estate and all that went with it. Provision – in due course – had to be made for the child.

'Do anything you like for him,' Eva said when the subject was finally broached.

So – she did not contact Dan. To do so, she felt, would have been to be kind to herself, which would have been unthinkable. If no one else would punish her for all she had done – not Alexandra, not Cousin Marisha, and hardly Aunt Lilya, exempt from all of it lying up in her room – then she had to do it herself.

In not writing back she was highly inconveniencing Dan, who needed to make his own arrangements before leaving Russia. Had he known what was going on he would have been within his rights to say that Eva was being selfish again in a different sort of way. He would have told her to give over wallowing in self-pity on the basis that it would achieve nothing.

But he would not have told her of the further horrors that were emerging from the Khodynka meadow affair. It was bad enough knowing them himself, understanding how such an accident could have occurred.

Deep hollows had been dug behind the festive huts making holes of up to eight feet deep. The soil in that area was sandy. It would have been hard enough to secure a foothold in it without the pressure of bodies. And into these holes many victims had fallen. Some had gnawed at the feet of others in their efforts to get out. Others had been flattened. Thirty bodies had been found at the bottom of a disused well where the planking had given way.

Moscow was a sombre city now – a city in deep mourning. It was hard to believe that, so recently, it had been the scene of gaiety and cheer. Not even the Tsar's gift of 1,000 roubles to each bereaved family had alleviated the gloom.

I will be glad to get away from it, Dan thought, when his reports had all been filed and he was waiting in vain for Eva's second letter. When it failed to arrive he vacillated, wondering whether or not it would be appropriate to intrude upon her. In the end the sheer gloom of Moscow drove him towards a decision.

He would go to Klyonovo, call upon Eva. If she were not happy about his being there he could always go away.

17

Many a time Dan had anticipated seeing Eva again, but never an Eva sad. This Eva's nose was runny and her eyes had a pinkish hue. Other than that, to his relief, she was the same woman to look at. It was her character that had changed.

She has been humanized, he thought. You would never think so, to judge from her letters, but she must have loved her dead husband to be so submerged in her grief for him now.

I shouldn't have intruded upon her after all, he berated himself; and here she is maintaining that she is pleased.

The friendly lady called Marisha was equally hospitable towards him. A lovely woman, Dan decided, and a wonderful comfort to Eva.

While they were all chatting on a conventional level, the women asking him about his work and how long he would stay in Russia, two tiny people came in to the room, a dwarf and a little boy.

A very beautiful little boy now regarding the newcomer with large, suspicious eyes.

Eva's son, kept out of her letters along with the other expression of love? But Dan was swiftly disabused of the wild thought. To be sure Eva's eyes followed the child – rather wistfully, Dan thought – but the boy ignored her, smiling instead at the older woman and climbing on to her knee.

'Who is *he*?' the child seemed to be asking.

Seemed, for he did not speak in French but in Russian: the language of the common people. And yet he was beautifully dressed.

'Who are *you*?' Dan wanted to ask him.

There was another story here.

When they were alone Eva told it to him, along with everything else, vomiting out the truth of her marriage and her ruinous affair with Karol.

'So, you see, I sent my husband to his death,' she concluded. 'And the child's mother as well.'

'Nonsense!' exclaimed Dan. 'You did no such thing! Your husband was not sent to his death, as you call it: he was killed in an accident along with hundreds of others. And as for the boy's mother, she took that decision herself. Blame yourself for other things, if you like – this obsession of yours with the de Burghs, for instance; your marriage to a man you didn't love; perhaps the poor judgement you showed in choosing this fellow Karol for a lover – but don't turn yourself into an executioner! Anyway, we all make mistakes in love. Shall I tell you some of mine? I warn you, it would take time!'

Eva laughed. Well, that's an encouraging development, thought Dan. She never did have much of a sense of humour in the past.

Maybe she will emerge from the tragedy as a human being in her own eyes, instead of a goddess or a queen. Maybe she'll learn to laugh at herself, instead of laughing at me! But he didn't know that, long before now, Karol had made her laugh.

'Are you going to see him again?' he asked suddenly.

'No, I'm not!' said Eva; as if horrified at the thought!

This assertion he had heard many a time from disillusioned lovers, only to be reversed on receipt of a letter or a visit from the one who had been shrugged off. It meant nothing, he told himself firmly. Within weeks, months, Eva could be back in Karol's arms.

That devil, he thought; although *he* – or their affair – has been the saving of her. That was his objective response. On a wholly subjective level he toyed with the concept of throttling Karol.

It was Marisha, not Eva, who asked Dan to stay on.

'She seems so much happier since you have been here – happier than I can remember her being for months,' she told him. 'Do you have to rush away? Can you not spend a little time with us in order to cheer her up?'

He was due a break from work.

'I think I could manage a week or so,' he said cautiously, 'if you're quite sure I should.'

In that period their old friendship blossomed again. There was so much to talk about, apart from the tragedy, that had not got into their letters. Rambles to share, like those of long ago.

On one of their walks together Dan raised the subject of the de Burghs – a safer one than Karol.

'What is your feeling about them now? Are you still so concerned about your status as Ulick's daughter?'

'That's all dead,' said Eva in the same sort of voice she had used when speaking of Karol. 'I'm no longer tied by those chains, Dan. I have broken them for ever.'

'I'm glad of that,' said Dan in a heartfelt voice.

'It's all buried in the past –' Eva insisted; and then she remembered the comparison Sasha had drawn between himself and her father.

Sasha's last, bitter words to her had been lost in the events of the past weeks. Now, with complete clarity, she recalled what he had said at the Yar.

'I should have been warned, remembering from whence you came. Was your mother as devious and unchaste? Your father seems to have known no more about women than me. Another cuckold – another fool like myself!'

'What's got into your head now?' Dan wanted to know.

'Nothing,' said Eva quickly.

Had she not affirmed her break with the de Burghs a couple of minutes ago? If she told Dan what Sasha had said he'd tell her to forget it.

And maybe she *should* forget it instead of wondering about it.

Was your mother devious and unchaste? But my father wasn't married to *her*, thought Eva, so how could he be a cuckold?

'What are you going to do with the rest of your life?' asked Dan before he left. 'Stay in Russia?'

With her wealth there seemed no reason why not. But Eva was shaking her head.

'Not for ever, no. I like the Russian people very much, particularly the ordinary people, but I don't belong here. I sometimes wonder where I do belong; but for me that feeling is nothing now – I always was displaced. I'll have to think – perhaps I'll come to London – but in the meantime there are things to sort out here.'

'I hope you do come to London,' he said to Eva.

He thought: *Damn it – I hope to God you come!*

Although half of Eva was still drenched in remorse, reminding herself that she should be suffering, the other half was appraising the new version of Dan who had emerged out of the past.

The reconstituted Dan was wiser and much more worldly than the old one – he had even spoken fluent French in Cousin Marisha's presence – but there was also in him all of the good that she remembered from before.

Images of their first meeting in Shragh, shared excursions in Dublin, came into her mind's eye. Why had she failed to appreciate his friendship then – why had she turned her back on his love?

If I had not chased after a dream of being a great lady, of being accepted as a de Burgh, she thought, how different my life might have been. And Sasha would be alive, maybe married to some more suitable woman, and Dusya would not have died.

But this was just to resume the process of self-castigation and Dan had already expressed his feelings on that. As he had about Karol. But there Eva knew more than Dan – the affair was truly over.

She should be taking action instead of feeling sorry for herself. For days Cousin Marisha had been dropping hints that Eva should sort through Sasha's papers in case there were instructions about the child in them. That would keep her out of mischief. She went to the room where Sasha's papers were kept.

True to form they had been methodically filed and packed away in boxes. Sasha might have been anticipating his premature death. Covers listed the content of each coffer – 'Documents relating to S. Pobedonostsev: Birth, Education, Immediate Family – Will.'

The will, although it confirmed her own inheritance, did not mention the child. Sasha's son – his only child – forgotten! The omission angered Eva, healed her wounds a bit. This, at least, was one wrong she could right. The estate must be made over to the child when he came of age. And in the interim he must remain at Klyonovo in Cousin Marisha's care.

That decided, did she really need to go through the remaining papers? Sasha had seemingly kept anything and everything relating to his family which had been given to him over the years. Bills and receipts, deeds of sale and old letters had been neatly put away in order of years, along with a yellowing copy of a flowery manifesto dated February 1861 which, when Eva perused it, turned out to relate to the end of serfdom: at the bottom of the letter an unknown hand had scrawled, 'At last, emancipation!'

But so many other boxes and their contents – surely dull! And dusty! She sat back on her heels, smothering a sneeze, and noticed the wooden chest.

It was quite small and intricately carved and fortuitously unlocked. She opened the lid. The box was lined with scarlet satin.

On top of a pile of documents was a heading in Sasha's writing: 'These are my grandmother's papers.'

But which grandmother, Eva thought at once: Alexandra's mother, or Sasha's paternal grandmother, Mariya, who fell for my own father?

I have never been able to find out any more about Mariya. Make it be her – please!

She reached into the box and lifted out the top layer of papers. The diaries were underneath.

There were five diaries. When Eva had opened the first, seen on the fly-leaf the inscription – 'Mariya, Her Diary, 1837' – she took them up to her room.

Eighteen thirty-seven. The year before her father, Ulick de Burgh, had first arrived in Russia.

The first entries made no mention of him, nor were they even dated. The year's events were laid out more like one long story than a series of short records. As she began to read what Mariya had written in that, her nineteenth year, Eva began to form an impression of a vivacious, strong-willed girl, a girl frustrated by her life. The initial entries had much to say about St Petersburg at that time; the writer in conflict with one or other member of her family; her little sister whom Mariya referred to in Russian as *nadoyedlivaya devochka* – bothersome little brat; the ball she attended that year at the Winter Palace, with detailed descriptions of the gowns worn by the women and their diamonds and robes and pearls.

The men, too, had caught the young Mariya's attentions, particularly one young man, an officer of the Guard, in his white cloth breeches, silk stockings, silver-buckled shoes and plumed black tricorne.

But as the year went by Mariya's interest in the young guardsman seemed to peter out. The men she met were dull, she complained – and the women even more so. 'We are only allowed to dress up for great occasions,' Mariya reported crossly. 'The rest of the time we are expected to be modest in good durable cloth and shawls while our menfolk can be dandies.' So the diary went on.

Then, towards the end of that year's records, Mariya livened up. 'Maman is all excitement,' she wrote. 'We are to have a new British ambassador although, in fact, he is Irish! But Maman maintains that he is a link with her English cousins all the same. His name is Ulick John de Burgh, Lord Clanricarde of East Galway, and we will be one of the first families whom he meets when he arrives in 1838. He is married with several children, two of whom are sons.'

To the young Mariya, Ulick de Burgh was a most beautiful man. He was over six feet tall, with broad shoulders and dark hair attractively waved around his face. His eyes were deeply set. She noticed his clothes at once – the long well-fitting coat which hung in graceful folds from the waist, the pale kid gloves, the Irish linen shirt.

Her young father stepped out of the text and into Eva's room, along with his dazzling wife. Lady Harriet, wrote Mariya, was 'also very beautiful, very clever and in-formed: a hard woman with a grand manner who likes to inspire alarm and – as her father was once Prime Minister of Great Britain – to demonstrate her wide political knowledge. In comparison to *her*, Lord Clanricarde is warm and kind and interested in everyone else, even in Valerya who tried – without success, I may say! – to engage his attention. My foolish little sister!'

There was much more along these lines as contact between the two families increased and with it Mariya's interest in Clanricarde and dislike of his wife.

'I think he has a need for my friendship,' she informed her diary after a couple of months. 'Lady Harriet is a shrew! I wonder what drew him to her? It was not to further his own political ambitions. They did not exist before the two of them met – or so he remarked at dinner.

Maman says that Lady Harriet has exquisite eyes and great expression – that a man would find her irresistible. Sometimes, I hate Maman . . .'

On the floor, at Eva's feet, Nábat had gone to sleep, his huge head with its arched skull resting on his large, compact front feet. She stroked him, finding in Mariya's diaries her father's love for dogs; the pride he had taken in a new horse; his admirer's descriptions of how handsome he had looked, dressed for riding, in a blue coat with gilt buttons, a buff waistcoat, tight leathers, and high buttoned boots.

Many descriptions of Ulick, but only one of his boys. 'They bear no resemblance to brothers,' reported Mariya, 'either in looks or demeanour. The older boy, named for his father, is the very image of Ulick, with that wonderful face. A fine fellow, full of mischief, the way a boy should be, and his father's favourite. The other one, Hubert, is nondescript and very small for his age.'

There was no further reference to the boys over the next year's entries, but many to Lady Harriet, and the growing friendship between Mariya and Ulick.

The opportunity had presented itself for the relationship to grow. Lady Harriet was frequently away over the next two years. In Moscow, it was reported – as was the fact that her strange behaviour caused her to be spoken of in St Petersburg society. Clanricarde was observed attending functions on his own. Whenever possible he and Mariya chatted on their own, but her attempts to lead him into romance did not meet with success.

Eva smiled, reading: 'I asked Ulick what the shops were like in London and where did Queen Victoria get her bonnets and dresses and furs and he told me that the most expensive goods can be bought in Bond Street and that the Queen is said to be very fond of clothes and to order them from Paris, although she is very conservative by nature. "I am not at all conservative," I said to him.

"In fact, I am quite outrageous, although you would never think it, to judge from how I am dressed!" '

My father, so often accused of pursuing women, thought Eva; but perhaps they hunted him.

In St Petersburg, at that time, the field was open for the chase. So Mariya maintained: 'Tongues are beginning to wag about the British ambassador's wife. In London – so it is said – where she was a leader of society, her early life was lived in a blaze of publicity and gossip. And I heard Maman and the acid-tongued Princess Bariatinsky talking about her two evenings ago in most disparaging terms. *Lady Harriet has been seen in Moscow with a man!*'

Who Lady Harriet's lover was Mariya did not know, only that he was 'half-Russian and of noble extraction', information gleaned from Ulick.

Unhappy, embarrassed by his wife's infidelity – so Mariya said – Ulick revealed his emotions to his young friend while her mother lamented the friendship. A girl had to be careful of her reputation. Mariya was over twenty and should be giving thought to contracting a serious union.

'It is Ulick's marriage that interests me – not the prospect of my own,' Mariya wrote indignantly. 'Ulick's humiliation. This evening he and I have spoken once again. He began by asking a question: "Haven't you noticed the difference between them?" "Between who?" I answered, wondering what was wrong. "Between my sons!" he responded. "Or what I refer to as my sons. Ulick and Hubert. You must have noticed by now. Everyone else has done. I should imagine that the dissimilarity between them has been the subject of several conversations at dinner! The fact that Ulick, in every respect, resembles his father – myself – while Hubert . . . Mariya, you are no longer a child. *Hubert is not my son!*" '

* * *

Hubert illegitimate! Rich, powerful, cruel Hubert, a bastard like herself!

Eva's initial reaction to this revelation was positively joyful. Many things now made sense. Why Hubert, who had no blood ties with Ireland, did not visit the estate; why, in a twisted way, he hated the Irish people; why there had been no portrait of him at the house.

Inevitably, too, she thought of her father, of his betrayal, of which Sasha must have known.

At some stage Sasha must also have read the diaries, or learned the secret in them from Alexandra, and decided it should be kept; perhaps asked his mother not to speak of it – only to blurt it out himself.

Hubert, too, had betrayed her father, thought Eva. Having been reared as his son, he had gone on to discredit Ulick's name – the great de Burgh name – by his appalling behaviour. The name to which he had no right.

Monstrous Hubert, who had been responsible for her mother's death on the roadside, and God knew how many others'.

Just by mischance, he had inherited money and a title and land, and abused all of it.

But monstrous Hubert was now in her power. In her hands she had the evidence with which to discredit him – to make him the laughing stock of London and everywhere else. The people of County Galway who had suffered under his domination could join in the general merriment.

'Think of that, Nábat!' Eva said to the dog.

Nábat merely looked melancholic, as St Bernards do when they are most alert.

This is a time for celebration, she said to him, not for grieving any more. A time for action. She had a project to carry out – the downfall of Hubert de Burgh.

She began to plan her campaign. It would require her going to London, but that she wanted to do.

Before she left she would copy out that part of Mariya's

diaries which related to Hubert and turn it into a form of an open letter to post perhaps in Hubert's club, whichever one he might belong to.

And she would persuade Dan to write an article about Hubert's illegitimacy in *The Times* of London which would be read all over the world.

The evidence was here – Dan need only reprint that, surely, to avert a problem like libel.

Meanwhile, it was a pleasure to sit in her room with Nábat beside her looking forward to the day when people would scoff at the so-called Marquis.

He, who had taken away the dignity of so many, was about to lose his.

Soon, soon, soon, thought Eva.

'I'm going to London, Nábat,' she said. 'But what will I do without you?'

18

The manager of the Savoy Hotel was courteous but insistent.

'I am extremely sorry, Madam Pobedonostseva, but I don't think it is within my power to accommodate your dog.'

'Why not?' enquired Eva. 'Nábat is house-trained and good-natured.'

'He is also – ' the manager gulped, 'also rather large. He weighs, I would imagine, over 150 lbs.'

'Well over,' said Eva proudly. 'Nearer 170.'

How difficult the Savoy was being, she thought, the manager saying: 'A small dog now –', his mind already made up.

There is nothing else for it, thought Eva, but to take Nábat to Dan's. He who was always so supportive towards her would no doubt help in this.

It was a pity that pressure of work had prevented Dan from meeting her off the ship, but at least she had his address.

'Never mind,' she said briskly to the manager. 'I shall make other arrangements for the dog. You may send my luggage up.'

Gesturing nervously, the manager implied regret.

'Of course, there is no objection to your keeping him here for a while . . .'

'Good. In that case, I'll have tea.'

This time round she did not marvel at the luxury of the hotel. Prosperity was no longer a novelty. She took her tea in the manner of one born with a silver spoon in her mouth.

A most exquisite woman, thought the manager,

worshipping her from afar, annoyed with himself for not being powerful enough to permit her dog to stay. She was obviously still thinking about that, nurturing her displeasure. A slight frown was marring the perfect brow and her beautiful mouth turned down.

Had the manager known that Eva was not thinking of his refusal but of Oscar Wilde, he would have been surprised.

Details of how the Irish playwright had been ruined the previous year had reached Russia at the time. Now she was going to disgrace Hubert, as Lord Rosebery had disgraced Wilde.

At the thought of his forthcoming humiliation she smiled to herself, and reached out for one of the Savoy's delicious cakes.

Perhaps she won't hold it against me after all that I rejected her dog, the manager thought, watching her eat and drink. As her even white teeth bit into her cake, he emitted a little sigh.

Dan lived in Fountain Court on the right of Middle Temple Lane, not far from the Savoy, so Eva decided to walk.

With Nábat on a lead, she strolled past the Aldwych to Fleet Street, thinking how marvellous it was going to be to see Dan again. He, her long-time ally, would praise her for unearthing the secret of Hubert's birth – be as excited as she was by what she now thought of as Eva's Plan of Campaign.

Anticipating his approbation and encouragement she reached the peaceful spot where Dan had his rooms. Trees grew outside the house, and a bench had been thoughtfully placed beneath them so passers-by could sit.

'You'll enjoy living here,' she said out loud to the dog. 'Dan will look after you very well, I am sure, when I'm not with you – which will only be at night. And soon, when I've done what I came to London to do, I will make plans for our future.'

Nábat, straining on his lead, did not turn around; but a young woman, overhearing Eva's words, looked at her oddly.

Eva did not notice her. She thought: 'Soon, very soon, Hubert will be disgraced . . .'

Good God, she's here, thought Dan, looking out of his window and catching sight of the top of Eva's head. Having expected to catch up with her at the Savoy her arrival at his rooms was surprising but delightful, although it caught him out in the act of changing his shirt.

Fumbling with its buttons, he went to let her in. But when he opened the door he found himself face-to-face with her half-recalled St Bernard.

'Dan,' she said, offering her cheek to be kissed, 'I've brought Nábat to stay with you. They wouldn't have him at the Savoy. Isn't that odd!'

'Very odd!' said Dan, kissing the cheek and privately wishing the dog to Hell and gone.

His rooms were not spacious. He hated to think what a large dog would get up to in them. How typically presumptuous of Eva to inflict the animal upon him, and how equally characteristic of himself to permit her to do it! *Why* did he allow his joy in seeing her again to override his judgement?

'It's late for tea. Would you care for a sherry?' he asked. 'Or would you prefer –'

But Eva, as he might have expected, promptly interrupted.

'I have so much to say to you,' she said. 'Come and sit down with me, and I'll tell you about my plan.'

'Is *that* your reason for coming to London, just to take revenge?'

Dan could not remember when he had felt more angry. He had often been tempted to lose his temper with Eva in the past, but never like this.

'What's wrong with you?' she actually said, to add to his fury.

He could hardly speak for rage. While he was struggling for self-control he went to the decanter and poured himself a drink.

'Are you annoyed?'

'You would be hard put to it to find an adequate word to describe how I feel!'

'But *why*? What have I done that's wrong?'

'I'll tell you,' he said in an even but furious voice. 'I'll tell you, Eva Dillon, and don't wince, because that's how I think of you. You come here, to me, as full of the damn'd de Burghs as ever! Look at you – set, not to build a new life for yourself, but to muddy yourself in the old! And sanctimonious into the bargain: carrying on about Lady Harriet and what *she* got up to! What were *you* doing in Russia, may I ask?'

'That's not fair!'

'And you think what you propose to do is?'

'Hubert deserves it!'

'I'm sure he does!' said Dan angrily. 'He deserves that and more, but what about the rest of those who will be implicated in the débâcle? What about John Burke's family? Didn't he have a son?'

'But it's *true*!' Eva cried. 'It's true! Why should I care about John Burke's son, if the man is still alive? My father's name was blackened. Isn't it time it was cleared?'

'Your father chose of his own accord to save his cousin,' said Dan. 'He made a conscious decision. He put another member of his family before himself. Do you actually think you have the right to reverse that view?'

'Why should my father's reputation suffer?'

Dan said brutally: 'He's dead! Who cares but you?'

'And doesn't it matter that my mother and I were put

out on the road because of Hubert, along with all those others; that my mother got sick and died?'

'And this way you'll reverse the past and bring your mother back? Let me tell you something, Eva Dillon, that will open your eyes wide! My family was also evicted for failure to pay the rent –from the farm you knew as Saunders' Fort. You're surprised? Let me tell you one more thing – or let you guess it. This happened before Hubert's time. So who evicted them?'

She said in a tremulous voice: 'My father put them out?'

'Or his agent,' Dan said. 'It is all in the past. It has nothing to do with now.'

He had been leaning against the window-sill, gazing out at the trees. On the bench beneath them an old man had fallen fast asleep.

In this tranquil place, Dan thought, writers, artists and poets have lived – William Blake and Havelock Ellis among them.

'Does what I found out have no significance for the tenants?' Eva asked, less certain of herself now.

'What matters to people in Ireland is that the landlord system is going. Times are gradually changing, Eva. You don't know how the battle for land is going in Ireland – even if it's not known as the Land War now.'

'The Land War – Home Rule. What hope is there for any of those ideals?'

'Plenty! Wait. We'll win our battle yet. It's as certain as it is that, one day, there will be revolution in Russia! The Irish people will get back their ancestral land. Hubert de Burgh, if he lives long enough, will be the loser yet. But why don't you let history and the politicians take care of that? You look to yourself, Eva. You spoke to me in Russia of being part of a spiral of destruction. Do you want to perpetuate that, wasting energy on destruction instead of being happy? What *do* you want?'

'I'm not sure any more,' Eva said sadly.

On the way to Dan's she had been buoyed by her venom – now she was worn out.

'Here,' said Dan, thrusting a glass into her hand. 'Drink this up.'

As she did so he asked himself if he was being unfair, too hard on Eva. Unlike himself, she was still not in possession of all the facts about Hubert – or many of them.

What do you really know about anybody? he thought. Mrs Handcock now – Pretty Kitty as she was called in her day – on the face of things, a skittish creature and yet . . .

John Delacour, she had called her son. *De la coeur*: of the heart. For all I know her relationship with Clanricarde's cousin might have been a wonderful love affair – one that broke her heart . . .

Eva was still sipping her sherry. Nábat, stretched out at her feet, emitted a tiny snore.

'Maybe I've been imposing too much of my will on you – or attempting to do so,' Dan said more gently. 'Although it was for your sake I did so. But it seems to me that perhaps you need to make your mind up yourself, after you've seen Hubert. Although I can't promise you that I will keep quiet – that I won't try to assist the process! Would you like to take a look at the old fellow?'

Eva's brown eyes widened.

'Do you know where he is now?'

'I know where he lives – in a flat in the Albany. On the second floor. I was once asked to interview him. In fact, he threw me out. I know his club: The Traveller and St James. And, of course, he has his seat in the House of Lords. I can find him easily enough.'

'What is he like?'

'You can see for yourself. I have a free day tomorrow. What do you think?'

'I'd like to see him,' she said.

* * *

The Albany was a courtyard leading off Piccadilly, on the north side, near its eastern end. Once the home of the Dukes of York, it had been converted into apartments.

'The editor of the *Saturday Review*, Douglas Cook, used to live here – and Lord Macaulay, along with over 6,000 books!' Dan said lightly.

His anger of the evening before had gone and he was more annoyed with himself for having shouted at Eva than he was with her.

It was a cold and damp day and most of Eva was invisible inside a cocoon of furs. Her pale face could just be seen under her furry hat.

Here I am, falling for her again thought Dan. Or was there ever a time when I was truly free of her?

But how changed is she, really – how humanized?

'You're sure he'll come?' Eva said.

'Oh yes,' said Dan, 'he'll come.'

He had no sooner spoken than a curious figure emerged from the entrance to the Albany.

'That's him – watch!'

The figure stopped, half-turned, made as if to go back into the flats.

'But he looks so small,' Eva said. 'And so *shabby*! Surely that's not him?'

'Believe me, it is. Those ill-fitting clothes he's wearing, the top hat, are probably second-hand, bought in some flea-market. Either that, or he's made them himself! Look, he's changed his mind again. He's walking towards us. Take a good look and you'll see that his cravat is tied with a piece of tape!'

The small bent figure drew closer and Eva was able to see the rusty frock-coat it wore, the frayed ends of its baggy trousers, the way its hat appeared to be held together by rough stitching.

Under its arm was an umbrella, folded up. The nearer it came the easier it was to see that its face was ugly and heavily lined.

'Dan – he looks like a scarecrow!'

'Worse than that, he smells!'

'You're sure it's Hubert?'

He said: 'Here's an anomaly: take a look again at his cravat. In it he always wears a valuable family jewel.'

'Was he always so – ?'

Pathetic, Eva was going to say, but how could you say that of a man who had put people out of their homes?

'So odd?' went on Dan. 'Hubert de Burgh is known in London as a miser and an eccentric. Don't think I'm standing up for him, but here are some facts. As a young man he went into the diplomatic service and was sent to Turin. At that time foreign attachés received no salary. It was a privileged appointment and they were expected to have private means. I should imagine that Hubert was always the scapegoat for his mother's infidelity. Your father gave him so little money as a young man that in order to survive he slept in a broom cupboard. God knows what he ate! And at the same time he must have been aware of the money spent on his brother, of how much your father loved *him*.'

'Do you think he knew about his parentage?'

'Probably. Your father wasn't famous for his taciturnity. There would have been quarrels. If he wasn't given the information directly I'm sure he overheard it.'

What is she thinking? wondered Dan, as de Burgh shuffled away. Suddenly he knew that his whole relationship with Eva rested upon the outcome of this encounter. If she can make this final break with the Clanricarde hold, get the de Burghs out of her system for ever, she will be free of fantasy, able to look at the world as it is, and accept its reality. Assess me as I am, instead of as how useful I might be to her in perpetuating her dream.

When Eva still did not speak he thought – I did not promise to be quiet myself.

It was hard to be casual about so important an issue, but he managed to say in a deliberately neutral voice: 'All that money and yet de Burgh is drowned in his father's hatred. He appears to have got nothing out of life but a collection of Sèvres china, so they say. No wife, no children to inherit the title. Not even the ability to enjoy his money. That man is so mean he smokes cigars by instalments!'

Eva smiled weakly. 'You're telling me that hatred is passed on.'

He said: 'Don't waste energy on attempting to hurt a man whose capacity for pain was all used up in his youth. More importantly, don't hurt yourself.'

She was still looking thoughtful when the two of them went to the Gloucester coffee shop in Piccadilly and ordered coffee and cake.

Around them smart women in the new, rather masculine chesterfields and three-quarter coats wore small hats perched squarely on the tops of their heads.

'I must buy some clothes,' Eva said, looking around. 'Do you know that you can send a telephone message these days from the Savoy to a shop, and an assistant will attend with a selection of models, designs and materials from Paquin's in a matter of minutes?'

But she sounded abstracted as she spoke, as if her mind were occupied by something other than clothes.

Dan munched his cake and contemplated the other women, all dressed up. Women were growing much more extravagant lately in their attire. But did they wear the latest fashions to impress their menfolk or in defence against each other? Were all the gaudy silks, the ostrich feathers and the black lisle-thread stockings only a kind of armour?

'You should wear bloomers,' he said to Eva. 'It would suit your personality to ride a bicycle and shock!'

That cheered her up. She laughed outright.

'I've had enough shocks to last me a lifetime. And enough excitement –'

'You'll get over that,' said Dan. 'And start giving trouble again. Go back to your artist maybe . . .'

There was always that fear.

'No, I won't,' said Eva, 'or even to Russia. I want to stay here.'

And she looked at him in a way that gave him hope. Before he could ask her to expand on this statement she said, even more encouragingly: 'But will *you* be here, or will you be posted abroad again?'

'I think I've had enough of being a foreign correspondent,' Dan said. 'I want to write on another level altogether. Settle my life . . .'

'Get married?' interjected Eva.

On her face was an expression of part alarm, the other part regret.

So she actually feels for me, Dan thought, scarcely able to trust the look.

Still he grabbed the moment.

'Only if *you* would have me.'

'Really?' she said, the expression on her face changing to one of radiance, then just as quickly to despondence. 'Not – surely – after what I have done?'

Dan sighed. Be careful now, he warned himself. You have wanted this woman ever since you have known her, but don't let yourself be blinded by her interest in you so the one unacceptable aspect in her personality becomes – temporarily – obscured.

After what I have done, repeated the guilt-ridden brown eyes.

He reached out for her hands.

'Not what you have done,' Dan said. 'Only what you threaten to do. I love you but I'm not an idealistic young man any more and this is not an unconditional proposal. I cannot live with you unless you get the de Burghs out of your head. You may think you have come far in that respect – and you have in many ways – but you have not progressed far enough for me if you are still obsessed

298

with the wretched Hubert. Hatred has played a big enough part in your life. So don't say yes if you're still thinking of exposing Hubert de Burgh.'

Epilogue

That spring of 1915 the turf-man was seventy-four years old. Or was it seventy-five? These days he found it difficult to remember, and his daughter, when he asked her, was no better than himself, saying she did not know.

'Would you not be bothering about that at all,' she said, 'and get yourself out of the house.'

Talking as if he was the child and she was in charge of his life! The turf-man sighed, indicating displeasure. She was a holy terror, he thought, and she only after planting her husband two months back.

'Wouldn't you think you'd be glad of my company,' he remarked, 'after being on your own all day? I don't know that I'm up to going out.'

'And you as hardy as a snipe that wouldn't tear in the plucking,' his daughter only said.

Still, he had to admit that she kept a heavy table and for that he was glad, for he could put back a huge feed on the strength of her ministrations.

'I'll go down to the lake so.'

But when he got out the door and went a few yards in that direction he paused and looked back at the house, marvelling at the restoration that his daughter had done. It was a fine place altogether but it hadn't always been so, with the holes that had been allowed to form in the thatched roof, and the broken overhang.

But its position had always been good. From the front door it was possible to see not only the lake, but Spa Island South, although when his daughter and her husband had found the place you couldn't see out because of the bushes and ferns and grasses that had been allowed to overgrow.

'Will you go *on*!' his daughter shouted at him from the house, seeing that he had stopped.

'I'll lambast you, so I will!' he mouthed, but nevertheless obeyed.

After a few more steps he was glad that he was out in the open, even if he would not admit it to Herself. The sky had only a few clouds in it and the lake was almost blue. While the sun shines and the wind blows the world will still be going, he said to himself, and it did not seem to matter that he was seventy-four or -five.

Having prowled around by the edge of the lake he turned back and went off on the boreen that led to Kylnamelly wood, marvelling at the peace of the place. Nothing much had changed there over the years. No war with the Germans affected the tranquillity of the lake.

And none of the things that were going on in Ireland, either – the Home Rulers being united on the platform of the United Irish League under John Redmond and the Gaelic League being formed, and the young fellows playing their own National Game.

Not to mention what had been happening in County Galway of late! The old man mulled happily over the facts, breathing the good, fresh air. The Congested Districts Board defeating the Marquis of Clanricarde and getting the land for the people at last for £238,211! And that after fighting the case in the courts for so many long years!

And then – this very month of April – the wicked marquis dead!

'Good riddance to him down there in Hell!' the turf-man rejoiced out loud, and a redpoll that was busy making a nest protested at the sound.

At that point in the proceedings, both to the turf-man's surprise and displeasure, no less than six figures materialized ahead of him on the boreen.

When they came more clearly into his line of vision he saw that they were a middle-aged couple with four teenage children, three girls and a boy.

His memory might be failing, but his eyesight was fairly good. And his perception. He noticed that while the man was casually attired in nondescript clothes, the woman was dressed up to the nines in a pale suit the hem of which reached just above her ankle. Not only was she wearing extremely high-heeled shoes, which must be crippling her poor feet, but she actually had a hat with a kind of a sweeping feather on one side of it perched on her pretty head.

Did you ever see the like? the turf-man said to himself, impressed nevertheless.

'Good day to yez,' he said as the figures drew even with him.

'Good day to you,' said the man.

But the turf-man was less interested in the man than in the woman, who did not speak at all. There was something familiar about her. Memory stirred, like a lazy cat stretching itself in the sun.

What *was* it about her? But memory was sleeping again. He was unable to recall.

Eva, her mind on other matters, did not glance up as the turf-man passed by. Even if she had it is doubtful if she would remember him in the context of having once stolen his cart.

'Dan,' she said, looking at her husband instead, 'perhaps we've come all the way from Dublin for nothing. Maybe the house has fallen to the ground by now?'

'More to the point, I wonder who lives in it?'

'No one who was ever part of *my* life, anyway,' said Eva, and the turf-man disappeared out of sight, into the heart of the wood. 'And someone who is bound to be better off than we were. Now that the people have been able to buy back their holdings under the new system, he's bound to own the place.'

'And with fixity of tenure ensured, *and* fairer rents

fixed and the right of free sale guaranteed,' Dan nodded. 'That's a relief all right. Listen, are you sure you can walk in those shoes? What madness made you wear them?'

Eva grimaced, caught out.

'Vanity,' she admitted, 'vanity and the desire to come back here looking like a lady! As if anyone cares!'

'But you still do . . .'

'Mama?'

A chorus of voices cut into their talk. Dan smiled, his concern for his wife temporarily glossed over in his pleasure in his daughters, the three of them, Muráid, Kate and Nell, ranging from seventeen to thirteen. One with Dan's brown hair and the other two so blonde.

Muráid the bossy one with her keen awareness of power and her need to rival her mother. Vulnerable Kate, always ready to build a protective wall around herself. Nell, with her burning ambition to make a contribution to the world. No wonder young Brendan behaved as if he felt swamped at times by femininity, giving way to often ill-timed or inappropriate bursts of indignant fury!

Saying he wished he was old enough to go off and fight in the war! That could still happen, Dan thought, if the war went on – if the Catholics of the south united their arms with the Protestants in the north, the way John Redmond said they would if Ireland herself was threatened.

It was one of Eva's worst fears. Only last night she had pointed out that the military authorities in England had accepted the services of a division of the Ulster Volunteers, forming them into a unit: that an Officers' Training Corps had been established in Dublin University.

He had shrugged, wanting to reassure her: 'Well, a similar tender made by the Nationalists' Volunteers has been refused, and the authorities have declined to permit a training corps to be established in Dublin University. Stop fussing, woman! Brendan is only twelve.'

303

And here was he, making a living out of writing books! But a good one, nevertheless. On each side of them the extraordinary green land, bounded by ferns, speckled by a myriad of wild flowers, mauve-hued, crept towards the blue lake. Pale lilac cuckoo flowers, stark blue butcher, its austerity softened by the gentians and wild geraniums amongst which it grew, delicate yellow and orange heartsease, bright yellow marsh marigolds and lethal yellowy-green Irish spurge which the poachers crush for the killing of fish and others use on warts. To the right of them the birch trees showed off their purple springtime bloom.

'There were birch trees in Russia, too,' said Eva. 'I used to look at them and think about this place. Once, there, I remembered what people here say about snow: "They're plucking geese in Galway." But now I don't care about snow. Why did you bring us here?'

He said, with the air of one who is about to disclose a great confidence, yet with trepidation: 'The house and the land are for sale. I've been in touch with the owner – a widow. She's very anxious to sell.'

'Dan!' she exclaimed and his worry faded away. 'Dan – it's a perfect work place for you and, of course, I'd want to come home.'

'I'd buy us a boat,' he said, 'and take you out on the lake.'

'Yes!' she said. 'Yes!'

The children behind them, they walked along the narrow, cow-spattered boreen. When they looked ahead at the lake they could see Bounla Island, and the land mass behind it.

And way across the lake to the left, Portumna castle . . .

She thought: The children, too, will be coming home. In their veins is the blood of the de Burghs.

'We'd have to rebuild the house,' Dan said.

And she pushed the thought away.